M000012066

shakespeare burning

CHARISSE MORITZ

Copyright © 2019 Charisse Moritz

All rights reserved.

ISBN: 9781086411072

Chapter 1

SHAKE:

No lie. I'd rather nosedive into a horde of flesh-eating zombies, wearing nothing but salt and pepper, than take one more step.

You think I'm exaggerating? Making too big a deal out of after-school detention? Since just lurking in the doorway, just sniffing the funk of odors from inside has my guts stuffed into my throat, you're wrong.

None of my seven fellow fuckups have spotted me yet, so I still have the choice. Either I head into the classroom and brave the same looks and whispers I've been dealing with for the last eight months, or I skip and might as well tattoo *delinquent* across my forehead. The purple-haired gal in the last row decides it. I'm outta here.

I ease into a retreat, execute a hasty spin and bash into something. A someone. A girl and she's no match for my bulk. I reach out, but she's shorter than expected, so my palm caps her skull like I'm testing for ripeness. And since my luck is worse than a wet fart, it's Cleo Lee. Shit, shit, shit. She's gonna make this extra awful, I just know it.

I hold perfectly still, hoping to minimize collateral damage, but this teeny-tiny mean little creature escalates from stunned surprise to DEFCON 1 in less than three seconds. She shrieks and flails at my chest, fingers snagging in a minor tear in my shirt and turning it into a rag I'll be forced to throw away. Thank you, Cleo.

Laughs erupt from inside. We're putting on a better show than the theater club's version of *The Jungle Book,* which is really saying something, because Brad Tesch ended up on the wrong side of a loincloth malfunction, flashed Baloo an eyeful of the Bare Necessities and his prickly pears became briefly famous on YouTube.

At least it can't get any worse. Right? Please? Except it can.

Whether by accident or on purpose, Cleo yanks at my shirt and flashes my naked belly to the whole wide world, right before she stomps my toes. I hear Allie Kindle, AKA purple-haired girl, shouting "Ermigawd! Ermigawd!" as I curl forward and bash my forehead off the top of Cleo's head. For the record, her skull could pulverize diamonds to dust. I'm probably concussed, which will be my excuse for possibly, maybe, inadvertently brushing the back of my right hand across her tit.

She's so angry she's hissing, cheeks so pink they glow and still tugging, tugging to untangle her hand and only managing to further destroy my shirt. This is going so well, we should sell tickets.

"Stop," I mutter.

"Me?" she screeches. "How about *YOU* stop pawing at *ME!*"

I now realize I'm touching her. That can't be right. But yeah, there's my big mitt, resting in the curve where her neck meets shoulder, my thumb reaching to the hollow at the base of her throat.

Way down in a dark mossy corner of my brain, awareness flares. It's the primitive reaction of a starved caveman catching a whiff of a Brontosaurus on the grill. Me want. Me horny. This is all about aching loneliness, and it's not getting fed.

I snatch my hand away, scrubbing my tingling palm against my jeans and she notices. Here's a little chestnut to keep in mind. Hand wiping directly after touching a girl is not recommended. Her eyes narrow in on me. Uh-oh.

No way the *it's not you, it's me* excuse is gonna fly, so I move to slip around her. I'm running faster than red boxers in a hot water wash, and I know what I'm talking about. I do my own laundry and am rockin' a T-shirt the color of Easter peeps.

"Where you going?" Cleo shifts between me and my escape, and even though she'd fit in a travel mug, her scowl is scary.

I could bully her aside but don't wanna risk touching her again.

"What's the hurry?" she pushes. "You too good for us, Princess?"

I chew my lip, because the guy who used to sweet talk his way out of trouble has nothing but bitterness in his mouth.

"Come sit! Right here!" That seismic blast would be Allie, shouting from inside, while patting her lap. On a scale of one to ten, her volume hits somewhere around fifteen. I've probably said all of four words to Allie Kindle since grade school. The same four words, over and over. *Please Don't Touch Me.*

I tense from neck to toes and Cleo doesn't miss a thing. Ya think she lets me off the hook? Surprise, surprise, little Miss Ray-O-Sunlight taunts me with a nasty smile and says, "What's the problem, sweetheart? Can't bare to slum it up with the ordinary losers?"

"You're the problem." Did I really just say that? Feel free to roll your eyes. This is more painful than getting nibbled to death by guppies.

"So sorry," she holds up her hands, actually laughs and I don't trust her. "Lemme just pull a red carpet outta my butt and cue the doves, because his royal High-Ass has arrived."

Since I'm dumb enough to think anything's gotta be better than tangling with Cleo, I wave my white flag and duck inside the classroom. I'm just in time to hear Allie call out, "Feel free to take your shirt off. Give us another peek at the goodies."

My face burns. Someone shoot me. I'm begging you.

I cross to the far side of the room and put five rows of desks between us. It's not enough. Allie's still ten feet too close. I could dress in drag and hide in poison ivy, and she wouldn't be discouraged.

For reasons I don't understand, Allie zeroed in on me in seventh grade and has become the MVP in a non stop game of embarrassing the shit out of me. Thanks to her, my buddies have endless ammunition to abuse me.

"Oh c'mon Cupcake," she whines.

Cupcake? There you go. I'm six foot four, two hundred pounds.

"I'm gonna wear you down," she tells me. "I'm going to wear your ass like a pair of earmuffs."

I don't even know what that means.

"Allie." Mr.Schwartzmeyer, our babysitter for detention, lowers his newspaper to give her the stink eye. "Contain yourself."

It would take a cement bunker, wrapped in razor-wire, buried in the earth's core, to contain Allison Kindle. Look up the word relentless in the dictionary. Allie's picture is right there next to it, cross-referenced with noisy and juiced to be alive. She's so giddy, I swear she burps sunshine. We do not belong on the same planet. I can't even remember how to smile.

Schwartzmeyer gestures at me with the sports section and his eyebrows squeeze together like a pair of mating caterpillars. "Sign in, Mr. LeCasse."

He pronounces it Le Case. That's wrong. My name's French, sounds like costume, without the tume. I don't bother to correct him, just like I don't bother to lift my feet as I trudge up to his desk. My sneakers scrape the dull anthem of the defeated.

5

After scribbling my name on a yellow tablet, I drop back into my seat, tip my head forward and hide behind my hair. Whoever said misery loves company didn't know jack shit.

I hear Allie, clicking her tongue as if she's calling a stray cat. I should stick to reading the graffiti on the desk but the crinkle of a wrapper has me glancing over. She waggles a half-eaten Snickers bar and my empty stomach sits up and begs. I tell myself dignity is more important than chocolate, peanuts and nougat, but I'm not sure I believe it.

Wondering what the hell nougat actually is, I lock eyes with Cleo. She's sitting with Allie but focused on me. How come she doesn't need to sign in on the yellow tablet?

She stares back with sharp, dark eyes. I notice one is bruised a faint purple. A thin silver chain thing connects the piercing in her nose to her left ear. This girl is a real-life combat fairy. She'd definitely kick Tinkerbell's ass

When I glare back, Cleo keeps right on looking. No change in expression. I'm pretty sure she stole the Oreos out of my fourth grade lunch box.

"What?" I snarl. Might as well stand up and beat my chest. Look up the definition of giant asshat in the dictionary, and there's my picture. Shame digs in deep, but I can't manage an apology.

Cleo turns in her seat to face me directly, props an elbow on the back of her chair and says, "How come the best looking guys are always the biggest dicks?"

6

Back up. Is there a compliment floating around in there? The old me would have had a field day with the big dick comment. The shitty me gets pissed off even though I don't give a flying hoho what she thinks.

"I have a theory," she tells me, and I can't wait to hear this nugget of wisdom. "Because everybody's always sucking up to you, you've never needed to develop a personality."

Says the girl who is as fun as jock itch.

"Don't even think about sucking on my boy toy," Allie blares at her, drawing another round of laughter. "Hey! Shake-n-bake! Hey!" Her voice cleaves my eardrums in half. I ignore her.

She moves one desk closer and pounds on it to get my attention. She has pink lipstick smeared across her teeth and sparkle blue eyeshadow crusted on her lids. She's so colorful, she should be hung from the ceiling and stuffed with candy. If it would shut her up, I might be tempted to blindfold myself and swat at her with a stick.

Relax. I wouldn't literally beat the girl with a stick. I'm not that big of a jerk. Once upon a time, I was actually a decent guy, with friends, a girlfriend, honor roll GPA and the whole list of super worthless shit. I've just sort of lost my way. That's the wrong choice of words. Lost implies me trying to find my way back. More accurately, my way has been obliterated.

"I gotta know. What happened with Westin?"

Allie's voice is a spotlight, and I am the main attraction. Even Schwartzmeyer lowers his newspaper. There is nowhere to hide. I keep waiting for everyone to move on to the next tragedy, but I'm an overachiever and no one can compete.

"Nothing," I mumble, hiking my shoulders to my ears.

"C'mon sugar-buns," Allie says to me and everyone within a twenty mile radius. "Tell me, tell me, tell me."

The thing with Mr. Westin actually happened at the end of English lit. He was jizzing over the *Glass Menagerie*. Doing the voices. Leaping, twirling, nearly impaling himself on his own boner, right up until he noticed my zoned out state. All of a sudden, it was my job to explain the bird motif.

FYI, it's not a couch pattern

So he stood me up, leaned in so close I smelled tuna on his breath and said, "I'm sure the faculty has shown a certain leniency due to your circumstances, but I am disinclined to facilitate your self-destruction."

Yeah, he's a douche of epic proportions, but he's right. The teachers cut me slack. It's a perk of my shit-suck existence, and everybody is on board except Westin, who then said, "What would your mother think of your conduct? I daresay she'd be disappointed to see her only surviving son…"

I've never been a violent person, never gotten in serious trouble, but I may have grabbed Westin by the shirt, screamed animal noises. Whatever. I made an idiot of myself, gave everybody more to talk about and have now been permanently ejected from English lit. I'm also stuck with two weeks of detention. Ten days, times forty minutes. That's four hundred minutes of Allie Kindle and Cleo Lee. The two of them are regulars in detention, and I'd rather spend seven hours plucking my groin hairs with rusty tweezers while listening to a lecture on the menstrual cycle.

I fold my arms on the desk, drop my head and try to sleep. The desk smells like sweaty erasers, wasn't designed for someone my size and teeters sideways on a gimpy leg. There's no good place to put my feet, and I consider trying to crawl under it, because even with a cracked seat pinching my ass, the chair is no match for Allie Kindle.

"Whatcha listening to?"

I've got buds in my ears, my music cranked, but can still hear her. Tribes in Africa can hear her. Hyenas are howling in agony.

"Hey!"

Her voice would definitely register on the Richter scale.

"Hey! Shake-a-leg! Helloooo!"

Her determination is Terminator level. I glance up. The female Schwarzenegger is now seated in the row next to me. The rest of the detention hostages glare at me as if everything about Allie Kindle is my fault. I don't understand her eagerness to draw attention to herself. My spine physically aches from spending the whole day trying to disappear. I finally mutter, "the Black Keys."

She wrinkles her nose with a disgusted, "Ew," then shoves her chest at me. I don't recognize the chick on the front of her shirt.

As fascinated as I am with Allie Kindle's taste in music, I check the clock. I just want outta here and every second freshly sucks. I'm pretty sure the minute hand is stuck. I watch it wobble on the seven. When it suddenly drops backward to land on the six, I clunk my forehead on the desk and find the very sore dent created by Cleo's skull.

"Cyndi Lauper," Allie informs me. I roll my head against the desk to watch her pull at the sides of her shirt and present it as a visual aid. "Have you heard the song She Bop? Do you know what it's about?"

Since I'm not fifty years old, I've got no clue and nope, not gonna answer.

"I listen to it on repeat and think about you." How nice of Allie to share that uncomfortable tidbit with the universe.

Squeezing my eyes shut, I silently plead, leave me alone, leave me alone, please, please, please. My misery is almost the same as masturbating. I'm ashamed of it, can't help it and don't want an audience.

I sit up, blow a breath hard enough to move my hair, and there's Cleo, still staring. What the hell is her problem? I'm not giving in this time. If she wants to play the staring game, fine by me. Bring it. I can do this all day.

I focus on her eyes. They are huge and the color of dark chocolate, the shit that's so bitter it shouldn't be classified as candy. Her lashes are super long, like on those creepy baby dolls that only blink when you turn them upside down. Maybe I need to grab Cleo by the ankles and dangle her. How is she going so long without blinking? I mean, come on. Is she an effing cyborg? She's staring at me like she's getting paid to do it.

Maybe her eyes were designed as an interrogation weapon by NASA. I'm half a second away from babbling all my worst secrets, and I wonder if she can see it. Guilt, anger and pain coat me like a permanent sweat and most everybody is scared off by it, as if my suffering is contagious.

Not Cleo. I look away first. I lose.

Chapter 2

SHAKE:

After detention, I end up across the street from my house. It's not my house anymore, but I come here to stare at it. It reminds me of why I hate myself and somehow makes me feel better. Confused? Join the club.

Mrs. Pendleton steps onto her porch with a broom in her hands and eyeballs me. She isn't sweeping. She's armed. I lived next to her for almost seventeen years, but she doesn't recognize me. Or maybe she does. My brother Hemmie ran over her corgi. There is a blind curve, and the dog was in the road. Captain Cuddles is still alive. My brother is dead. Mrs. Pendleton is still pissed.

I push buds into my ears, flip my hood and start walking. My town has one stoplight. Life here is about as exciting as watching cows piss on flat rocks. Yup, I've actually done that. Along with four-wheeling, tubing and tractor pulls. Welcome to Armpit USA.

Closing in on my Grandma's house, catching sight of her in the front yard, I'd sell off my pinkie toe to have somewhere else to go. Not the big toe. It's not big toe level bad. It's just that eight months ago, when she claimed me at the police station, I overheard her say to Sergeant West, "What am I supposed to do with him?" So now I'm the thing that inhabits her basement.

She's got her back to me, digging under a pine tree with a rake. I ease one foot onto the front step of her very small, painted blue house before she speaks up.

"School called. They tell me you're dicking the dog."

My Grandma swears. All the time, in weird ways, and since I don't really know her, I'm still getting the hang of it.

"Not showing up," she clarifies. "For days at a time. Seems to me, you decide to do something you do it. You wanna be a dropout, quit. You wanna graduate, go to school. Pissing on both sides of the fence just leaves no place dry to stand."

Huh. I can quit school? That's an option? Freeing up those three months until graduation would give me plenty of time to … I got nothing. My level of pathetic is staggering.

"I dropped out," Grandma goes on. I know this. My mom used to beat me over the head with the story. "I was getting as much out of it as an extra asshole. But that's my life. Not yours."

I make a meal out of my lower lip and wait for her to dive back into my shit. She doesn't disappoint.

"According to your principal you shoved some English teacher, which can't be right, because I'd like to think you have better sense than a titless cat."

I can't think of anything to say, so I just stand there and perfect my imitation of a titless cat.

"Called me at work."

Four words and the universe skips a beat. Woodland creatures go still. Grass quits growing. My balls shrink.

I once dropped my phone in the toilet. After eating one too many tacos from a food truck. This moment is worse.

She makes another long swipe with the rake, dragging across semi-frozen dirt, churning up brown, mushy leaves leftover from last autumn. She shakes the tines, kicks at them and lets me stand there. I know better than to vacate. I know better than to let anything bother her at the bakery.

Oh so slowly, she gives me one hard glance over her shoulder and says, "Vivian Sanderson seems to think she farts priceless advice."

Vivian Sanderson is the high school principal and apparently has nothing better to do than pick at the scabs of my existence.

"I can't get calls like that at work. You know that right?"

I nod, but my grandma's no longer looking, so I grunt a quick, "Uh-huh."

"Don't expect me to pull miracles out of my ass. You're on your own."

Two females, less than an hour apart, ranting at me about pulling something outta their butts has to be some kind of record. Now I panic, thinking this is the moment, the one I've been expecting but am not even close to prepared for, when Grandma tells me I can't stay with her anymore. I've got nowhere else to go.

She pins me with a stare. Her blue eyes are heat seeking missiles. Her hair is a gray helmet. She is six feet of combat-ready, scary Grandma, and I curl my shoulders, hoping to make a smaller target.

"You've got food, shelter." Her voice is as rough as the scratch of her rake. "I'm doing my part. Whatever else, you gotta speak up. Tell me, Shake, what do you need?"

I hope I'm not required to actually answer. Because I can't. I don't know what I need.

Her eyes pound me for another second, wait for me to crack and peel me like a soft-boiled egg. I'm a sticky mess on her doorstep by the time she finally shakes her head, grumbles something under her breath that is either "Christ Almighty" or "Cry Salt Nightly" and then goes back to raking.

I escape inside, retreat down to the basement and forget about the low ceiling on the stairs. I learn that if I bash my skull hard enough, I curse in French. The pain feels good. It gives me something to think about that hurts less than just being me.

What do I need? What do I need? The question comes back like hiccups. If I could figure out the answer, maybe … I don't know, but it seems important. I drop to the floor and hit the push-ups, repeating until I'm a trembling puddle of sweat. I still don't know what I need. Other than a shower.

Are you bored with me yet? Just hang in there. It gets way better. After the shower, I eat a jar of pickles. Dill pickles. I know. Total madness. I choose them because the jar is dusty and maybe Grandma won't miss it, then wash the fork and put it away.

I should grab a rake and help my grandmother, but she might feel the need for conversation. Since the words trapped in my mouth would scare the stripes off a zebra, I'm stuck with myself for company. And I fucken hate being around me. Seriously, I'd rather hangout with an incontinent narcoleptic, and no, I'm not going to explain those big words. Look 'em up.

So I head out and just walk. I kick a few pebbles. Stumble over a crack in the pavement. Narrowly avoid stepping in dog shit. Wrestle an alligator. I made up that last part. But I am fighting my conscience, does that count? And yes, I know I'm a whiny bitch.

I walk until my legs go stiff and the sun sinks, stopping finally at the top of three cement steps facing a black door. Hard music bleeds from the edges. I find Rex on the other side. Rex is a short, furry cube of muscle who wears flannel over T-shirts, stained jeans and work boots. He is the brother of Cleo, former best friend of my dead brother, and I can't quite look him in the eyes.

Ask anyone. They'll tell you my brother was a druggie asshole who washed out of college and made a career of living in the family basement. I'm not sure if Rex dragged Hemmie down or if they met at the bottom, but I blame Rex. Cuz I remember Hemmie from better days and don't want to believe he was the scumbag everybody says.

Rex is the security at the door, the line of defense against underage drinking and the reason I get in with my brother's ID. He slaps my back like we're fulltime buds, and the music sucks me in. It's manic and pounding and loud enough to promote brain damage. My feet stick to the floor, and the air is musty enough to taste.

The place is called The Crypt. It's dark, gritty, and a wonderful subterranean shithole. There are five people hanging out, looking as permanent as herpes. I sit at the bar and get a beer. The old me wasn't much of a drinker. This me is learning.

A kid from school who looks forty, Bruce, drops down next to me and buys me a Screaming Orgasm. It sounds like something I'd like but tastes like ass, and Bruce spills most of his on his shirt. Bruce then spends way too long on a story about some two-legged dog he saw on the internet. I wonder which two legs, front or back or one of each, but he isn't sure.

Bruce eventually gives me a sales pitch, and I pull out my wallet. We then wander to the men's room and each swallow a pill that looks an awful lot like mouse poison.

Not so long ago, I was the varsity hockey captain, leading scorer and on the verge of a scholarship offer. Now, I could roll dead into the ditch and no one would notice the lack of me until the stench and vultures drew attention. Tonight, leaving the Crypt almost defeats me. I bang off the walls, monkey crawl, and after three tries and both hands working at it, manage the door handle. Staggering across the sidewalk, I look left, then right.

What do I need?

Chapter 3

CLEO:

He has a small birthmark behind his left ear. I sometimes stare at it in homeroom. It's shaped like a state. Illinois. I Googled it. But that was before, when his hair was short.

He's currently a mess splattered on the sidewalk. I squat down next to him, debate over leaving him there, but can't make myself do it. "C'mon, Sasquatch. Time to go."

I curl one arm around his waist and grab his bicep with my other hand. Besides our awkward wrestling match outside detention today, when he wiped the feel of me off on his jeans, I've never touched Shake LeCasse before. I'm not gonna tattoo the date on my boob or anything, but my heart jumps like a Mexican bean. I'm not disappointed. He feels warm and solid, and smells of beer and fabric softener. I know this because I take the time to sniff him.

Have you caught on yet? Pay attention. This is important. To me anyway. I didn't mean any of the nasty stuff I said to Shake earlier today. I'm like one of those people who's never owned a dog and gets all weird around them. Except, Shake is the dog in this scenario, and I've got no idea how to pet him.

Heaving upward, I battle to straighten my legs under his weight. There's a lot of him and not very much of me. To handle this much bulk, I should have rented a moving van. The dude is so ridiculously big, he probably beeps when he backs up. So when his arm lands across my shoulders, I dip forward quicker than a robin spotting a worm.

"Hey!"

He plops a massive hand on top of my head, and I'm suddenly wearing an octopus as a hat. For the second time today.

"Hey!" I try again.

He lifts up his right foot, waggles it, and says, "My feet are fucking huge."

I squeeze tighter. He's unsteady and OK, yes, he just feels really super good. I may never get this chance again and plan to make the most of it. I sort of wish I could crawl right inside him and burrow deep. I am the parasite. He is the healthy host.

"You know what they say about dudes with big feet," I tell him.

"Big shoes."

"Nope. Try again."

"Big toes."

"Sure."

"Big socks."

"Whatever."

"Big steps."

"Jesus," I snap. "Quit already!"

He points at my boots and says, "Arose your fleet."

His name is Shakespeare. He not only takes AP courses, but until this year, held a top ten spot in our senior class. So maybe this conversation is above my IQ level, because I don't know anything about my fleet or how to raise it. But when his hand drifts upward, pointing at my boobs, and the drunken mess says, "They're tiny as shit," I hope to hell he was asking about my feet. As in, "Are those your feet?"

"Your fleet can kiss my ass." I tug on him. "Let's go."

"Where?"

"Home."

He shakes his head. "Not what I need."

"Home, dude."

He gives me another slow head shake and suddenly drops to the pavement, landing on his ass. Since I'm hanging on, and still squeezing like my life depends on him, it turns into a whole Jack and Jill thing, with him breaking his crown and me tumbling after. My left elbow takes the worst of it.

I push away, trip over his ginormous fleet and nearly fall again. "Goddamnit! Screw this."

I only came to The Crypt to bitch out my brother for stealing my toothpaste, hoping he'd throw me a couple of bones. Shake can find his own way home. Or not. I don't give a shit. So what if Mr. Popularity spends all night on the cold sidewalk? So what if the cops pick him up? So what if he wears his jeans better than the Mona Lisa wears a smile? He is nothing but trouble in a pretty package and definitely out of my price range.

I groan and glance back.

Shake sits on the ground, forearms on his knees, head in hands, looking broken. Oh fuck a duck, why is he so stupid hot? Why do I feel responsible? I know the answer, but I'm still gonna fail this test. Sucker that I am, I trudge back.

"C'mon."

"Don't need your help," he slurs.

"Obviously. C'mon. We'll just walk." I finally get it. He can't go home. No place is home. I know all about that. "To Minnie's house."

He looks up at me. His eyes are the color of those blue freezie-pops I used to eat as a kid. They are wet and hopeless and it scares the hell out of me.

"To Grandmother's house we go," I singsong.

I even hold out my hand, palm up, as if I'm offering grain to a skittish horse. Then I wait. And wait. Trying not to scream, "hurry the hell up!" at a guy I'm trying to rescue. But I'm not known for my patience and the less witnesses the better. And c'mon, the spin cycle at the laundromat doesn't take this long. So I finally blurt, "Holy monkey balls, let's go already!"

This magic phrase gets him to his feet. Slowly to his feet, because despite my tugging, huffing and puffing, there is no rushing Shake LeCasse.

We walk together. He walks. I jog. At his full height, he bumps his head on the moon and I often get mistaken for a fifth grader. His gigantic steps weave from left to right, and I'm getting the hang of dog ownership. He's sort of like walking an oversized puppy determined to sniff everything. I'm glad he's wasted. He's not quite as scary, doesn't seem to mind being with me and probably won't remember tomorrow. I decide, before the end of the night, I will touch his hair.

"I had a screaming orgasm," he tells me.

"Impressive."

"With Bruce."

"Not cool, dude. Better keep that to yourself."

"Keep what?"

"What you said."

"What did I say?"

"About Bruce?" I try. "Your screaming orgasm?"

"Nope," he blurts. "Haven't gotten laid in months."

Color me surprised. I'll be tucking that little tidbit away for examination at a later date.

"How many months?" I fish, but he's distracted by cracks in the sidewalk, quantum physics or ... How the hell should I know what goes on inside that curly blonde head?

We walk the rest of the way in silence. His grandmother's street is lined with well-kept, cookie-cutter houses and dark windows. I smell flowering lilacs and hear the whispers of bats overhead.

Minnie starts her ovens in the middle of the night, has definitely left for the bakery already, so we're alone, and I'm relieved and anxious and a little sweaty, hoping I put on enough deodorant and definitely overthinking this. We're not walking down the aisle together.

Shake manages to get us in the front door, leads the way to the basement stairs and then stands too close while I swipe at the wall for the lightswitch. His breath hits the top of my head like something out of Jurassic Park. I catch the switch and trudge downward. Halfway down, the T-rex bangs his noggin off the low ceiling, bumbles into me and nearly sends us both face first to the bottom.

"Christ on a cracker!" I snarl. He mumbles something I don't understand, then dances awkwardly sideways. I dodge his flailing arms and hug myself.

I don't like basements. Even though this one smells nicely of laundry detergent, they are usually the happy home of big spiders.

There's boxes of his grandma's stuff pushed against the washer and dryer to make room for a twin mattress on the floor. In a corner is a plastic tote overflowing with guy clothes and crumpled shopping bags. Everything Shake owns is less than eight months old. Everything. He woke up one morning with the clothes on his back and whatever was in his pockets. I think of my own stuff and decide it is different for him. He had everything.

He sits on the edge of the bed, his knees bent up grasshopper-style. I check out his tangled navy blue sheets and feel slightly naughty, like I'm peeking into Santa's bag on the twenty-fourth. I should go. Before I do something crazy, maybe mess around with the wasted hottie. But that sounds more like a once-in-a-lifetime chance than a problem, so I linger.

Shake catches hold of my fingers and sort of smiles. His lips are full, a little pouty, and the stuff of high school girl legend. No lie, I once heard three cheerleaders spend an entire forty minute study hall talking about nothing but his mouth and his kisses. I was so fascinated, I considered taking notes. He also has straight white teeth. I remember him in seventh grade with braces, but haven't seen his smile in a really long time, and never for me.

"Shoes," I tell him.

He offers an enormous foot. Lucky me gets the job of plucking the knot outta his laces. I could row downstream using his sneaker as a canoe. Once his shoes are off, he suddenly stands, unzips and steps out of his jeans. His ten-mile-long legs are nicely muscled with just the right amount of blonde hair. He wears boxer briefs from Gap and his socks don't match. I may someday use this information to piss off Dripass-Deanna.

Snagging the hem of my shirt, he tugs me close and stares down. I look way up and wonder what he sees. I am not something he has ever bothered to look at before. I don't blame him. I am the social equivalent of pocket lint.

Fingering the chain looping my nose to ear, his lips tip crooked. "Weird," he says.

This is beyond weird. It's so far beyond weird, it should be studied under a microscope and tested for harmful side-effects. Racing pulse. Shortness of breath. Dizziness. A sudden urge to slide palms over naked abs.

"Shirt?" I say, testing my power, and he peels it off. I am suddenly a winning contestant on a game show. I bounce in place but stop myself from clapping. This is the best day ever. His naked chest is everything I've imagined. Maybe better. Definitely better. And I've devoted a lot of time to that mental picture. I'm happy to report, the reality offers up all sorts of flat muscles, interesting ridges and mysterious hollows I'd like to get to know better. It will take time, but I'm prepared to give my all to the job.

Shake drops onto the bed, reaches for me and hell yeah, I jump right on top. He's so long and lean and hard, he is my own personal liferaft. I'm definitely floating, wondering at the places this boy could take me. Which is silly, because this ride won't last long and at best, he'll abandon me on the shores of a bad reputation. At worst, well, I don't wanna think about the consequences I'm flirting with here.

I'm just stoked to finally get my hands in all that blonde hair. It's soft and thick and curls around my fingers like strands of pale July sunshine. I grab fistfuls, and he kisses me so deep, so fast, the world must be ending at any second.

His kiss doesn't last long enough. Ten years wouldn't be long enough, but he's in a big hurry. He pulls off my shirt, shorts and tights as if we're playing beat the clock. He's not careful. I worry he's going to rip everything, so I help him. Maybe I'm in a hurry too. I need to stay far ahead of the voice of reason.

Once he's peeled me down to my bra and panties, he rolls me over and tilts his head into a hungry kiss. His tongue sweeps into my mouth, and holy hallelujah, Shakespeare LeCasse takes my breath away. His mouth lives up to the hype, and even though I've never been a big fan of beer, the taste of it on his tongue is pure heaven. I want to make him my steady diet.

With one very large hand pressing at the small of my back, his other slips under my bra, finds what little treasure there is, then chases right down to dip fingertips under the waistband of my panties. We are officially entering uh-oh territory, and I'm without a map, all tangled up in the heat of his mouth and still tingling from the light tug he gave my nipple.

The guy is too blitzed to take off his own shoes, but he's got what feels like four extra hands and they're not wasting time. He's turned me into a complete melting mess, and I'm really tempted to just go with it. Except, he's got no idea it's me in his bed. He's horny. I'm here. I'm kind of OK with that, kind of not and can't decide who's taking advantage of who. Whom? Whatever. Him. Me. Match. Gasoline. I will get burned in the end.

"Wait, wait," I mumble against his lips. It takes a while to slow him down. I'm not convincing. "Wait." I push him onto his back and straddle him. I feel his hard-on through my panties and am tempted to make bad choices. Let's just say he's a very big boy in every way.

"Take it easy." I grab his wrists and pin them against the bed. If I let them roam again, I'll cave. "You've done enough damage for one night."

His eyes open slowly. They are so blue they remind me of pictures of faraway islands. I wish I could dive in and find him. This boy is lost.

I let myself kiss his lips. Just once more. Twice more. A third cuz I'm greedy and his mouth is really something. His full lower lip is tastier than a red velvet cupcake.

"I should go," I whisper. "You'll be OK?"

"No," he says back.

His eyes fall closed on a sigh. I slide my hands back into his curls and lay down on his chest so I can hear his heartbeat. Funny how they all sound the same. Even the broken ones.

Chapter 4

CLEO:

I never sleep for long stretches, so I wake early. I take a shower and use Shake's soap, shampoo and conditioner, and it's weird, rubbing his scent all over me. I spend more time at it than I should. I also help myself to his toothbrush and toothpaste. Seems like it should be OK after last night.

I make myself eggs and toast. There's cinnamon-sugar for the toast, milk for my coffee and nobody beats my ass for making noise. I'm sopping up yolk when I hear the sasquatch. Actually, I hear the alarm on his phone. I set it for him. And yes, I creeped his phone. He has eight billion unopened texts from Dripass-Deanna, various teammates and somebody named Rat. I resisted the temptation to delete all photos, texts, and evidence of Dripass. I didn't even send her a selfie of me curled up in bed with him. Mainly because no one can know I was here. But still, I deserve a medal.

His alarm rings and rings and rings, and then maybe he falls out of bed because there's a heavy thump. He is loud coming up the stairs and finally staggers into the kitchen, looking rumpled and unfairly adorable in his underwear.

Shake stops when he sees me. He is definitely surprised but not good-surprised. More like when you find a raccoon in your garbage. I think he'd like to shoo me away but is worried I might bite. He's right.

He stares, and I stare back.

I don't like having him between me and the door to the outside. He's so goddamn big. Hulk-sized. I brace myself for whatever he's planning to dish out, clutching my fork, but he just disappears into the bathroom and slams the door. The toilet flushes, water runs in the sink and the shower starts up. He drops something and grumbles.

I finally start breathing again. I finish mopping up the last little bit of runny yellow goodness with my toast, sip my coffee with my feet propped on the table and wonder if life can get any better. My answer comes out of the bathroom in a towel, and I think he should only wear towels from now on. His hair is wet and dripping. His eyes are patriotic. Very red white and blue. His skin is the color of death after its floated in a pond for a few days.

"What're you doing here?" His voice croaks a bit.

"You were too wrecked to get home last night."

He thinks this over. "So?"

"Brought you home. Duh." I singsong the last part, cuz I'm mature like that.

"You spent the night?"

"What was your first clue?"

"Why're you still here?"

"So you wouldn't feel cheap."

"You can go now."

"School, dude. We're both going."

"I'm going back to bed."

"Is that an invitation or should I just wait?"

He frowns, definitely pissed but with no idea how to get rid of me.

"That's my shirt," he points out.

"And your underwear."

"Jesus."

He drags back downstairs, thumps his head on the low ceiling, swears and comes back wearing a pair of jeans hanging loose and low off his hips, with a black T-shirt stretched thin across his broad shoulders. I catch the combined scent of deodorant and his freshly scrubbed skin and spit collects in my mouth. He didn't comb his hair. Somehow, it works for him.

He stands there, expecting something, but who the hell knows what. So I wait, then roll my hand and wait some more. This boy is slower than dialup internet. I finally snap, "What?"

He huffs and curses, snatches my plate and mug and drops them in the sink with the pan I used to fry my eggs. He squirts dish soap into a stream of water, washes and rinses, then sets everything in the strainer. When I say, "Hey Susie, are you almost done playing house?" he looks like he might crush my bones into dust with his bare hands.

"Hey, whatever, but I can't be late," I snipe, pretending I'm not the least little bit afraid of him and almost believing myself. "Mrs. K fucking hates me, and Sandersuck's favorite pastime is dicking me. And I just figured, after the shit show you put on yesterday, even your golden ass would need to be on time."

Mr. Pissy Pants is still unhappy, but we leave together. He wedges his hands in his pockets, stares at his feet, and his every step eats up seven miles of sidewalk. I trot to keep up. I feel like Dorothy. Maybe Toto. Did you ever notice Toto looks sort of mangey?

"When we get to the Wizard, don't forget to ask for a brain."

He gives me a weird look.

"You're the scarecrow," I say. I bet he's lost twenty pounds since last summer. "Eat a friggin sandwich."

I've got my flannel tied around my waist. I fish around in the pockets and score a half-smoked butt and lighter. I take it as a sign of a good day ahead.

The second I fire up, Shake barks, "Put that shit out."

"Piss off."

He stops walking. "I'm not smelling your stink all the way to school."

I walk backward, flick him off, then swing around and leave him behind. My goal was to get Shake LeCasse to school, but I'd just as soon not walk with him. Things are different in the light of day. We should not be seen together.

The buses have already unloaded by the time I get there. I toss my butt in the grass by the flagpole and thread through the front doors with the stragglers. The narrow infected-snot-colored halls of our small school are thick with bodies, ripe with smells and segregated into a cliche of cliques.

I'm at my locker, doing a whole lotta nothing, when Shake walks by. He's way taller than the rest of the inmates and easy to spot. Especially with a swarm of freshman girls trailing him, all giggling and taking turns reaching up to touch his blonde curls. I'm not sure if he doesn't notice or doesn't care.

Dripass-Deanna and Blair-Bitch put an end to it, flying up like a pair of storm troopers and shooting death glares until the freshies slink away.

Let me explain the awfulness that is Deanna Daniels. She has a koala face, Disney-princess hair, enormous boobs, a teeny-beanie waist and perfectly rounded, beach-ball ass. Her hobbies include tottering around on high heels like a hooker in training, jetting off on exotic vacations and getting everything she wants. Except Shake. I don't know if he counts, because she had him for a while.

I affectionately refer to her as Dripass because of a wonderful kindergarten memory.

Dripass corals Shake toward her locker, located exactly opposite the hall from mine, which offers me a daily gag fest. She now shoves her boobs against his arm, makes a pouty puss and says, "You never came over to work on the study guide yesterday."

I half-heartedly pretend to fish for something on the top shelf but am ninety percent invested in eavesdropping.

Shake doesn't answer or even look at her. His expression is one part annoyed and three parts zoned out. She doesn't take the hint and now starts yowling at him like a cat in heat. Any second now, I expect her to pee on him. "You know, I could pick you up in the morning, on my way to school. It's no problem. We can ride together. You're on my way."

No, he's not.

"I saw you," Blair-Bitch tells him. She is Deanna's minion, a total ho bag, and when I got her name for secret santa in fifth grade, she tossed my gift in the garbage. Without even opening it. Not that I'm bitter. But it wasn't easy stealing an elf ornament from the gift shop.

"It looked like you were walking to school with Cleo Lee," Blair-Bitch announces with a giggle. An actual giggle, which is only cute for two-year olds. "You might want to get a tetanus shot."

Can I just say I'm impressed by her three-syllable vocabulary, even if she did pronounce it, "tet-tit-anus."

"Oh Gross," announces Dripass. She is looking right at me, taking in the NY Dolls shirt I'm wearing. Shake's shirt. I watch the realization settle into her and wag my imaginary tail with pleasure. Her eyes are as toxic as drain cleaner.

I wave at her with my middle finger and mouth, "Suck it." Turning away, Bruce is there. Right there, because the moron has no respect for personal space. Or personal hygiene. I literally bounce off his smelly chest.

"Shit, Bruce."

"What's that about?"

"What?" I echo, but I know what.

"You got something going with Hemmie's brother?"

I roll my eyes so hard I almost knock myself down. "As if."

"I saw you last night. You left with him."

"You didn't see shit."

"Looked pretty friendly."

"You think a goat looks friendly. Which explains that rash of yours." I start away, but he jerks me back by the arm, and his breath could curdle milk.

"You got an itch," he tells me. "LeCasse ain't the one to scratch it."

I ignore the flare of panic and say, "I keep telling ya, scratching just makes it worse."

Chapter 5

SHAKE:

We are alphabetized for homeroom. Allie Kindle sits two rows from my seat. When I walk in, she yells, "There's my candy bar. Come melt in my mouth."

Everybody laughs. I turtle my head and ignore her. She is the only person, on my first day back to school, who treated me as if nothing happened. I appreciate it. I just can't tell her, can't encourage her, because she's already planning our wedding. No joke. She showed me samples for the bridesmaids dresses and asked if I like salmon better than blush. I'm not sure if salmon is a color or if blush is a type of fish.

I head towards my desk and realize Cleo Lee sits behind me in homeroom. How did I not know that?

She wears my NY Dolls shirt as a dress with a flannel shirt twisted into a belt. Her black tights are ripped at the knees. Her black boots are scuffed with holes. She's got a dozen studs in each ear and that chain-thing from nose to cartilage. I swear she chopped her hair with a weed whacker. She's also, according to her, wearing my underwear. Fan-fucking-tastic.

She watches me with her giant dark eyes as I take my seat. Has nobody told her the staring thing is friggin rude?

Thinking about her freaks me out. I wish I knew what I said and did with her last night. Can't really ask her and maybe better not to know. I kind of remember my hands on her tits, maybe even down her pants, which can't be right. I have not willingly touched another human being since the funeral.

Hold up. I had my hand on Cleo before detention, soaking the warmth out of her skin. But that was an accident, not gonna happen again and not worth thinking about.

When the bell rings, I bolt. I don't want Cleo talking to me, maybe saying some shit about last night. I don't want to explain to anybody how she ended up using my toothbrush this morning, and I know she did, cuz it was wet when I got to it. I can't take another reason for everybody to stare and talk about me.

The next few hours are brutal. I drag ass from class to class, doing the minimum, trying not to make eye contact or speak to anybody, working hard to avoid friends and teammates and just hoping to be invisible. I don't need their pity, their help, their fucking anything. I keep thinking that if I'm a big enough asshole, everybody will let me sink to the bottom in peace. But there's a reason I made friends with these people to begin with, and I'm not successful.

Deanna Daniels, aka double-D, grabs my arm on the way to World Government. She is so pretty, so familiar, it half kills me to look at her. She somehow spreads her perfume all over my shirt, and I'm stuck smelling her for the next hour, which gets me horny, angry and beyond miserable.

Sam and Terek catch me in the hall before Physics. They are my right and left wingers. Everyone called our line Shake, Rattle and Roll. I used to think that was cool. It's been eight months since I hit the ice, since I made time for them, and it seems like years.

"Hey, Dicknut!" Terek, aka Rat, yells at me, getting a warning cough from Mr. Frankel, the biology teacher. "Sorry, sorry," Rat offers, then immediately blurts, "How far did Sanderson crawl up yer ass for that shit with Westin?"

"Language," Mr. Frankel tries again but without much effort. He knows it's a lost cause.

"The Flats. Tonight," Sam cuts in. He's a little soft, looks way too much like Seth Rogen and wears knit hats all the time. He's got weird hair.

"Yeah?"

"Gonna be titties." Rat grins. He has a chipped tooth. Hit by a puck. His mom's been threatening to get it capped. "Adam scored his dad's tent, so I mean that literally." He cups his hands in front of his chest, just in case I didn't catch on. "Literal titties."

"Yeah?" I realize I've already said that. It's all I can manage.

"We could use you on the ice," Sam tells me. I know this. I've seen the scores. "Coach is so desperate, he bumped Drew to first line center."

"Every faceoff," Rat adds. "He basically takes a big steamy shit on the ice." He demonstrates with a squat then pretends to stick handle the imaginary offering.

"You coming back or what?" Sam presses.

I shrug. "Grades and shit."

They don't buy it but let me go. I'm ducking into French when Blair corners me and tells me Deanna is hurting for me. She says this as if my former girlfriend is the love child of Nelson Mandela and Mother Teresa. Since I heard Deanna and Adam have been hooking up, I figure she'll survive. I'm not worried about her.

I'm worried about me. Everything hurts, especially my ass, so I'm thinking I fell on it at some point the night before. I am in danger of vomiting at all times, and if one more person gives me the pity clap on the back, I'm gonna punt their nuts.

I drop into my seat in French class and close my eyes. My dad was born, raised, and lived in France until he married my mom. He spoke French to me and my brother most of the time, so this is the one class I still do pretty good in. Only pretty good, because I don't show up that often. And once again, I'm without textbook, notebook and pencil.

Since conjugating verbs is less interesting than hemorrhoids, I find the silver lining and am deep into a nap when I get called to the main office. I trudge down the hall, digging crud out of the corner of my eyes and wondering what the hell. I've made it to school two days in a row and even got here on time today. Since I feel like extreme suck, I should get extra credit.

Mrs. K shows me into Mrs. Sanderson's office. My high school principal sits behind her desk with pearls around her neck and a get-your-shit-together scowl on her face. Coach Mullen stands beside her and looks uncomfortable. The last time we spoke was at the funeral, when the whole team showed up in their jerseys.

I park my ass in a hard plastic chair, elbows on the armrests, hands clasped together and let my knee bounce.

"Hey Shake," Coach says.

I nod. I get it. Yesterday, I went after Mr. Westin. Sanderson figures I need an outlet for my aggression. Time to get me back on the ice. Principal Sanderson is starting to piss me off.

Don't get me wrong. I love hockey. I miss it. But I can't be part of a team anymore. I can't get revved up for a game that doesn't mean squat. I can't step on the ice when I know my parents never wanted me there. Enjoying it now, it's like they didn't matter, like I'm benefiting instead of suffering. Since suffering is the only thing I can do for them and less than I deserve, I devote all my time to it.

Coach says my name. My eyes flick to his. He then starts in about blowing off steam, the discipline of hard work, the support of teammates, yada, yada, yada, and more assorted horseshit.

I stare at a poster on the wall. There's a chicken and an egg, with some idiotic slogan about how being first is less important than being relevant, and it reminds me I'm starving. I'd eat either that chicken or the egg. Maybe there's a buck or two wadded up somewhere in my locker? Except the granola bars from the vending machine taste sorta like ground up toenails. Not that I've eaten toenails.

Whatever Cleo made for breakfast smelled amazing. Which reminds me … Cleo Lee is currently walking around school in my underwear. That knowledge shouldn't give me a chubby, especially sitting in the principal's office, but it's been eight months. A warm breeze gets me stiff. Did she find a clean pair of boxers? I need to do laundry.

I realize the office is silent. Coach has run out of words. Principal Sanderson is staring at me, frowning. She's looking at my hands, curled into white-knuckled fists on my thighs. I must've zoned out. Again. I've been doing that a lot lately. I guess it's better than going ape shit every time I get cornered, which is the alternative.

I force my fingers to loosen, stand up, look Coach in the eyes and say, "I'm not ready." I will never be ready, but I keep that to myself.

He says, "Good enough. When you are, you'll have a spot."

We shake hands and pretend we solved something. I head for the door. Sanderson sputters, "Hold on. Wait a minute, Shake. We're not done here."

I don't even slow down. This fuse has been lit, and I need to take myself away from innocent bystanders. Behind me, I hear Coach say, "Jesus, Vivian. Leave the kid alone. He'll figure it out."

Hurrying to get the hell out of there, I step into the hall outside the office and literally slam into Miss Jones. I probably outweigh her by ninety pounds so she staggers and flaps in a circle like a confused pigeon.

"Oh my goodness! Oh Shake. Well, you are the person I'm on my way to see." She laughs and adjusts her skirt, touches her glasses, smooths her hair. It doesn't matter. She always seems about to take flight.

I figure she is Act II. Yup, Sanderson is seriously pissing me off.

"I'm late," I mumble, pulling away.

"Wait, wait, wait." She plucks at my arm. "I know you've been skipping music." She waves her hands, shakes her head and her glasses slide back down her nose. "It's OK, at least for the time being. That's not, at this point, the issue. I was thinking maybe you'd like some time in the music room. You know, by yourself. I could, if you like, arrange that, the music room, for you."

My dad was a concert pianist. He traveled all over the world. He insisted my brother and I play, and hockey was only tolerated so long as it didn't interfere with piano.

I hate it. I've always hated it. My fingers are too big, my patience too short, and sitting at an instrument for hours at a time, bores me comatose. To be honest, the thought of playing piano is a grenade tossed into my cheerios.

"I know..." She closes her eyes and takes a deep breath. "You are at present without a piano and perhaps ..." Now she looks me in the eyes and says, "I believe, well I'm convinced that you NEED to play. You need it badly."

What do I need? I keep asking myself. Miss Jones thinks she has my answer.

She waits. She expects us to celebrate this epiphany together, maybe with the Snoopy dance. She smiles, squeezes her hands against her chest and squirms in preparation. My throat closes tighter than a pinched straw. The roar in my head is deafening, and it's clawing to get out.

I am without a piano because I am without everything. So thank you Miss Jones for bringing it up. Why not just stab me in the nuts with a knitting needle, because I'm now thinking about things I shouldn't. Things I've compressed into a tight ball and shoved to the very back corner of the vault. Like my dad teaching me to play, his long fingers resting over mine. Mom making up lyrics when my brother and I practiced, singing about artichoke sandwiches and missing socks and purple hedgehogs. And she liked to dance to piano music, always grabbing me or

Hemmie to partner her, insisting I dip her over my arm and calling me her sweet boy.

I experience the pain of being turned inside out. I am an open wound and can't catch my breath. Words I should not say rush into my mouth, hot and toxic, and I start gulping like a goldfish in a sandbox. Spots explode behind my eyes, and I'm either going to pass out or puke. This is definitely not what I need.

Chapter 6

CLEO:

I hold a tennis racquet in one hand, a cigarette in the other, and look lovely in my gym uniform. The stained tank and boxers, stolen from my brother, are the envy of all my friends. Friend. I have exactly one, and for unknown reasons, Allie thinks I'm cool.

I stand propped against the exterior bricks of the high school, outside auto shop. The bay doors are open and I hear guys inside, rotating tires or juggling mufflers or some shit.

In case the racquet didn't give it away, we are playing tennis in gym. Mostly, we take turns swatting the ball over the fence and fetching it as slowly as possible. I walked away from the courts when no one was paying attention. I've got about twenty minutes until I need to head back.

Before I ditched, I made sure to swat a ball at Dripass. Hit her right in the bubble butt. She accused me of doing it on purpose. Why else?

I drag deep off my cigarette and nearly choke when Shakespeare LeCasse steps through the bay doors. He's more surprising than spotting a unicorn running wild. He stands in a patch of sunlight with his back to me and kind of twitches. His fingers stretch and clench. His shoulders bunch. He breathes too fast and starts chanting, "fuck, fuck, fuck."

I wonder if I should slink away, when he suddenly bends over, hands on knees and pukes.

Gross.

When he's done, his body still heaves, and he makes a weird noise, like when you get soap in your eyes. I have no idea what to do but would rather avoid getting crushed by the angry giant. I take one step toward the bay doors and he wheels around and catches me there. Crap.

I've seen him look this pissed once before, at a hockey game. Some guy slashed him in the back of the knees. All of sudden the helmets and gloves flew off, and he pounded the poop out of that other guy.

He points at me, his eyes shiny and furious. Either that or he's on the verge of tears. His hand trembles. His blonde curls make a wild halo around his head. "Leave me alone."

I've learned how to take care of myself. I typically run or hide or both. When trapped, I fake it. So even though I nearly pee the boxer briefs I pinched from him, I snort a laugh and step up. "You leave me alone. I was here first."

The big, scary sasquatch leans over me and his shoulders grow wider with every breath. Holy shitbirds. I might bop him with the tennis racquet.

Instead I say, "You can touch my titties if you want. That made you happy last night."

He stares at me for a really long time and fear makes me shiver. Then he tips his head back and mangles a laugh. There's a touch of crazy in that laugh, and I think he's hiding a sob underneath it. I'm ready to hightail it when he wraps his arms around himself, flops against the brick wall and slides down into a crouch.

Hyper aware of the sound of his breath, the heat rolling off him, and his amazing smell that should be bottled and sold, I stay put, finish my cigarette and flick the butt. I need to head back to gym, but I don't. I stand beside a boy who's crumpled up like an empty wrapper and wonder what to do about him. It might help to say something but what? We are so different, I might as well walk on all fours.

Except for his brother. We have Hemmie in common. I shouldn't tell him that, can't tell him the truth, so we say a whole lot of nothing to each other. When the bell rings, we drift away.

Chapter 7

CLEO:

I see Shake again in detention after school. He walks in and the room temperature rises by ten degrees. I immediately feel flushed and fidgety. He's a living, breathing ray of sunlight, and I'm an ant under a magnifying glass.

Allie welcomes him with an old song by the Divinyls, singing about touching herself at such volume there should be an orchestra to accompany her. Her voice may crack windows in neighboring states. I don't know why she shouts, but she has no other level. The school has tested her hearing seven ways from Sunday. I think they should test her mom's hearing.

Schwartzmeyer peeks above his newspaper. "Allie, please desist with the singing."

"I'm doing my best. I swear," she tells him. "But it's dangerous to hold it in too long."

"That's pissing," I tell her.

"For me, both singing and pissing are bodily functions."

"And better without an audience."

She nudges me, nearly knocks me out of my chair, then points at Shake and lowers her voice so only people in Canada can share this secret. "My catnip looks bad."

Her catnip looks worse than bad. I've seen roadkill look happier.

"I was hoping we could figure out our honeymoon destination," she tells me.

I shrug. "I hear Niagara Falls is nice."

"You know that guy Bruce?" Shake suddenly asks.

It takes me a second to realize he's not only talking but directing his question at me. This is new.

"That guy Bruce," he repeats.

"He's a dickweed."

"Where can I find him?"

Shake is a mess. Bruce is a dealer. I do the math. "Can't help you."

"Can't or won't?"

"Nothing in it for me."

He stares at me for a long moment, but I know he's done. The walls are right back in place, shutting him inside a silent box where no one can reach him.

I remember when he owned this school. His smile, his voice, his laughter was everywhere, and everybody wanted to be near him. He was that rare specimen who stands on top of the popularity heap without stepping on anybody to get there. Now, he folds his arms on the desktop and drops his head. He's such a lost puppy I almost change my mind. But it's not like Bruce is hard to find. If he really wants to wreck himself, he'll get there without me leading the way.

Then Allie squeezes her generous self into the chair in front of his desk and taps him. I should have seen this coming.

"Don't," I tell her. But she's not listening. Allie likes to help people. Doesn't matter if she's helping them destroy themselves. And this is Shakespeare LeCasse, a guy she's worshipped since middle school. If he wants to jump off the roof, she'll hold the elevator just to make him happy.

He peers up through his hair.

"Whaddaya need?" she asks him.

"What do I need?" He takes a breath and his eyes roll up, as if the question is going to be on the final exam. "What do I need?"

Allie nods at him. I huff, look away and sit on my hands so I don't do something stupid. Like grab this idiot boy by the collar and shake him.

"Anything. I'm a, I'm a, ah." His voice cracks, and his eyes stretch around the edges, like he's so filled up with bad shit, he's about to split wide open. He is painful to witness, and I don't want to be here any longer.

"No worries," Allie chirps.

She carries a purse the size of a lawn and leaf bag. Every now and then her mom goes a little nuts and donates all their stuff to the Salvation Army, so Allie keeps everything she cares about with her at all times.

She stacks a snorkel mask on the desk with a hair brush, slippers and a pair of scissors. She shouts "Aha," as she unearths a baggie of assorted pills. As I said, her mother goes a little nuts so there's lots of meds around. Since mom tends to over medicate, Allie hoards them. I can't explain the snorkel mask.

"Zoloft, Paxil, Prozac, Trazodone," she lists them off. "I hope you're not picky about expiration dates."

I glance at Schwartzmeyer. He's hiding behind his newspaper, practicing for his retirement, when his transformation into a soulless robot will be complete. What an assturd.

"Allie don't," I hiss. My intervention is more pointless than tightening my shoe laces before throwing myself in front of a speeding train.

"Here!" she says. "Try this one."

Shake doesn't ask what it is. He swallows the pill and plants his forehead on the desk. What a colossal disappointment. He pisses me off. Allie pisses me off. Schwartzmeyer pisses me off. Hangnails, billboards, and people who budge in line piss me off, but mainly it's this situation right here.

Shakespeare LeCasse is not supposed to be in detention with girls like Allie and me. He's not supposed to poison himself, sabotage his future and end up a piece-of-shit like every other guy I know. I just can't decide how much of his downfall is my fault.

Chapter 8

SHAKE:

Whatever Allie gives me, mellows me. I sleep through detention and wake up hollow, as if I've been scooped out like a Halloween pumpkin. Not the greatest feeling but I'll take it.

I should thank Allie, but as shitty as it is, I just want to get away from her and Cleo. We seem to be on the verge of making friends, and I've done my best to get rid of those.

I duck out and wander over town. I debate grabbing a burger or something, but I'm too lazy, too broke and my stomach is risky.

I pick up bread and eggs at the grocery store to replace what Cleo ate and find out eggs come in different sizes. I wonder if it has something to do with the size of the chickens. The giant eggs cost more, so I settle with medium eggs, then walk to the drugstore. I am at the counter, buying deodorant, shampoo and razors, when the bell over the door jingles. The old guy behind the register points at the door and yells. "You don't come in here! One more step, I call the cops."

"That's bullshit." It's Cleo.

"Your choice." The guy holds up his phone.

"Go blow yourself." She flicks him off two-handed, and the door shuts behind her with another cheerful jingle.

"Lovely," the guy mutters. "Sorry about that."

He rings me up, hands me my change, and the smile slides straight off his face. He's suddenly recognized me. I used to hit him up every year to sponsor the hockey team. He'll probably tell his wife about me over dinner tonight. They'll feel shitty for a few minutes, feel lucky for a few, then watch TV until bedtime.

"You take care, son."

I nod, snatch my bag and clench my teeth so tight my ears pop. When I push through the jingle of the door, Cleo is waiting, leaning against the building, smoking a little stub of a cigarette. Why is she suddenly everywhere? I wonder if she followed me.

"I need toothpaste," she tells me.

"Great to know."

"Travel size."

I just look at her.

"You owe me, Sasquatch. I got you home last night."

I don't want to think about last night. Not the least little bit. I don't know what the hell happened, but I'm treating it like Vegas.

"Go away," I tell her.

She steps in front of me and says, "Is it a lot of work being such a giant dick? Like, do you take special classes? Practice in the mirror? Wear a rubber on your head? Cuz as a giant dick, you're downright impressive. Maybe even one of the biggest dicks I've ever met. Can I get your autograph?"

I tower over her, give her my meanest scowl and lower my voice, "Get lost."

"Is this when I wet myself because I'm so scared?" She even makes her eyes all big and shivers with her hands up. All ninety pounds of her and I consider just trampling her, but she's like one of those little ankle-biting dogs and won't quit. I settle for an eye roll and head back inside.

To the guy behind the counter, I mumble, "Forgot something." Within three minutes, I'm back on the sidewalk.

I hold out the bag, wait for Cleo to reach, then jerk it upward. She jumps, but I'm a head taller than the rest of the population and she's not allowed on the big girl rides at the amusement park. I enjoy watching her jump. I'm acting like a dick BECAUSE she accused me of being one. I don't know what that says about me.

When she tries to kick me, I shield my junk and toss her the bag. "You owe me a dollar and fifty seven cents."

She snags the toothpaste and drops the plastic bag on the ground. "I said travel size. I can't hide this. Rex'll steal it in five fucking seconds."

"You're welcome." I scoop up the bag. "You owe me a buck and change. Pay me and go away."

"Dude, I'm tapped." She wiggles her fingers. "There's a reason that assbag doesn't want me in his store."

Who is this chick? What have I done to snag her attention? How do I get rid of her?

I walk away. She trots after me. She carries a brown lunch bag. It would almost be worth making nice if she's got food in it. My stomach growls just thinking about it.

I finally say, "I want my shirt back."

It's the only shirt I've had longer than eight months. It's the shirt I had on the night IT happened, and I can't bring myself to wear it or throw it away. She must have dug to the bottom of my everything to find it. Seeing her in it kills me a little bit.

"C'mon." Cleo jogs ahead, glances back and says, "Or not. Your choice, Sasquatch. I'll just keep your crappy shirt."

I follow her along Main Street. Every time I get close to catching up, she jogs ahead. Since I refuse to play tag with her, I trail ten feet behind, like her personal stalker, all the way back to the grocery store. I am that desperate to get my shirt back.

She circles around to the rear parking lot, beyond the dumpster, onto a sketchy dirt path leading into the woods. I hesitate for half a second, but what am I worried about?

She leads me through waist-high weeds, between scrub trees, along a scuffed trail that takes us all the way down to the water. The creek is wide and mostly shallow here. If it rains enough, we get some minor rapids, and I've floated down a few times in a tube. On the opposite bank I see the elementary school roof above the trees. On this side, there's thorn bushes, some giant rocks and a bunch of empty bottles and old wrappers. I'm not impressed.

I spread my hands. "So?"

Cleo drops her flannel on the ground and peels off my NY Dolls shirt. She stands in my underwear, which is way too big for her, ripped tights, wrecked boots and a used-to-be-white bra held together by at least three safety pins. Not quite the matching lacey bits Deanna wears, but since there's tits, I'm interested.

Probably better not to stare at her, but I can't seem to stop. I see the hint of her nipples through the bra and realize she's freezing cold. I think that, then wonder what she'd feel like under my hands. I sort of remember from last night and picture wrestling around with her, which starts my dick twitching, so I bite the inside of my mouth hard enough to squelch it.

Cleo holds out my shirt. "Want your underwear?"

"What? No!" I snag the shirt.

She smirks, then picks up her flannel and shrugs it on. A few minutes go by with neither of us saying anything. I don't know how to bail.

She seems to be thinking something over, then finally asks, "Wanna see something?"

Imagining what else there might be to see, I'm strangely eager.

She rattles the brown bag then sets it down on the ground and pulls out a muffin. I recognize it as an apple pecan muffin from Grandma's bakery and wonder how she got it. They're expensive. I hope she's going to give it to me.

Cleo breaks it into pieces and a pair of mangy dogs inch out of the brush. Then another and another and some cats. An orange tabby has a stub of a tail. A black one is missing an eye and has the meow of a lifelong smoker. The dogs are so skinny, I could play their ribs like xylophones, and they smell bad. It's the world's ugliest petting zoo.

I sit on a big rock and watch. The animals are not happy with me. They look from me to the food but eventually ease up to Cleo.

She crouches down and pets and whispers and smiles. This is a new version of Cleo, but I don't know what's different.

"This is Lucy," she introduces a cat. "And Charlie, Violet, Sally." She names each one, but I'm not keeping track or paying attention to the animals. I'm watching her. I've never noticed how cute she is before. She has a pointy little chin, sorta puffy lips and those ginormous eyes that make her look like she should have wings and carry a wand. I imagine her pixie dust like acid rain, scorching everything in her path.

She stuffs a piece of muffin in her mouth with a groan that catches my attention, then feeds the dogs and cats the rest. I wonder what else she has in the bag, consider getting in line, and would really like to hear her make that throaty, sexy sound again.

"Different ones show up all the time," she tells me and her lips curl up at the corners.

This version is Happy Cleo. Her smile changes her into somebody almost tolerable.

"You do this a lot?"

"When I can scrounge food for them."

I nod, rub at the back of my neck and wait a pair of seconds. "How come you got me home last night?"

"I wanted your underwear."

"Why'd you stay over?"

She looks at me with hard eyes. "So I'd have something to write about it in my diary."

"Why'd you stay, Cleo?"

"Jay-zus, get over it already. It was late. I was tired, didn't feel like walking back and what of it? Did you miss a period or something? Cuz I promise, your cherry is safe."

Did I say she was cute? My mistake. She is nothing but a test of my temper. I blow a breath and hear my voice sharpen. "Not why I'm asking."

She upends the bag so the crumbs spill on the ground, gives a last round of ear scratches and gets to her feet. Her flannel is just long enough to hide my stolen underwear.

"Cleo?"

She looks at me. It's not easy but I tell her, "Thanks. For helping me out."

She hesitates a beat then flips me off before walking away.

Chapter 9

SHAKE:

I am heading to Grandma's, carrying my NY Dolls shirt and bag from the pharmacy, when Rat's Ford Fiesta rumbles up next to me. He calls it The Twat. The Twat is the ugliest car on the planet and sheds rust worse than dandruff.

Rat is obnoxious on a horn that sounds like moose farts. Sam, in the passenger seat, yells, "Get in fucktard."

I hesitate, panic a little but can't come up with a way out. How bad can it be? So I cram in the backseat with Drew and this kid named Thad, who is kind of a dick, and they both bitch over me taking up too much seat. One of them smells like a twelve-year-old girl. I sniff and tilt my head toward Thad then Drew.

"It's Rat." Sam swivels to hook an arm over his seat and look into the back. "He smells like Kotex with wings."

"It's Lavender dude," Rat cuts in. "Got hired at the mall. I sell lotions and potions to hot moms."

"Why?" Drew wants to know.

"Pay attention, Shit-for-brains. Hot moms. They wanna smell like lavender."

"So why do you smell like Cinderella's puss?" Thad snarks.

"Just my dick. And it's LAV-EN-DER, dude. Like fucken catnip, I'm telling ya." He glances in the rearview. "Hey Thad, you seen my flippies?"

"How the hell would I know where your friggin shoes are?"

"Cuz I left 'em under your mamma's bed last night."

They all laugh. I don't. The whole car goes quiet.

Sam smacks Rat across the back of the head and growls, "Dude, not cool."

He ducks and says, "Aw, shit man, my bad."

"Don't worry about it," I mumble. I don't care if they razz on each other's mothers. I'm not some sensitive wuss. I just don't know how to laugh anymore.

It's awkward for the whole drive to the Flats.

The Flats is what it sounds like. A big flat spot. The Twat bounces and bottoms out over a dirt track. It take us through cornfields and up to a worn patch of grass on a hill. Cars are parked at angles, and there's probably fifteen kids here already, standing around a fire with music blasting. The beauty of the Flats is no houses for miles in any direction.

We unload two cases of beer from the trunk and each grab a bottle. The beer is warm. The night is chilly. The mosquitos are hungry and find me delicious. It never used to bother me.

Nights at the Flats are a big deal. Back when I cared, my friends and I planned these things weeks in advance, trying to lay hands on tents, beer, and girls. Not necessarily in that order, and for me, I had to work around my parents, which meant coming up with a believable lie. I usually got busted and ended up grounded. I was grounded that night, eight months ago, so I should have been home to change what happened, but I wasn't.

I dangle a bottle from my fingertips, lean against the Twat with one foot hooked over the other and am anxious to leave. I haven't hung out since last summer, and I'm the elephant at the party. Everybody's eyeballing me, trading whispers, and nobody dares have too much fun. Not with me here.

My wingers flank me. Rat stands on my right, forever smiling and showing off his chipped tooth. Sam's on the other side, wearing his knit hat, and maybe he's the smart one.

It's too early in the season for this. I'm shivering but can't make myself go near the bonfire. Bad enough watching smoke twist into the sky, hearing the pop of wood burning, but I can smell it too. The smell reaches right down into my gut and rearranges things.

"When're you back in Westin's class?" Sam wants to know.

"I'm out for good. I spend the period in the main office."

"Gonna hurt your GPA."

I don't tell him my GPA cannot be hurt. It's dead, buried and grass is growing over it.

"Man, Westin's a total tit-wad," Rat says on a laugh then touches his nose. "And you're a friggin gorilla. Caught your elbow and I've been snotting blood ever since."

I should apologize. I should thank them. If they hadn't grabbed me, I'd be in a world of shit right now. If nobody stopped me, I might still be pounding Mr. Westin. But I can't bring myself to say anything to the two guys who fed me countless goals, held my head when I puked tequila and carried my brother's casket.

The fire shoots up a handful of sparks, and I flinch back. I am right on the verge. Using a swallow of beer, I try to wash everything down.

"How's living with Grandma?" Sam asks.

I shrug.

He nods. I wish he'd stop trying so hard.

"You know you can crash with me," he says. "It's cool with my parents. My sister's away at school. You can have her room. We'll hang out and shit."

I look over at Rat. "How bout you? Can I bunk in Tia's room?"

"If you go anywhere near my sister, I will cut off your testicles and feed them to Sam."

Rat has a dog named Sam, which makes things interesting. I never know if he's talking about the Sam standing next to me or Sam the dog.

"Seriously, Shake," the Sam standing next to me keeps pushing.

"I'm good," I tell him.

"No you're not." He shakes his head, tips his beer to his lips. We say nothing for a while. Then Sam tells me, "I got accepted at Niagara."

I nod and mumble, "Cool."

"You apply anywhere? Done anything?"

I don't answer.

"For fuck's sake, Shake," Sam blurts. "Get back on the ice. Show up at school. Hang out. Do something!"

I can't come up with anything to say.

He's heated. His eyes glare, and he rocks from toes to heels. "Coach talked to you, right?"

I manage another nod.

"Shit man, we're your teammates," Sam growls. "We got your back. Always have. You say the word, we do it. Whatever you need."

There it is again. *What do I need?*

Sam waits a second then says, "What the hell are you doing, hanging out at the Crypt with those dirtbags? Fucken Bruce and Rex? Seriously? And Blair saw you cozied up with Cleo friggin Lee."

"She's hot," Rat blurts then holds up his hands, grinning. "Hey man, I'm just saying. I bet she bangs like a rabid wolverine."

Sam shakes his head. "Jesus Rat."

"I'm tellin' ya dude, take a moment to appreciate that little heart-shaped ass for the sake of the spank bank. I've got her ranked fourth all time." Glancing at me, Rat tips his chin and asks, "You tap that yet?"

Before I can say anything, he elbows me in the ribs and calls out, "Hey Blair! Blair!"

Deanna, Blair and some other girls are dancing to a song I don't recognize, hips rolling, hair swinging, putting on a show for the clueless dudes standing around watching them.

Blair flounces up to us. "What?"

Rat has capped his index finger with the stub of a hot dog. "Can I stick my weenie in your buns?"

"Oh gross!" she shrieks, but she's smiling. "What are you, like ten?"

"Are we talking inches or years?" Rat is both juvenile and disgusting, which makes him awesome.

"LeCasse, where you been?" Thad steps in front of me. Since we rode here together and I'm still standing next to the Twat, I don't feel the need to answer.

"You see this?" He's wearing his jersey. He pinches the fabric and stretches it sideways. "Senior year man, and we barely made the playoffs."

Since freshman year, we've been expected to win states as seniors. This was our year. Last summer, it was all coming together. But I don't even own skates anymore.

Rat snags Thad's arm. "Lay off dude."

"Nah man." Thad shakes him off. "Fucken captain of the team and where's he been? You seen him around?"

"He's right here," Rat tries again.

"Bullshit."

"Not bullshit. Look. He's literally standing right here."

"He bailed on us."

Thad is hammered. He's a dick at best, but the thing is, he's right. Everybody else has been thinking it. Nobody's had the balls to say it.

"Brothers," Thad tells me, leaning in so close a dot of spit hits my cheek. "Fucking bros, man."

I shove him. "You're not my fucken brother."

"Whoa," Rat cuts in, one hand on Thad, one on me. "You're both pretty. Play nice."

I point at Thad. "Not my fucken brother."

"C'mon Shake," Sam wedges between us. "Not here. Not now. Get your shit together."

"Whatever," I say. I reach through the open window of the Twat and snag my shirt and bag of deodorant. Somewhere along the way, I lost the bread and eggs. "I'll catch you guys later."

I step away and Rat follows.

"Thad's a prick," he tells me. "Forget him."

"Doesn't matter." I trudge through damp grass, pissed about my sneakers getting wet, pissed at Thad, just plain pissed over nothing and everything.

"You're hanging out, right?" Rat keeps right on trying. The dude's been right with me since mosquito level hockey. "C'mon man. We'll get loosened up, have some laughs and shit."

"Next time."

"There's no designated D. Nobody's driving."

"I'll walk."

"Dude, it's like ten friggin miles."

I set my beer on the ground, wave him off and walk away.

"Shake!" Deanna chases up to me. "Shake, wait up." She runs like a Baywatch chick. All the right things jiggle and she knows it.   "Where are you going?"

"I can't be here, Dea."

"Wait a sec." She tugs at me until I stop and face her. Her shirt is tight and transparent and she's cold. She's also deep into the wine coolers, smells like bonfire, and I can't stand to be near her.

"What about me?" She looks up with soft eyes. Her hands slide up my chest.

"Not now, OK?"

"You never call or answer my texts. Everybody's asking me. I don't know what to tell them." Her voice is riding a wave of emotion and I'm not sure where we're headed, but I know I don't want to go there.

"What about me, Shake?" she whines. "Don't you miss hanging out with me?"

I shrug and step backward. She moves in, hands on again.

"Just ..." The words stick in my throat and I have to try again. "I gotta go."

I drop my hands to her waist, thinking to push her away, but she tilts her head and whispers, "No worries, Shake. I know you're messed up, but I can help. We'll crawl in the backseat and forget about everybody else. Maybe you can be happy for a little while."

I hate being this asshole guy. If I could just wipe all the shit from my head, maybe I could pretend to be me again. Maybe I could feel good without feeling guilty.

I wrap my arms around her. She lifts up on tiptoe, and I sink down, kiss her, and we fit together the way we always did. All I want to do is hold her for a little while. Except she smells like fire. It's all over her. I taste it. And it takes me back.

I remember running down the street, sneakers slapping pavement, sirens wailing, breath tearing from my overworked lungs. I see red lights flashing, a thick plume of smoke and a huge orange glow. Then I smell my whole world burning and start screaming. But whatever I imagine in that moment, the reality is so much worse.

What do I need? To forget.

I am suddenly squeezing my skull in my hands. There is this terrible sound, like a werewolf getting castrated, and it's coming from my mouth. It's coming from my toes and spewing over everybody and everything. The whole party is coated in my misery.

Shit. Shit. Shit.

They all look at me, horrified by me. This is why my mouth stays shut. This is why I stay away. I don't fit with these people anymore.

I see Deanna sitting on the ground, looking scared, and reach toward her. "Did I?"

I sense something coming at me. Something big and fast. I swing around and Adam punches me in the face.

Chapter 10

CLEO:

I don't mind having nothing to do. It just sucks having nowhere to go. And it's super cold out. So I walk and shiver and try not to get seen.

I head downtown, but with the cops crawling Main Street, I move on to the park. It's dark and empty, so I sit in the swings, smoke a cigarette and stare at the stars. I don't give a flying shit about stars, and they sure as shit don't give a flying shit about me. But I make wishes anyway.

I wish it was warm enough to sleep outside. I wish Allie's mom wasn't psycho again, so I could crash there. I wish a lot of things, just to waste time, but when my fingers go numb, I've got no choice. I make my way to the yellow house, hoping it's late enough.

I stare at the front door for a second, working up the courage. It's the only way in, the only way out. There's a big crack down the middle of it. Anybody who knocks here is desperate enough to pound the shit out of that door.

I open it just wide enough to slip inside without squeaking the hinges, then wait a few seconds, holding my breath. The living room is off to the right, kitchen up ahead. I hear the TV turned loud. There's one path to my bedroom, and I'm exposed as I inch past the living room. My heart bubbles right into my throat, but I make it into the kitchen. I'm hungry. That's nothing new, but I know better than to search for something to eat.

My room is ten steps away. Nine. Eight.

"Hey!"

I freeze at the sound of his voice.

"Cleo!"

I don't move.

"You gonna make me come get you?"

I peel my feet off the sticky linoleum. My boots weigh a thousand pounds, but I force them to the edge of the living room, to where the carpet starts. The brown shag is bleached yellow where the sun hits it, rubbed bald in spots and hides more food than I could ever scrounge from the kitchen cupboards. The vacuum cleaner broke over a year ago.

Randy is a fungus growing in an orange armchair the same color as his hair. Beer cans pile at his feet. An ashtray overflows by his hand. There's burns, butts and ash circling his perimeter. He's mom's boyfriend, even though she took off three months ago. She'll find her way back. She always does. Most boyfriends don't stick it out, and I keep waiting for this jerkwad to get the hint.

"Where you been?" He holds a beer and a cigarette in the same hand, his version of multi-tasking, and points them at me.

"Just out."

"I fucken know that. Where?"

Bruce snickers. He's a lump on the couch with my brother. There's a bong on the coffee table and the whole place smells like weed, somebody's burp, and litter box. We've never owned a cat.

"Downtown."

"Whatcha got there?"

I hold up Shake's grocery bag. "Eggs and bread."

He stares at me, eyes squinty and bloodshot, lips curled inward, and finally says, "Tell me."

"Tell you what?"

"What the fuck you're doing with Hemmie's kid brother."

I glance at Bruce. He looks away. That shit.

"What about him?"

"I warned you to stay the hell away from him. Thought I made it crystal."

I squirm at the memory, fear bitter on my tongue, but say nothing. I look to Rex. He's totally wasted, eyes glassy, mouth hanging open, and he's never much help anyway. So I wait, hoping, hoping, hoping Randy forgets me. He turns back to the TV. There's explosions, tires screeching, gun blasts. Bruce laughs and says, "Did you see that?" What a moron.

I ease backward.

Randy points at me again. "I asked you a question."

I don't know the question. I panic and my voice rises into a squeak. "What?"

"What's with the LeCasse kid?"

I shake my head. "It's nothing."

He pushes to his feet. I trip backwards. He drops the beer, lets it spill on the rug and lunges across the living room, grinding potato chips under his shoes. "Stay away from that kid. How many times do I gotta say it?"

"Nothing's going on."

"Where'd you go last night?"

"Nowhere."

"Nowhere? Is that what you fucken said? You sure as shit weren't here."

He doesn't give a stinky crap where I was. Probably didn't notice until that dinglebutt Bruce told him. This is all about Shake.

"I didn't tell him nothing," I blurt. "I swear."

I watch Randy's hands, but he's too fast. He slams a flat palm into my chest, and I fly backward, landing on my ass. I'm still catching my breath when he's on me, his fingers latching onto my left wrist and dragging me up. I drop the eggs and bread and claw at his grip, even when his other hand squeezes the back of my neck. The heat and smoke of his cigarette are right against my cheek as he drags me across the linoleum.

Chapter 11

SHAKE:

After the fight with Adam, no one is begging me to stay at the Flats. It's a long-ass walk back to town, over two hours, and my brain chews itself down to a bloody nub.

I swing by the Crypt, feeling desperate. Since neither Rex or Bruce are around, I can't get in and can't buy anything to round off my edges. I have no idea where Allie lives but wouldn't go there anyway. She might measure me for my tuxedo.

I end up where I always end up. The night is empty and weirdly quiet, like maybe it's been waiting for me. I stand on the sidewalk in front of 14532 Willow Drive. There is not much to see. The house and garage are gone. Everything collapsed into the basement and most of the debris has been hauled away. Twisted, dead trees mark the edge of the property. There is no grass. The ground is scorched and nothing grows.

When the fire started, my family and everybody else on Willow Drive was asleep. Nobody reported it for a long time. The fire burned so hot, it melted the tires off the neighbor's car.

I step into the road and precisely dissect the center line with my sneakers. The blind curve is off to my right. I close my eyes and wait for it. A thrill of anticipation tickles my gut. Balancing on this stripe of yellow paint is as close as I get to peace.

What do I need? Peace. Please, please, please let me find just a little bit of fucking peace.

I hear clunky footsteps.

I know those steps. She sounds like she's playing a game of whack-a-mole with her heavy boots. She's still wearing the ugly flannel. The tights are gone. Cleo Lee stands on the sidewalk, her back to me, and stares at my yard as if it hypnotizes her.

I watch for a second, but she's not moving. So I march right up on her. "What're you doing?"

She jumps and spins around with a thin shriek.

"Why're you showing up everywhere?" My voice is way too loud for this quiet neighborhood, but I don't like her here.

She tucks her chin and says nothing.

"Hey!" I say it sharp and regret it. She's a miniature girl, and I am a giant bully.

I expect her to flick me off, but she just hugs herself, shivers like a wet mouse and glares up at me with bottomless eyes. What the hell am I doing?

I stalk away, thinking about the gawkers. People showed up for days after the fire, piling up flowers and lighting candles. People who wanted a piece of the misery, to somehow insert themselves into it and take away something they lack. People who don't know jackshit about it.

I glance back at Cleo, watch her shake in her dumbass boots, and I suddenly don't want to be alone. "I'm freezing my nuts just looking at you," I tell her. "C'mon."

She falls into step beside me and jogs to keep pace. I shorten my steps by half, and it takes twice as long to make it to my grandma's. It must take her forever to get anywhere.

I lead her inside the house, then don't know what to do with her. She smells weird. Everything about Cleo Lee is weird. So why did I bring her here? Maybe because she is so frustrating, she makes me forget the insanity in my head. Kind of like slamming a hand in the car door to get over an amputated toe.

We stand in stupid silence way too long.

"I need a shower," she announces.

I nod and say, "OK. Yeah," because I am the king of cool. Christ, to be anymore pathetic I'd need to hold out a cup and beg her for spare change.

"Can I have that?" she asks, pointing.

I'm still holding the NY Dolls shirt and bag from the pharmacy. I hand them over, and she leaves me standing like a goober in Grandma's living room. She also leaves the bathroom door open.

I hear the shower. Worse, I picture her in it. I wonder if the open door is an invitation and then wonder what the hell to do about it. So I pace slow laps around the kitchen table.

Cleo Lee is not my type. She's all hard edges and mean. Then I remember what Rat said, about the rabid wolverine, and I can't think about much else.

I stop pacing. I listen to the quiet and realize the shower quit. My feet move before I think about it.

I skid into the bathroom doorway. I'm in such a hurry I bonk off the frame, hurt my shoulder and stagger sideways. I am out of practice and coming off as smooth as road rash on a porcupine's ass. Down boy, I tell myself. Then I get a glimpse of her and my tongue rolls right out of my mouth.

Cleo's wrapped in a yellow towel, dark hair wet and spiky. Her skin is flushed and her mouth is a pink bud that would look perfect sucking me off. No hard edges anywhere.

This is another new version of Cleo. Soft Cleo is not the girl I know from school and not the one who feeds strays by the creek. I hope this version is horny. Since she's naked under the towel, I'm feeling pretty good about my odds until she says, "Got any food?"

Soft Cleo is hungry.

"Um sure."

There are small bruises the color of ripe plums on her shoulders and throat. They match the fading black beneath her eye. Since that's something I'd talk over with my mom, I'm not going there. I can't handle anymore, can't afford to give a shit. So I spin around and abandon her in the bathroom.

I can feed her. That's all. That's it. I rifle Grandma's cupboards for dusty stuff and come up with a box of Pop Tarts that probably expired about the time I learned to walk. I add a bag of marshmallows and a can of chickpeas. I could come up with a more disgusting combination, but not without a lot of effort and imagination.

I consider grabbing something better. My grandmother's kitchen is crammed with everything from junk food and microwave dinners to fruit and granola. I could replace whatever tomorrow, but Cleo disrupts my thoughts. She steps out of the bathroom, wearing my T-shirt right down to her knees. She looks so tasty, I'm only capable of staring and breathing heavy.

Dropping her flannel and stuff on the floor, she proves there's nothing under the shirt, then sits cross-legged on the chair. I'm suddenly a little overheated. And impressed. No way could I sit like that.

"You look like shit." She tears into the box of Pop Tarts, wolfing a whole one before coming up for air. "Fight?"

I shrug. Eight months ago, no way Adam would've gotten the jump on me. But I've shrunk down, lost weight, lost strength and have nothing left to fight for.

Cleo rips open the marshmallows and pops one in her mouth. She makes a funny face, and I expect her to bitch about the food. Instead she caps three of her fingers in marshmallows and eats them off one by one. Her cheeks puff up like she's gathering nuts for winter.

"Looks like you lost," she says around a mouthful.

I take a seat, adjust the crotch of my jeans, swipe my palms against my thighs and stab a fork into the chickpeas.

"Who?" she asks.

"Huh?"

"Jesus. For a guy named Shakespeare, you don't got dick to say." Cleo's eyes dive right into mine. "Who pounded your ass?"

"Adam. And he didn't pound my ass."

"Turner or Harris?"

Adam Turner plays the tuba and wears bow ties to school. He sews them himself, and I heard he's taking his mom to prom. I give her a look.

"Hey." She holds up her hands. "How do I know which Adam schooled you like a puss?"

"Harris. And he didn't school me like a puss."

"Why?"

"Cuz I'm not a fucken puss."

Cleo rolls her eyes, shakes her head. "Why'd Adam make you his bitch?"

Why did I bring her home with me? Oh yeah, cuz she's as fun as slamming my hand in a car door. Repeatedly.

She smiles a bitter little smile. "Dripass."

I have no clue what she means.

"You went up to the Flats, right?"

I nod and wonder why she never shows up at those parties.

Cleo curls her fingers for the chickpeas, and I hand her the fork. My knuckles are crusted with blood. I'll probably get an infection from Adam's goddamn teeth. I test my cheek with my fingertips and find it sticky and swollen.

"You need ice," she tells me.

I figure needing ice would prove me a puss, so I don't budge.

Cleo suddenly pops up and helps herself to Grandma's freezer. She's in there before I can stop her. The freezer is jam-packed with community Tupperware, from the eight billion people who dumped food on the doorstep for three solid weeks. Why the hell people think losing every member of my family would make me crave endless amounts of lasagna is a mystery to me.

I cringe, expecting Cleo to ask why we have it, why we don't eat or toss it. I honestly don't know. We just don't. But after only a little hesitation, Cleo grabs a handful of ice and wraps it in a dish towel. "Here."

I watch her bare feet move around the kitchen. I focus on the way my T-shirt hugs the curves of her round little butt. Her ass is a revelation. Never noticed it before and I've been missing out. Thank you Rat.

She pours two glasses of tap water, adds cubes and plunks them on the table. She seems to be on board with my hands-off-Grandma's-stuff policy.

I touch the towel-wrapped ice against my cheek and it stings like a bitch. I bite my lip to keep from hissing. She already accused me of being a pussy, and so far, with the way I've been acting around her, somebody might as well chop off my balls, because I don't deserve them.

Cleo polishes off the chickpeas and goes back after the marshmallows.

"Open," she says.

I open my mouth. She tosses. I catch. The marshmallows have fossilized into something less edible than styrofoam. I hold one up. She opens and I throw. It bounces off her nose.

"You gotta aim," she says,

"You need a bigger mouth."

"No one's ever told me that before. Other than marshmallow catching, why would I want a bigger mouth?"

I tilt my head, touch my tongue to my upper lip and wait.

She gets a little pink and snorts. "Somebody thinks a lot of himself."

"You did want my autograph. For being such a giant dick."

"I stand by my opinion. Throw another one."

She catches my second attempt. I set the ice pack on the table.

"Hey, Sasquatch, put that back on your face."

Sasquatch? WTF? I wince as the cold touches my ragged skin. And then, for no other reason than maybe my brain's mission is to sabotage my chances of every getting laid, I blurt, "You stole the Oreos out of my lunchbox in fourth grade."

Pay attention. Maybe write this down. If you're desperate to get in a chick's panties, accusing her of stealing should be avoided. And probably, since she's the only other person in the room, don't point at her like a total tool.

Cleo, strange creature that she is, smiles back at me and her little nose crinkles. "I also stole your Ninja Turtle action figure."

"Donatello? No way!" I sit up straighter. This is huge. That Donatello came with a removable shell, glow-in-the-dark vial of ooze and ... OK, OK, back on track. "You know I blamed Thad Bates for that, right? I got in all sorts of trouble for punching him in the face. I gave him a bloody nose after gym class."

She nods. "Yup, and he deserved it. Thad told everyone I stole his little sister's shirt off the clothesline in their backyard."

"Did you?"

"Well yeah." Her inflection calls me an idiot for asking. "But that's not the point."

I wonder what the point is.

"Thanks a bunch, Cleo. I got sent to the office. Got my XBox taken away for a week. My parents drove me to Thad's house, made me apologize and ... " I trail off because I can't catch my breath. Because my lungs have suddenly deflated like a pair of leaky pool toys. Because I know better than to travel down memory lane, where nothing but nightmares live.

Cleo watches my face. I know I'm obvious and expect her to tell me how sorry she is or some stupid shit like that. We sit in silence for about five seconds, before she asks, "Can I sleep over or what?"

"Um ..."

"Nobody'll know."

I can't come up with anything to say. She's the human equivalent of whiplash.

"Hey, screw it, whatever." She's instantly on her feet, bristling and growling like a kicked cat. "Dripass'll get pissed. I get it. I'm gone."

"Dripass?"

"Deanna."

"What?"

She huffs. "I call her Drippass."

"To her face?"

"As often as possible."

"Why?"

"Um, cuz pissing her off is my favorite hobby?"

"No. Why Dripass?"

"She ass squirted her chair in kindergarten, and I want to make sure she never forgets that priceless moment."

I snort. I can't help it. Yes Deanna, aka Dripass, would have an effing cow if she knew Cleo was here. But since Dea's probably curled up in Adam's tent, what the hell.

"Stay if you want," I tell her.

"Yeah?"

"Yeah."

She nods, pinching off a smile between her teeth and bouncing a little on the balls of her feet. Soft Cleo is happy. That was easy. And probably a big mistake. Too late to take it back now. She's already grabbed her stuff and disappeared downstairs.

I clean up the kitchen, duck into the bathroom and brush my teeth. Cleo definitely used my toothbrush again. I splash cold water on my face, wash off the blood and check myself in the mirror. My cheek is purple, swollen and seems about to give birth to an alien lifeform. It's got a heartbeat all its own. I test it with my fingertips. Hurts like a mother. That's not why I'm still hiding in the bathroom.

There's a girl in my basement. It's been awhile. There's a real possibility of embarrassing myself. I'm not just talking about sex. But I could be talking about sex. I need to get my ass downstairs.

Leaving the light off, thinking about yellow towels and her little pink mouth, I crack my head off the friggin overhang and trip down the last few stairs, arms flailing, swearing, auditioning for the staring role of Godzilla stomping Tokyo. I am an ass.

When I finally get control of myself, I make out Cleo's shape in my bed, curled up tight and facing the wall. Asleep? Hiding her laughter over my bumblefuck down the stairs? Scared of me? Please don't let her be afraid of me.

I crave her warm little body, even just to hold her. But who knows what she wants or might expect from me tomorrow. I can't give her more than right now. I'm alone all the time by choice, for good reason, and just having here is throwing me off balance.

Why her? After all the girls who've attached themselves to me these past few months, just begging to pat themselves on the back for fixing me, why Cleo Lee? More than half the time, I'm sure she hates me.

With no clue what I'm doing, I strip down to my underwear and slide under the covers. There's not much room. I lay on my back, arms behind my head, and debate touching her. Cuz you know, even if she hates me, there's still a possibility of messing around.

The whole rabid wolverine comparison is a good thing, right? She won't bite the shit out of me? What about how small she is? Will I split her in half? I bet she'd feel tight as a keyhole. Goddamn, I gotta think about something else.

I picture her standing in front of my house on Willow Drive and wonder what's up with that? And what's the deal with the bruises? Talk at school blames Allie. There's stories of her and Cleo cat fighting, teachers pulling them apart and throwing them in detention. Which is weird as shit. And not my problem. Can't be my problem. Cleo in nothing but my shirt is what I've got.

I am not going to sleep anytime soon.

Sleep got me through the last eight months. I am often unconscious for twelve-hour stretches, but lately, I've been dreaming, mostly about my mom. Sometimes it's good. I get to see her again, hear her voice and pretend it's real. Most of the time, my dreams are a screaming hell, and either way, I wake up wrecked and the rest of the day is the true nightmare.

So not sleeping is OK. But I can feel Cleo next to me. I've got a situation and no way to hide it.

I try thinking about toe fungus, sweaty jockstraps, and earwax. I consider running back upstairs to jerk off. She curls tighter and her stellar ass bumps my leg.

Fucking hell.

Chapter 12

CLEO:

I wake up to Shake twitching. Hands, legs, even his eyelids tweak. He makes noises. Unhappy noises. Whimpers. Moans. It's bad.

I'm spread on top of him like butter on toast. Don't know how or when that happened, but since my mouth tastes like a wet monkey, thank my lucky stars I woke up first.

Easing out of bed, I put on my crusty clothes from yesterday and use his toothbrush. I hurry. I shouldn't be around him, can't get caught here and might end up in a world of hurt because of it. Which didn't bother me last night, when I went all stray hound and begged for scraps, a bed, and wouldn't have turned down a belly rub.

I steal his hoodie because it's raining and I want it. It's big, soft, smells like him, and I have a long walk. I lace up my boots, adjust the hood and bail. The street is quiet and spooky with fog. I jump puddles, press buds in my ears and listen to the Alabama Shakes. Yup, I also stole his Ipod. I like his taste in music.

I make my way to Minnie's bakery. I start super-sucky early on Saturday and Sunday mornings, cleaning floors, shelves, windows, toilets, everything nobody else wants to do. Sometimes I help unload the delivery truck, fold napkins or write daily specials on a huge chalkboard. If I'm really lucky, I get to bake.

A buzzer sounds as I shove through the back door, into a storage room full of a sugary sweet smell. I have my own locker with my name on it. It's only a piece of tape with CLEO written in Sharpie, but it's the only space I've ever had that's all mine. I keep stuff in there, stuff I'd rather not lose, like money, a photograph of a smiling family and my new tube of toothpaste. I add the Ipod to my collection.

I tie on an apron, grab a broom and join Minnie in the kitchen. The sun is still asleep, but she's been at work for hours and hours already. My nose tells me she's making white chocolate, raspberry muffins. I think she grinds up angels, unicorns and fairies to make the batter. Remembering the stale marshmallows and chickpeas for dinner, I can't decide if Shake isn't allowed to raid the fridge or has really weird taste in food. I'm tempted to drop to my knees and offer up my firstborn for a muffin.

"You're wet. You're late," Minnie snaps.

I glance at the clock. "I had to walk like ten frigging miles in the pissing rain. And you're wrong. I'm not."

"Late and about as useful as a knocked-up nun."

"I'm not goddamn late."

"Must have been in an awful hurry to get here. Forgot your pants."

"I'm wearing pants." I lift up the hem of the apron and hoodie to prove it.

"Those don't qualify."

"My ass is covered."

"Only because your ass is scrawny. You're only a quarter the size of a normal person. I should only pay you a quarter an hour."

"That doesn't even make sense. And since I'm one of only three people on the whole entire planet who can stand to work for your nasty ass, you gotta be nice to me."

"I am being nice."

"This is nice?"

"Any nicer and you'll be so overwhelmed you'll shit nickels."

"If I could manage to shit nickels, I wouldn't need to work here."

We bitch back and forth for the better part of two hours. When Minnie's two other employees show up, we take turns ganging up on one another. I love it. I don't get to bake, but I run the counter, which is almost as good. My shift ends and I duck back into the storage room to do my homework.

I may be a trashy loser, but I get good grades. I have a plan to graduate, get an apartment, work at the bakery full time and hopefully start taking night classes at the local college. I will get out of the yellow house.

When I finish my assignments, I hang out until Minnie tells me to be a normal teenager and leave. She has to tell me more than once. I've got nowhere better to be. Actually, I have absolutely nowhere to be.

It's still raining. I take a bag of stale muffins and feed myself and my strays. I stop at Allie's, but she's on her way to a group meeting with her mom. She loves group meetings. Free snacks and coffee, lots of people in need. So I chill at the laundromat. I check the dryers for stuff to steal, but there's nothing decent, so I just sit in a dirty plastic chair, watch the clothes tumble and listen to Shake's Ipod.

I wonder what to do about him. I should do less than nothing. Just like everybody else. But Shake is getting worse and getting there faster. If I tell him about the night of the fire, will it help or hurt? It doesn't matter. I can't tell him. Not ever. Just hanging out with him is a risk.

Chapter 13

SHAKE:

I spend my Saturday walking around town in the rain and decide I'm sick of being broke. I hit the ATM, buy weed from Bruce and smoke until I'm baked crispy. In the Pathetic Olympics, I'm setting world records. Move over Michael Phelps. Kiss my ass Usain Bolt. Look for me on the Wheaties box. I am an unbeatable, gold medal dipshit.

I can afford it. See, I've got a sizeable bank account. I don't like to think about the reason for it, don't like to touch it and sure as hell shouldn't be spending it on weed. Good thing nobody gives a shit.

When I'm sure Grandma's asleep, I duck down the stairs and after bashing my goddamn skull on the overhang for the hundredth time, spend an hour tearing the basement apart, hunting for my Ipod. I find my NY Dolls shirt on the floor and push it back to the bottom of my stuff. My stuff is not really my stuff. My hockey gear, clothes, books, and everything I had burned up in the fire. This is just generic shit piled in a tote. The important things are irreplaceable.

I grab the tote and fling it across the room, satisfied when it bangs off the dryer and spills. Then, in a moment of utter basement silence, as I pull on my hair, I remember a quote from Shakespeare, from when Mom and I used to trade them back and forth. "When sorrows come, they come not single spies but in battalions."

Collapsing on my bed, digging my knuckles into my eye sockets, I let them trample me. All of the sorrows. I don't fight back. I welcome every blow, let them stomp the living shit out of me, and there is nothing but pain. Mom. Dad. Hemmie. The loss of them is a crushing weight. I can't breathe. I can't carry it. My chest caves in. But I have nothing else. I've been torn apart and patched back together with jagged bits of guilt and anger and memories that torture me. It all finally explodes behind my eyelids, pours down my face and stings my split skin.

That's when Grandma tests the durability of the stairs. She charges down them, shaking the rafters, carrying a full basket of laundry, humming a Beatles tune, with no idea of the shitshow waiting for her.

I bolt to my feet, look left and then right, confirming there's nowhere to go. I'm wasted, crying harder than a lost two-year-old and breathing like I'm trying to blow out birthday candles. Hello humiliation. You are my new best friend.

Grandma drops the basket, makes a squeaking noise and half falls against the washer. She actually cups one hand over her mouth and presses the other against her heart.

I swipe madly at my face, then ram my hands in my back pockets. I don't look at her but keep busy gnawing on my own tongue. We say nothing for a good long time. I'd rather she catch me jerking off than this.

"Holy jumping june bugs, Shake." She grips the washer, propping herself upright. "What the hell ran over you?"

"I'm OK."

"No. No. Goddammit. You're less OK than non dairy creamer."

I just stand there, not sure what that means or what to do. I've definitely pissed her off, but I don't know how to fix it.

She eventually inches closer, holding her hand out as if to a feral cat and inspects my cheek. Her fingers hesitate a half inch short of touching me. I'm waiting for it, wishing for it, even tilt my head toward her, but she drops her hand and looks away, like she can't stand the sight of me. I don't know what she's thinking. I know she doesn't want me here. I'm screwing up her life but am pitiful enough to have nowhere else to go.

I swallow a whole bunch of wet and wait.

She takes a deep breath, then says, "I've got three questions. Think carefully. Tell the truth."

I nod.

She stares into my eyes for a long second. "Are the cops going to knock on my door because of this?" She gestures at my face.

"No."

"Should I call the cops because of what happened to you?"

"No."

"Do you need medical attention?"

"No."

She stands another minute, nods twice, then suddenly turns and storms back up the stairs.

Chapter 14

SHAKE:

In my dream, I'm a little kid and my mom, dad and Hemmie are right there, within reach, but every time I try to touch them, I get burned. They tell me, "Be brave." But I can't hang on, can't tough out the pain, and they slowly crumble to ash. Not real hard to figure that one out.

My phone wakes me. Not the alarm but a call.

I snatch it up. "Wha..." I take a second to hack up something as foul and sticky as a gerbil covered in tree sap. I try again. "What?"

"Shake? You're late, hon, and Principal Sanderson is waiting to speak with you. Can you get yourself here?"

"Huh?" My wires are still fried from the dream. If I mash my face into the pillow, I wonder if I could suffocate.

"Shake?"

Do you think I could hold my breath long enough to pass out?

"Shake? Are you there, hon?"

"What?"

"This is Mrs. Kline? From the main office? We need to get you to school. Can you do that, hon?"

Monday. I lost Sunday in a haze of burning weed. Shit. I throw on jeans, shirt, sneakers, and walk to school. I'm beyond late, and Mrs. K has to buzz me in.

She is very short, very round, with pencils jabbed into a hairdo balanced on her head like a water jug from Kenya. She is a dead ringer for the office secretary from Ferris Bueller. One look at my face and Mrs. K is all over me.

I promise her I've received medical attention, although I'm not sure ice from Cleo qualifies. I swear I've received pain medication, and I think weed from Bruce should qualify. I assure I'm fine when I'm deep in a soul-sucking hell.

She directs me to a chair beside her desk to wait for Principal Sanderson to get around to me. I wonder why I busted my ass just to wait on her ass, but I slouch down and chill.

Mrs. K clears her throat. She holds a tin of cookies.

"Help yourself." She winks at me.

Once in awhile, my grandmother brings cookies home. They are perfectly shaped, perfectly golden brown, with weird names like Milano, biscotti, lebkuchen. I'm never sure if they are up for grabs, so I don't eat them. Mrs. K's are not from the same cookbook. These lumpy turds are all different sizes and burnt on the bottom. They are something I haven't had in a very long time.

My mom couldn't bake for shit. It didn't stop her from trying. She made a really disgusting chocolate chip I truly loved.

I reach for one. Mrs. K beams her approval. I have trouble thanking her, my voice all wet because I am a giant pussy slobbering over a goddamn cookie. I sort of want to grab the whole tin, cradle it against my chest and scream, "Mine!"

Sanderson calls me in. I stuff the cookie in my mouth and half choke on it.

When I plop into the familiar plastic chair, Sanderson stands in front of me, leans back against her desk with arms folded and says, "No more excuses, Shake. I'm done playing around. Look at me and make sure you're listening."

I stop just short of snorting and rolling my eyes. This is a new tactic for her but old for me. My dad perfected the hard sell. Try getting your ass chewed in French.

My mom was the opposite, all flyaway noise, and she and I had some killer shouting matches. More toward the end. Constantly toward the end. Over grades, college, me wanting a car, her wanting me at the piano, me begging for a life, her setting down rules to keep me from wrecking it.

She and Dad couldn't decide what went ratshit with Hemmie but saw one last chance with me. So they piled on the rules, expectations and consequences. I didn't understand the consequences. So now I've got all the freedom I ever wanted. I traded my family for it and never even got to say goodbye.

It's never going to change or get any better, any easier, and I'm so completely fucked that I can't imagine living day after day like this.

What do I need? An end.

"Shake!"

I realize Sanderson has said my name at least twice. I must have zoned out again.

"Where'd you go, son?" She looks down at my hands.

They are clenched in my lap. I force them flat and swipe sweat from my palms.

"Are you all right?"

I jerk a nod. She hesitates a second, just looking at me, chewing the lipstick off her lower lip. If she calls me son again, I'm gone.

"Should you see the nurse?"

I swivel my head back and forth.

She takes a deep breath, straightens up and gets her game face back on. "You're forcing me into a corner, Shake. It's my job to keep you on the right path, whether you're here at school or off the grounds. Your behavior outside of school has been brought to my attention. Underage drinking. Possible drug use. Fighting." She ticks them off her painted nails. "And I ..."

"Who told you that?"

She tilts her head. "This is about you, Shake. We need to get you straightened out, back on track. Talk to me. Tell me where you're at with everything. I went out on a limb not suspending you after the incident with Mr. Westin. I'm trying to keep you in school, protect your future. Work with me here. Let me help you."

"This is fucking bullshit!" I jump to my feet. "Who told you that?"

"Hey, hey, hey. Enough with the language. Let's cool down." She holds up her hands as if this is an old Western and I'm robbing her. "I need you to sit."

I loom over her for a moment, breathing hard, this close to fucking losing it. Not a good idea, so I drop back down, clamp my mouth shut and stare at my hands. They've balled into fists again. I pry them open and make a quick mental list. It's no secret I was at the Crypt and the Flats. Anybody could've ratted me out. Thad? Adam? Deanna? Sam? Probably not Rat.

"Shake." Sanderson snaps her fingers in front of my face. It's super aggravating. "I'm on your side."

She waits. I don't want her on my side. We aren't choosing teams for friggin kickball. I want to be left alone. How hard is that? Did I lose a goddamn coin toss? Why am I her pet project all of a sudden?

"Let's start with your assignment. How are you coming with that?"

Assignment? I just look at her. I need to know who's been talking about me.

"Am I to assume you didn't complete the reading or write the paper I asked for? That was the agreement, after the last incident. I thought we were on the same page here."

Same page? We're not even in the same book. I can't even remember what I was supposed to read. To quote Mrs. Sanderson, I'm going to go out on a limb here and guess it was something totally pointless. But what do I know? Maybe writing a five hundred word paper would've had me so juiced with happiness I'd be jizzing rainbow sparkles right now.

She huffs and rubs the crease between her eyebrows with her fingertips. Why is she so annoyed? I'm the one who got tattled on.

"You have a fifth period study hall," she clarifies like I've forgotten my schedule since yesterday. "For the next little while, you're going to spend it in counseling talking with Ms. Robbins."

I tip my head back and breathe out. Fuck me.

"Starting today and non-negotiable," she adds on. "Cooperate with Ms. Robbins and we'll leave your grandmother out of this for now."

Hah. She's not fooling me. Mrs. Sanderson doesn't have the stones to call Grandma. I don't blame her. Neither do I. We finally agree on something.

"Now," she goes on. "Before you get to class, tell me one positive step you've taken to deal with the negative emotions you've been experiencing."

What the actual fuck is coming out of her mouth right now? Is she kidding?

She taps a long nail on her desk. "C'mon, Shake. Don't force my hand. I'm trying not to involve the authorities. Give me something. I offered suggestions the last time we spoke. You remember?"

I draw a blank.

"We talked about the right path?"

I blink.

"Finding a productive outlet?"

I poke at my lip with my tongue.

"Shake?"

Oh Christ, she's not going to let it go.

"I ... uh ... yeah, I've been hanging around, um, abandoned animals. You know, strays. Feeding them and sh... stuff."

"At a shelter?"

"Something like that."

"Well that's great." Her face lights up. She's surprised but digging this. "I'd like to hear more about that."

I nod a few times. I've got nothing else. She waits. So do I. I'm not sure what we're waiting for, but it gets skin-crawling awkward. Are we expecting a surprise guest or something? Doesn't matter. I'm back to wondering who's been talking to Sanderson about me, getting pissed off all over again, when she finally says, "Well, OK. That's a start. A good start, I think." She claps her hands, twice. "Ms. Robbins will expect you fifth period."

She releases me into the wild like an infected lab rat.

Chapter 15

CLEO:

No Shake in homeroom. I skip gym, hoping, but he never shows at the wall outside auto shop. I keep looking for him. I'm a little ashamed of myself but almost resort to hunting down Allie. As his most dedicated stalker, she usually knows right where he is. Maybe we should put a bell around his neck, tag his ear, put him on a leash, something. Cuz the boy is running wild and headed for trouble.

I finally spot him in the hall before fifth period, and I hate to admit how ridiculously relieved I am. Wrinkled blue T-shirt, jeans hanging low on his hips, blonde curls all over the place, and he didn't shave. He's such a hot mess, I get sweaty from just a glimpse of him. It's not just me. His scruffy face literally stops girls in their tracks and causes pile ups in the hallway. Even the nasty bruise on his cheek doesn't dim the light that is Shakespeare LeCasse.

All day long, everybody's buzzing about the fight at the Flats. Adam's mouth is swollen and an eggplant seems to be growing out of his ear. There's a wild rumour about Shake throwing a screaming fit and knocking Deanna on her ass. I would have bought a front row ticket to see that. I'd like to record it and watch in slow motion.

Dripass holds court as the reigning Queen of Slutsville. She tells her skanks-in-waiting a fairy tale about how Shake and Adam fought over her. She even gets weepy over Shake, over how he's so broken and needs her more than ever, and she's totally there for him and aren't they just the douchiest love story since the Notebook?

I consider stabbing her with my pencil. I would aim for a boob and hope to deflate one. I imagine it sounding like a really long fart.

"Did you hear?" Allie shouts at me when I flop down in detention. She's in full drama mode. The girl is fearless. I've seen the finger pointing, heard the jokes and witnessed the overall meanness she's put up with since first grade. Allie fights back with more colors, more volume, more everything. She gives the haters endless ammunition and somehow survives. She even smiles back at them. I don't know how she does it, but she is my hero.

"Hear what?" I ask.

"Shake! What kind of sick animal harms that face? Crushes a rose? Pulls the wings off a butterfly?"

"The butterfly still has his wings."

"How can he fly, how can he flutter, when the world keeps knocking him down?" Her voice climbs into painful territory. "Why is nobody helping him? Looking after him? What's wrong with his friends? What's wrong with US? All I've been thinking about is the menu for our reception!"

"Allie, please," sighs Schwartzmeyer. He rubs his temples. "In respect of this being a Monday, for the sake of my sanity, let's take it down a decibel or two."

"This is too big to keep quiet, Mr. Schwartzmeyer. This is a tragedy, and I can't just do nothing. I feel a personal responsibility."

He sighs. "The last time you told me that, I believe Jennifer Lopez announced a breakup."

"Exactly! I knew you'd understand. Ermigawd!" Allie clamps both hands over her mouth when Shake meanders in. The high-pitched yowls of a harpooned seal squeeze out of her.

"You're killing her," I tell him.

He signs in at the front, then surprises me by plunking down in the desk closest to Allie and me. He is all long arms and legs, and the chair can't contain him. I can't imagine what it's like for him, taking up so much space in the world, never able to go unnoticed.

Allie grabs his hand, pulls it to her chest and starts singing about turning back time, taking back hurt and who the hell knows.

"Cher?" Shake tugs his hand free.

"You recognize it!" She's orgasmic in her joy.

He leans in, licks his lower lip, then asks in a quiet voice, "Can you help me out again?"

"No!" I snap. They both look at me. "She's not your personal goddamn vending machine."

Allie flaps a hand at me. To him, she says, "Are you feeling awful bad?"

"I'm not doing so hot." He puppies his baby blues and adds a pouty puss, which is basically the same as feeding her roofies. "I was hoping you'd take care of me."

"What a shovelful of shit!" I'm so pissed I pound on the desk with both hands. "I can't believe what a douche worm you're being right now!"

"Miss Lee," Schwartzmeyer barks. "You are not scheduled in this classroom. I only allow you to join us because you're somewhat helpful in containing Miss Kindle. But if you disrupt my detention, you're gone."

I clench both fists between my thighs to keep from flipping him off. But my feet stomp. I can't help it. Everyone in the room deserves a hard kick in the ass. Especially Shake.

"What?" Shake demands.

"None of your business!" I resort to the tell-off of a second grader. I stop just short of sticking out my tongue.

"You don't have to be here?" His giant hands flaten on the desk and he leans toward me.

I just glare at him.

"What the hell?" Now he sits back and throws those mitts in the air. "What are you doing here?"

"We've got a deal," Allie confides. "She keeps me company because I..."

"Allie!" I cut her off. "Don't be spilling stuff to this numbnuts."

"He could help you," she tells me. "And you could help him. How have you two not figured this out yet? You're like ketchup and pickles."

"What?"

"Not so tasty on your own. Way better together."

"Which one of us is the pickle?" I need to know.

"Just tell him Cleo."

Shake, proving himself the ultimate king of the numbnuts, whispers to Allie, "I love secrets." And I swear to Christmas, he honest to god flutters his lashes.

"Holy shit buckets!" I screech. I'm nearly purple and crawling over my desk to get at him. "Really? You're willing to gift-wrap your balls for meds?"

"That's it," Schwartzmeyer snaps. "You're out for the day Miss Lee."

"Allie shouts all the time!"

"For as long as her name appears on my attendance, I'll weather that storm. But you do not fall under my job description. Goodbye Miss Lee."

If there's anything worse than sitting in detention when you don't need to, it's getting thrown out the one time you do.

I take one last second to point at Allie and warn her, "Don't tell him anything. Don't give him anything."

Chapter 16

CLEO:

I sit in the grass by the flagpole, under a sign that says *No Smoking On School Grounds.* I am smoking and proving a point. Nobody gives a shit.

There's a crappy drizzle falling from the sky. I'm cold, wet, and worried. My guess is three seconds. That's how long it took Mr. Sexy Sasquatch to charm meds, snorkel and my secrets out of Allie.

Ditching the butt, I pop to my feet when I see them, but check for witnesses before stalking over.

"Did you tell him?" I go after Allie first.

"Yep," Shake answers with a sloppy smile. A smiling Shake is as odd and scary as an ingrown toenail. Wonderfuckingful.

I am already kicking at the ground and launching F-bombs at the sky when Allie shouts, "I didn't tell him! I didn't say anything! I swear."

I stretch on tiptoes, grab Shake's hair and yank his face down to mine.

"Hey! Ow! Ow!" he screeches.

"You gave him shit," I snap at Allie. "His eyes are all muddy."

He rubs his scalp.

Allie hangs her head. "He needed it."

"Fine. Good. What do I care?" I turn and stomp off. I even throw my hands up, making a performance of it. Meryl Streep is a hack. I am Oscar worthy. "Shakespeare LeCasse is not my problem. I'm done with this. You can have him."

"Really?"

"Look at him!" I wheel around and march back.

Shake's grin spreads so wide he may dislocate his jaw as he nods at me and says, "Wolverine."

Oooh-kay.

"I like him like this," Allie whines. "Can I keep him if I promise to look after him? And pet him? Just the thought of petting him is hatching my ovaries."

"Your hamster died young Allie."

"Let's hope Shake is more durable."

"How many did you give him?"

"He's having a bad day."

"How many?"

"He's very hard to say no to."

"Allie!"

"Just two. It's OK. My mom takes two sometimes."

"That's not OK. That's actually very bad and probably dangerous."

"Maybe three," she admits. "He asked so nicely. He's very polite. He let me touch his hair. And he smells amazing. Have you sniffed him? He smells like angel food cake floating in a mountain stream. I can't decide if I want to eat him or bathe in him."

Weird. Weird. Weird. And just getting weirder as Shake blurts "Rabid wolverine," while nodding at me.

I poke him in the chest. I hurt my finger. "What's with the wolverine shit?"

"You," he says.

"Me? I'm the wolverine? You're saying I look like a

wolverine? A rabid wolverine?"

"It's more ..." He pauses. Grass grows. Civilizations crumble. Acorns mature into full grown trees. I consider pinching his nipple really hard. "Behavior."

"Oh that's way better. I just act like a rabid wolverine. You need to stop before I beat you to death with my boot." Someone kill me now. "Do you have a frigging clue what you're doing right now?" I snarl at him.

The sasquatch looks around.

"Don't ruin it," Allie tells me. "He needs to float for a little while, or he's going to drown. Do you understand? I just gave him a temporary life raft. I'm hoping he'll drift a little closer to shore."

"No! You went too far," I argue, because my mom floats away sometimes, takes forever to come back, is never quite the same, and I'm stuck with a snot rag named Randy. And Shake is better than this. I'm counting on it. "He's not like us, Allie. He doesn't belong with us."

"He does now."

That's when Shake figures out he's holding hands with Allie. He tries to yank free, but she snatches him into a hug. I've experienced that hug. It's a cross between a really scary pillow fight and the thing that crushes cars into cubes. I hear cracks and pops from Shake's spine, and he makes the sound of a mink getting shaved. When her hand drops to his ass, he really starts to struggle. But he's just gotta ride it out. According to Allie, everybody's better off after a really good hug, and there's no getting away until she gives up. By then, he's pale and shaky on his feet.

Allie sings some asinine song about spinning round and round at full volume, grinning at Shake as she turns in a surprisingly graceful circle.

"Allie," I hiss. I can't be seen with Shake, and she's bringing the circus to town.

"It's Britney Spears," she tells me.

"You're making it difficult to be your friend. What do we do with him?" I jerk my thumb at our pet clown. He stumbles while standing still. "We can't exactly turn him loose like this."

"I gotta get home to take care of my mom. Unless he fits in my purse, I can't take him."

"No, no, no." I shake my head, trying to back away. It's broad daylight. "I don't want him. I can't want him. You know that. And this is your fault."

"Cameron Diaz," she tells me.

"What?"

"That's not right. Wait a sec." She takes a deep breath, scrunches up her face and tries again. "Trout diaz? Carp diaz? That thing about a Latin fish?"

"Carpe diem?"

"Yup. That's you. Be the fish."

"I can't be the fish Allie. I can't get caught with him."

Shake wanders off during our argument, feet scuffing the sidewalk, head sagging against his left shoulder. I should let him go. Why can't I?

"Be HIS fish," Allie says. "This is your chance to grab hold of something better. You deserve it and so does he. You're welcome for whatever happens next."

"What are you, the dalai fucken lama?"

"Consider me your fairy god lama, full of magical advice." She wiggles her fingers in a wave, and as she heads in the opposite direction, calls over her shoulder, "Just like Cinderella. May the force be with you."

"That's Star Wars!" I shout back. Grrrr.

Chapter 17

SHAKE:

"What?" My eyes snap open and I'm confused as hell.

"How many fingers am I holding up?" Cleo straddles my lap, facing me, giving me the middle finger.

"What're you doing?" I cringe back.

"Keeping you awake. For three fun-filled hours. A job I didn't want by the way. So you owe me."

I think about this. My feet are firmly planted, but my head is a lost helium balloon floating up, up, and away. And my face stings. Not just the side Adam pounded on. The other cheek is downright hot.

"Did you just slap me?"

"Huh?" She crinkles her nose and tilts her head. Her innocent routine could use some work. I'm not buying it.

I kind of remember getting slapped. The sharp sound and definitely more than once. "Did you? Slap me? Like a bunch of times?"

"Hold your breath and wait for me to get back to you."

She's more annoying than an itchy rash.

"Where the hell are we?" I glance around. We're sitting in the backseat of a wrecked car. I'm facing forward, with Cleo perched on my thighs. Her spectacular butt is kinda bony. The air smells damp and moldy. There's a thick layer of old leaves under my sneakers, a bumblebee banging against the windshield and maybe something dead under one of the seats. Goldenrod grows up all the way around, taller than the windows, and the sun is setting in death throes of pinks and purples. It's way later in the day than it should be.

"By the creek," Cleo tells me. "Beyond that spot where I feed my strays."

"Whose car?"

"Don't know. Don't care."

"How's it here?"

"Rex left it here."

"Why?"

"Stole it."

"And?"

"Didn't wanna get busted with it, so he ditched it here. Over a year ago. Nobody's found it. But it's either too cold or too buggy to sleep here ever. And if you ask another question, you'll need to read me my rights first, and I'm gonna want a lawyer."

I wonder why in hell anybody would sleep in an abandoned car with a busted window but don't dare ask. Cleo's sort of a prickly pear, and I'm not completely with it. Maybe I'm missing something, and I don't want to do anything overly moronic.

We sit and listen to the bumblebee get super angry. I close my eyes and catch the sounds of birds, maybe the rush of creek water and distant traffic.

Cleo slaps me. Hard enough to crank my head sideways.

"Hey! Ow! What the hell?" I grab her by the shoulders and shake her a little. "Stop doing that."

"Stop being such a giant toadwart!"

"How am I a ... uh, what did you call me?"

"You keep nodding off. All wasted on that nasty shit. How am I supposed to know what could happen? What if... what if..." Her eyes bulge. She's halfway hysterical.

"What could happen?"

"What if you don't wake back up?"

That doesn't sound so bad. Say it with me slowly. Oblivion. I like the word, the way it rolls off the tongue.

What do I need? Oblivion.

Cleo seems to know what I'm thinking, and we glare at each other. I'm still gripping her arms. I ease up but don't let go. I don't trust her.

"I'm OK," I tell her. I'm not sure it's true. That's a lie. I know I'm not.

"Do you want to die?"

My mouth works, but I can't manage an answer.

"Say it," she snarls.

"I'm not trying to kill myself."

"That's not what I asked."

"It's the best I can do."

We're back to the silent stare. She's an expert at it. Her sharp dark eyes see way more of me than I'd like. But she seems mostly OK with the shitty me I am now.

"I think," she says slowly. "You just gotta get by. Don't look ahead. Stop looking back. Just figure out what you need to survive this minute and then the next. That's what I do, and it mostly works."

What do I need? That's the million dollar question.

I want to tell her that medicating myself is my way of getting by, but I know it will piss her off. She might slap me again. For the sister of a drug dealer, she has a surprisingly low tolerance. For a guy who hated what became of my brother, I am surprisingly eager to embrace his lifestyle.

"Wanna listen to music?" She digs an Ipod from her pocket. I recognize it.

"You stole my IPod?"

"Borrowed."

"So you were gonna give it back?"

She rolls her eyes. "Don't be an idiot."

I don't know if that means I was getting it back or not.

Cleo scoots closer, which rubs her ass across my crotch, and I woof like a startled dog. She snorts a laugh and offers me a bud. I slouch way, way down and she rests her forehead against my chest, her hands on my shoulders. We share, one bud in her right ear and one in my left, and listen to Edward Sharpe and the Magnetic Zeros.

She's touching me. I feel each one of her fingertips, the press of her chest and puff of her breath. I smell her hair and might be imagining the light thump of her heartbeat against my belly. My whole body tingles as if waking up after an eight month sleep, and it's both exciting and painful. I am as tempted to push her away as pull her close. In the end, I don't know where to put my hands.

She's wearing boys basketball shorts down below her knees. They're shiny green and butt ugly. She's sticking with the tired flannel, and her clunky boots are planted on the seat, one on each side of me. Her outfit makes no sense and no difference. I've seen her in a towel. I'm liking the shape and feel of her bony ass in my lap.

I take a chance. I place my palms on her knees. She tenses. I wait, count three Mississippi's, then slide my hands up her legs, inside the shorts, over her thighs. She keeps still, so perfectly still she must be holding her breath. I can't decide if that's good or bad. This version of Cleo is a mystery. But she doesn't slap me again, so I'm encouraged.

Except, we've got a problem. I'm too tall for the backseat of a compact car. I'm all bent up and my legs are unhappy. Everything starts to ache and cramp. I try to ignore it. My fingers are right there. Right effing there. Just brushing the edge of her panties, so close I feel the heat of her, but I'm in serious pain. If I don't adjust, I risk paralysis.

I shift, which dislodges the earbuds and unsettles Cleo, but I slide so my back is against the door and my legs are on the seat. I'm still bent but not folded up like a paper fan. I maneuver Cleo so she's lying on her back, between my legs, with her head under my chin. She huffs and squeaks and swears while I manhandle her, but once we're settled, she seems cool with it.

I reposition the bud and then rest my hands on her stomach. Now I've got better access, but I'm starting over. After a few more Mississippi's, I slide my fingers back and forth, working my way under her flannel. My hands are big, especially compared to her. I span her rib cage, wondering how her organs fit into such a little package.

My fingers are poised for the jump to her tits, when Mystery Cleo says, "I knew your brother."

I go still and say nothing for a long minute. "How?" My voice sounds as if it's coming out of a ten-mile tunnel.

"He was friends with my brother. And with me. We hung out sometimes."

"Hung out how?"

I feel her shrug. "Hemmie was nice to me. He was fun, you know, and he talked about you sometimes."

I don't know what to do with that information.

"The world breaks everyone, and afterward, many are strong at the broken places," she says softly. "Hemmie taught me that."

I recognize it. Ernest Hemingway said it.

"Hemmie said your mom taught literature at the college. That she liked to quote Hemingway to him and Shakespeare to you, and she always called you by your full names. He told me you read, like all the time, and remember everything, cuz you're smart like her."

I wish she'd tell me more, but I can't bring myself to ask. My brother and I weren't close at the end. She probably knew him better than I did. And that leads to a question I don't want to ask.

"Will you tell me one?" she says.

I need to swallow before I can speak, and it's not easy. "One what?"

"A quote. From Shakespeare."

I squeeze my eyes shut. I only ever did that with my mom. "I don't do it anymore."

"OK." She sounds disappointed. I think of how easy it is to make this girl happy and call myself a douche.

We are quiet for a few minutes, the music drifting into one ear and silence pouring into the other. I'm tensed up tighter than the spring in Shaquille O'Neal's mattress.

Then Cleo starts swirling her fingertips over my thighs, so soft I can barely feel her touch. But I do feel her. Something has changed. For some weird reason, maybe because of the way she treats me, gets all up in my face and calls me on my shittiness, she is the only one I can stand to be around. She is the only one who can stand to be around me.

I don't zone out when she's around.

After awhile, I finally tell her, "In the world I fill up a place which may be better when I have made it empty."

Chapter 18

CLEO:

It's growing dark and the cold is settling in.
We're on the verge of seeing our breaths. I don't care.
At all. Because I'm sprawled on Shakespeare
LeCasse with his hands on me. In what universe have
I landed? Suddenly up is down, left is right, my
thoughts are a spiral and my heart is out of control.

Unfortunately, since I mentioned Hemmie, his
paws haven't moved. I shouldn't have said anything. I
thought it might help, starting a conversation about his
brother, and maybe I was hoping to let some of the air
out of my bloated, guilty conscience. Talk about a
backfire. Shake shut right down on me.

Question. If I don't offer the truth, is it the same
as lying?

I slide my fingers up and down his thighs,
learning the shape of his muscles like it's totally OK to
touch him however I want. Like he belongs to me. For
this one moment, maybe he does.

I repeat the Shakespeare quote in my head. I
hope I remember it right. It's beautiful and incredibly
sad. While I'm floored that he shared it with me, I've

now moved beyond the point of flirting with disaster and am officially dating it.

"Wanna get food?" he asks.

There are only two of us in the car, but he must be asking someone else. I say nothing and assume he'll realize his mistake.

"Cleo?"

"What?"

"Food?"

My mouth works for a moment or two before I produce actual words. "No money."

"I'll buy."

"Are you being nice to me?"

"Maybe."

"Why?"

"I'm wasted. And hungry." He shrugs. "And I owe you."

This is exciting stuff, but I can't walk downtown with him. There are limits to my risk taking. I'd be safer running in traffic blindfolded and carrying sharp scissors.

"We could grab some burgers or something," he offers, sounding hesitant, as if he expects to be turned down.

His moment of vulnerability is my moment of insanity, because I hear myself saying, "Pizza?"

"Good."

"Get cheese. No pepperoni. Pick it up. I'll meet you back here."

"Wait. What?"

"Pay attention. Just cheese dude. We'll meet up."

"Why?"

"Cuz I don't like pepperoni."

"No. Why meet?"

"Keep up Sasquatch. I don't like meat on my pizza."

"Not meat. Meet. M...E...E...T."

"Are we still talking about pepperoni?"

"If I'm paying, pepperoni is non-negotiable," he decides. "I'm asking why we can't just go together."

"Cuz you didn't buy me a corsage and rent a tux. And I got shit to do. Put on your big boy pants. I'll catch up with you."

"What shit?"

"Regular shit," I snap. "None-of-your-business shit."

"Bullshit. With all your practice you should be better at lying." He pushes me upright, jerking the bud out of my ear and adjusting so we're facing each other. "What's the problem Cleo?"

I don't look at him as I feed him a teaspoon of honesty. "Me. You. Not a good idea."

He tilts his head down to catch my eye and his hair flops in his face. God I love those fat blonde curls. I want to pull them straight and watch them bounce back. I want to feel them slide through the spaces between my fingers while I devour that mouth, which is frowning in a really adorable way.

"Explain it to me, Cleo. What's going on right now?"

"Nobody wants to see us hanging out together."

"So this is about a bunch of nobodies?"

"Dripass?"

He half smiles. "Not an issue."

"Maybe not to you."

"You've already slept with me. Twice. Getting pizza is no big."

"Aren't you hilarious?"

"I'm just trying to keep your hands off my underwear."

"I may pee myself you're so funny."

"It's food. I'm hungry. No big deal. So?" he prompts.

I just stare.

"OK then." He digs out his phone, finds the number in his contacts, and orders us pizza. He probably grabs food with his buddies all the time. No big deal.

Not the same for me. I go hungry. A lot. I feed on whatever I find, beg or steal. I answer to a ballsack named Randy. My world is a puddle of shit, and Shake is stepping in it. I could just refuse. I could ruin whatever is happening right now. But I won't. I'm not sure if I'm crazy, greedy or just plain stupid.

So we walk together, through the center of town, right out in the open. I hide in Shake's shadow and twitch and startle and watch for faces or cars I might know. Shake pays, carries the pizza and leads me straight to his grandma's house.

I skid to a stop out front. "What about your grandma."

He shrugs. Still no big deal. "She's probably asleep."

The key is in a fake turtle. Shake unlocks and let's us in. We trudge downstairs. The sasquatch forgets to duck and smacks his head off the overhang.

"Goddamnit." He rubs his forehead, muttering, "Every friggin time," then tosses the box on the bed. "Napkins," he says and jogs back upstairs.

In the basement, by myself, I bounce on my toes, and chant, "Whathahell, whathahell, whathahell?" Because, seriously, what the hell am I doing in Shakespeare LaCasse's bedroom? Why would he want me here? No one wants me here. Which could land me in a buttload of trouble. And what am I hoping for? A fuck-you very much before Shake forgets I exist?

Shake comes back with a fistful of napkins and two glasses of tap water. This time, he crouches way down to avoid bonking his head off the overhang. If he sees me freaking, he ignores it. He sets the glasses on the floor, plops down on the bed and tears into the pizza like he's been living off chickpeas and marshmallows for weeks. He will eat a large pizza by himself if I don't grab a share. So I kick off my boots, crawl onto his unmade sheets and sit cross-legged. I snag a slice, can't remember my last meal, but remember why pizza is the greatest food on earth.

I flick pepperoni aside, then cram hot cheese and tomato sauce into my mouth. I try not to make chewbacca sounds as I gnaw a hunk of crust down to a nub. I nab another slice while still swallowing the last of the first and catch Shake staring at me.

"What?" I spit sauce at him.

He just waggles his head with an almost smile.

"Let me guess." I lick cheese off my upper lip. "Dripass eats two bites of pizza and is totally stuffed. I bet she picks at it like it's a scab on somebody's ass."

I demonstrate. He laughs, and for a second, I feel really good about myself. Then he panics a little and presses his lips together so tight, they nearly disappear. I don't think he lets himself laugh anymore.

"Just so ya know," I tell him, "Your princess scarfs down her weight in peanut butter and Doritos when she gets home."

He reaches for the last slice.

"Hey, hey, hey. Hands off Sasquatch. That one's mine."

He makes a show of dangling the slice over his mouth and taking a ginormous bite.

"Seriously?" I snark at him. "You're cool with being a giant, selfish dick?"

"Anytime you're ready for that autograph, just ask."

"Not fair."

"You're like a quarter my size. You get a quarter the pie."

"Your grandma said pretty much the same goddamn thing. Boohoo, what a crock of shit."

He's got the slice tilted in midair, just hanging there, the cheese starting to slide. "My grandma? How do you…"

"Watch the cheese," I warn.

"You know my grandma?"

"I work at the bakery on weekends."

He just stares at me, not blinking.

"Hemmie got me the job." I point, cuz he's still not paying attention. And c'mon, it's the last slice. "The cheese dude."

"How did," he starts, then drops the pizza back in the box. I snatch it. He lets me have it without arguing. "Hemmie got you a job?"

I nod.

"At my grandma's bakery?"

I nod again. His slowness to catch on makes me wonder how hard he bashed his head coming down the stairs.

"How did that happen?" He sounds testy. He scrubs at his fingers with a napkin and then crushes it into a tight ball. "My mom and grandma barely spoke to each other. I never even knew her. I still don't know her. I'm just the thing she got stuck with."

"Hemmie liked her." I hesitate, then admit, "Your parents were rough as shit on him. He helped out at the bakery, and Minnie was just OK with everything, you know?"

"No. I don't know." He tosses the napkin and stares down at his hands. His fingers clench and stretch, clench and stretch. He looks lost. Like he's eight years old and the only kid on the planet who missed out on the secret decoder ring hidden at the bottom of the cereal box. I really want to hug him.

"Hey," I speak around a giant mouthful of pizza and drop the crust in the box.

Shake glances up.

I pull the ring off my nose, tug the other off my ear and dangle them by the chain. "Fake. Couldn't afford the real shit. And I was chicken. Oh, and I can't drive either. No car. No license. Nobody to teach me. And I've never eaten at a restaurant with actual waitresses."

He blinks at me. I should shut up, but I don't.

"You know, like where they come to your table and take your order and shit? I've never done that. I've never been in a different state, touched the ocean or ice skated." I'm babbling. I don't know why. I guess there's the hope that sharing embarrassing secrets might make him feel better, get him focused on something else. Maybe it's stupid.

It's definitely stupid. I am beyond lame. I might as well describe the regularity and heaviness of my monthly flow. Just to scare him spitless.

He stares blankly at me for a second, and my face is hot by the time he almost whispers, "I might have Miley Cyrus on my IPod."

"Please tell me it's Hannah Montana."

He nods. "Rat's fault. He did it, but I never deleted it. I might kinda like it. Don't tell Allie."

"I have to."

"No."

"This is too good. She'll be so happy."

"I'm a little afraid of her."

"Be very afraid. She has plans for you, and I know her snorkel mask is involved."

We smile at each other, and it's doofie and wonderful. For about two seconds. Until I see him lose focus. His eyes dull, his mouth flattens, and I know it's coming the instant before he pisses all over our fun.

"What's with the bruises?" He points at me, his big finger stabbing in my direction. There's an edge of nasty in his voice. This sabotage of our good time is deliberate, and I want to punch him in the throat.

"Don't," I warn him.

"Everybody at school blames Allie. But it's bullshit, right? That's the secret. She wouldn't hurt a fly, but she sits in detention every day, covering for something or somebody else."

I shake my head, close up the greasy pizza box and push it aside. For every one step forward, this guy takes two steps backward, and he's giving me vertigo. "Just stop."

"Why were you on Willow Drive Friday night? What's that all about?"

I slide my legs off the bed. Suddenly, the boy who's got nothing to say can't shut up. The stubborn ass isn't gonna quit.

"It's because of Hemmie, right Cleo? You said you hung out with him, and he got you a job. So what's the deal with you and him?"

"There's no deal." I stick my feet in my boots, stand up and shuffle toward the stairs. I'm outta here.

"Tell me," he growls with an extra helping of obnoxious scooped on top. "Did you fuck my brother?"

Well isn't this fun? I can't believe he went there. Too bad he doesn't come with a reset button. Like a busted video game, I could try turning him off and back on. Instead, I'll just pull the plug.

I hold up my middle finger and get one foot on the stairs. He lunges across the room in two gigantic steps, catches me by the arm and spins me around. My feet tangle in the laces of my untied boots. I'm going down, so I grab the bully to save myself, slip, flail, and knee him in the balls. Hard. He says "Oomph," and we drop in a heap. The back of my head clunks off the cement floor and Shake slams on top of me. He is bigger and slightly heavier than a charter bus full of NFL linebackers.

I squeeze my eyes shut, gulp air for a few seconds and after I adjust to the pain radiating through my skull, finally whisper, "You suck."

Shake lays half on me, knees pulled in, hands cradling his junk. I should feel a little bad, but I don't.

"Just cuz you've slummed around with me a few times, you don't get to be a jerk to me," I snipe at him. His hair gets in my mouth and I spit it out. "Buying pizza isn't a free pass to judge me."

He holds completely still and makes the same sound as a snake getting boiled in a soup pot. OK. Now I feel bad.

I open my eyes, and he's right there, inches from my face, looking down with those uber blues. His pain shimmers on the surface.

"You're right," he whispers. "I suck. I'm sorry Cleo."

That mouth of his could read the toxic shock warning on a tampon box, and I'd be all over it. It's the lower lip. That delicious lower lip. I start to wrap my arms and legs around him, mimicking some sort of slutty tree sloth. I am already puckering for an amazing apology kiss, when he eases awkwardly to his feet and leaves me dumped there on the basement floor.

Chapter 19

SHAKE:

I sit on top of an ancient picnic table in Grandma's backyard, in danger of getting splinters in my ass. I dip into my essentials kit. My essentials kit is a ziplock bag of weed, papers and a lighter. I proceed to roll an expert blunt. All the piano practice is finally paying off. My fingers are downright dexterous. Or maybe I'm just becoming a well-practiced delinquent. Whatever.

It is eight months after the fact. They say time heals all wounds. It must be meant to be taken literally. Like paper cuts or getting kneed in the balls. Because I still think of my parents and brother every fifteen seconds. It doesn't hurt any less. When I smile, I feel nauseous. Laughing too hard might kill me. Joking with Cleo in the basement dumped such an avalanche of guilt on my chest, it crushed me.

I'm not doing well. I know this, but it doesn't matter. My life affects no one. I am nobody's son. No one's brother. I have nothing to prove or offer. Cleo is learning this the hard way.

She climbs up on the table to sit cross-legged and scowls at me. This is another new version of her.

Silent Cleo. I remember the sound of her head cracking off the basement floor and my stomach flips over. I wonder if my gorilla tactics have left her with a concussion. That's her payback for being nothing but good to me.

After abandoning her in the basement, I expected her to bail. I hoped she would. I don't want any more opportunities to hurt her. Maybe I look enough like Hemmie for her to pretend. Maybe she's hanging with me because of some weird loyalty to him. Which is totally twisted, because if I wasn't such a selfish prick, he'd still be alive.

I suck smoke into my lungs and hold it until my brain softens. This weed, bought from Bruce, smells like a homeless skunk wearing gym socks and tastes about the same. But it's potent, so I'm a satisfied customer.

Silent Cleo pulls a cigarette from her flannel, lights up and gives me a look that dares me to say something. Aren't we a pair?

A sliver moon dangles above our heads, and the night is cold and damp. Dew seeps into my jeans. Cleo hugs herself and smokes. Her eyes are sharp as blades and dig at me with her every sideways glance. I'm not sure if she's pissed because I'm an asshole or because I'm getting wasted. I'm not quitting either one, so it doesn't really matter.

I drop back to lay across the table and stare up at the sky. I wish it would smother me. After a few more hits, the skunk weed settles my brain. I am ready to tell her what the whole town probably knows, but I've only said out loud once, at the police station. Even then, I wasn't completely honest.

"The night of the fire," I begin and feel her twitch beside me. "I was grounded for mouthing off."

I remember it, the lecture from my parents. They'd had enough of my irresponsibility and attitude. That's what they told me. I couldn't wait to get out of their house, out from under their everything. That's what I told them. That was our last conversation. It led to my house arrest and sneaky escape. I've replayed that last day in my mind about eight zillion times, sifting through the details like broken shards of glass. I keep trying to somehow glue them together, make something useful out of them, but just manage to cut the living shit out of myself.

"I snuck out," I tell Cleo. "Climbed down the trellis outside my window and walked to Deanna's. Her parents were gone for the weekend. Rat, Sam, and some guys from the team were hanging out with a bunch of girls. I had a couple beers, messed around with Dea and ended up falling asleep. The dubmfuck trifecta."

I set the joint between my lips and suck, talking on the exhale. "I was supposed to be home that night. I should have been there. I could have gotten my mom and dad and Hemmie out." My voice shreds apart, so I don't say anything more. I don't tell her the rest. The way I stood in the street that night, watching the flames take everything I loved. How I screamed, cried, and was totally friggin worthless.

"What makes you think you could have changed anything?" she asks.

"What makes you think I couldn't?"

Cleo twists around to look at me, but I keep my eyes on the moon.

"When your mom and dad figured out you weren't home, you know for sure, it made them happy. They knew you were safe. Think about that."

I examine my dwindling joint and tap off the ash. Taking a hit, I let the smoke drift out and give shape to my words. "Have you ever burned yourself Cleo? On a hot pan maybe? Hurts like holy fuck. That's what I think about."

"You know," she whispers slowly. "It was probably smoke inhalation that …."

"Don't," I snarl, pointing a finger like I'm training a dog. "Just don't."

She pulls her knees to her chest, becoming a tight little knot and rocks back and forth. I think I hear her sniffle. I've given her a concussion and made her cry. I'm on a roll. Maybe I should call her fat, then go to her house and kill her kitten. God I suck.

I squeeze my eyes shut against the smoke from a last pull off the joint. It burns my fingertips and I crave the pain. My whole body, every little piece of me has twisted into somebody I don't recognize. I can't fix it.

I don't know how long we stay there, saying nothing while crickets fill in the silence. I am stoned and not good company. I'd like to go stand in the road on Willow Drive but don't want Cleo with me. I'd like to exhaust myself with chinners and push-ups but don't want to prove myself a total weirdo. At least having her here keeps me from dissolving into sobs. It's a thrill a minute, and we share the miserable loneliness of being side by side and yet a million miles apart until her shivers get too distracting.

I climb off the table and lead the way to the basement. I don't invite her to stay. She doesn't offer to leave.

I strip down to my underwear, kick my dirty clothes in the general direction of the washer and flop on the bed. She strips down to bra and panties and helps herself to my NY Dolls shirt. Then she climbs right over top of me and wiggles her round little ass into the space between me and the wall. I feel her warmth, the movement of her breathing and imagine getting lost in her. It's really goddamn aggravating. I squeeze my eyes shut, fist my hands in the sheets and don't let myself reach for her.

Chapter 20

SHAKE:

I have no plan for school. My phone says otherwise. The alarm rings, rings, and keeps right on ringing. It's some kind of girlie ringtone I've never heard before, like a fairy tea party just broke out in the basement with me. FML.

I slap my hand along the floor beside the bed. No phone. No Cleo. I blame the second for the first. I stumble out of bed and track the alarm to the very top of the stairs. Nice try Cleo.

Diving back under the covers, I sleep for twenty perfect minutes before the phone goes off again. A call this time. I slam it against my ear and mumble, "Whatthafuck?"

A flustered Mrs. K calls me hon and convinces me to head to school. For her, I'll play nice. Yesterday, she welcomed me to my mandatory fourth period English Lit in the office with a juice box and those gummy fruit snacks. She even punched the straw into the juice for me.

I'm too late to make homeroom. I nap through the last half of World Government and puddle drool on my desk. I work on a sliver in my thumb during

Physics and watch a squirrel out the window during French. It's a productive day. For the squirrel. For me, not so much.

Fourth period, I step up to Mrs. K's desk. She smiles as if she's genuinely delighted by my forced presence, calls me hon some more and nudges a bowl of candy toward me. I hold up my earbuds, and because I'm a complete weasel, have no trouble lying to her.

"Yesterday," I say. "When I was in Mrs. Sanderson's office, I found these under the chair. Whoever was in there before me must have lost them."

She reaches toward the buds, smiling as if I've sprouted wings and a halo, completely oblivious to the pitchfork I'm stabbing into her back. "Why thank you hon. I'll make sure to return them."

"I'll take care of it." I pull the cord out of her reach. After prying them from Cleo's sticky fingers, I'm not sacrificing my buds again. "I don't mind," I tell her. Aren't I helpful? I even force my mouth into the shape of a smile. "Do you remember who was in the office first thing yesterday morning?"

The way I figure it, whoever was sitting in Sanderson's office, in the plastic chair before me, ratted me out. Right after that, Sanderson checked attendance, realized I hadn't made it in and asked Mrs. K to shag my ass out of bed. I just need a name. The name of the rat so I can beat it to death. I wait for Mrs. K to hand it to me.

"That would be Cleo Lee."

Chapter 21

CLEO:

I am in detention. I'm here so often I've memorized Mr. Schwartzmeyer's wardrobe and worn my chair into a wooden mitten for my butt.

When Shake walks in, Allie shouts, "There's my bicycle! I'm gonna ride your ass with no hands!"

I snort, cuz c'mon, that was a good one. Shake ignores her, slaps both palms on my desk and leans into my face. Now I flinch backward.

Shake LeCasse is pungent. Wrong word. Shit. I'm definitely gonna blow my vocab test. He actually smells obnoxiously wonderful, is more snuggly than a blanket still warm from the dryer, and I want to wrap him around me.

The word I'm searching for is potent. There's just one not-so-little problem. He's so angry his eyeballs vibrate. If looks could kill, worms would already be feasting on my carcass.

"Having fun, Cleo? Messing with me?"

Uh-oh. That's a dark, scary voice and something hot and slimy germinates in my stomach.

"Is this some big game to you?" he goes on.

I begin to sweat. Allie is silent. The entire universe cringes away from me.

"I know what you did." His words crawls down my spine and bite. I'm pretty sure they're going to leave a mark. "Sanderson threatened to call my grandmother. I'm in counseling with Mizz fucken Robbins because of you. Do you think I need that kind of trouble? You think I don't have enough to deal with? Sharing a pizza isn't a free pass to judge me. Isn't that what you said to me?"

"Mr. LeCasse," Schwartzmeyer calls out. "Sign in and take a seat."

Shake doesn't budge. He stares at me for a long second. Now that he's chewed me up, it's time to spit me out. I wait for it. He doesn't disappoint.

"Stay. The fuck. Away. From me."

I once heard a screwdriver put through a garbage disposal. His voice sounds like that. I am the screwdriver.

Shake jerks away and signs in at the front. He then drops into a chair on the opposite side of the room, sticks his buds in his ears and pretends to sleep. I know he's faking it. His muscles are squeezed into hard bumps. His one knee jackhammers. I wonder what he's listening to and wish I'd hung onto his Ipod. At least I still have his hoodie. I can use it to cloak myself in shame.

Allie stares at me then swivels to Shake. "Can't you be the one guy who isn't an asshole! I had high hopes for you."

I shake my head and mumble, "Don't." It's better this way. Even if this is a big bowl of turds with sour milk poured on top.

Over the next forty minutes, Allie works at me like I'm a stubborn pickle jar. She tries everything, but I don't answer her questions, don't share, don't have an excuse for what I did.

I am a tattletale. The lowest lifeform. There's cockroaches, slugs, pond scum and then there's me. I should live under a rock, in a garbage dump, in Siberia.

My eyes sting, my vision goes blurry, but I still stare at Shake's wild blonde curls and notice how his hair lightens at the tips. I sniff and swallow, leaking like I've been used for target practice and study the strip of skin where his T-shirt hikes up and his jeans slide down. I collect details and know I will never be allowed to touch him again. Just yesterday, he quoted Shakespeare. He trusted me with something he only ever did with his mom and I wasted it.

Each minute takes an hour. Shake bolts the second the bell rings. I walk slowly because my heart is now filled with rocks, and I have trouble carrying it. I manage to shrug Allie off and send her home. I am a shitty friend. She'd like to help and make me feel better, but I'm busy paling around with guilt and misery.

I skip my regular stop at the bakery, proving I'm an all around rotten person by abandoning the strays to hunger. I don't know what to do with my crappy self, so I just wander through town and scuff my feet. I kick an empty Pepsi can down the sidewalk for a while and come across a lost quarter but decide someone more deserving should get to pick it up.

I should never have trusted Sandersuck. She acts like she cares but it's only about the students worth caring about, which includes Shake. Not me. So when I confided stuff about Shake, and she promised to keep it quiet, I should have known the kumquat would throw me under the bus. I just wanted her to do something for him. I can't tell Shake the truth, so ratting him out was the only option I could come up with. I tried to get him some help, and now Shake hates me. The world is right side up again, which blows.

I drag my sorry ass to the yellow house. After this shit-tastic day, there's no place I'd rather not be. Bring on the suck.

I kick off my boots, retreat inside Shake's hoodie and curl up on a futon mattress that is stained from whoever had it before me. It smells like feet and is decked out in Batman sheets I feel bad about stealing from the laundromat.

I mentally pick through my garage-sale existence and realize I am less valuable than my stinky mattress, which actually smells more like crotch than feet. I am nothing anybody wants or needs. I'm lucky I don't fit easily into a garbage bag. Yes, I'm throwing myself a pity party, but I'm right.

Only Hemmie ever gave a shit. I miss him so much, sometimes the world stops, and it's impossible to breathe. Hemmie looked out for me, and for his sake, I should be stepping up for his little brother. I don't want Shake to be another thing I miss and feel guilty about. Too late.

Quiet tears slide down my face. Even in an empty house, I know better than to make noise. I know better than to fall asleep, but I do anyway.

"How stupid are you?"

I startle awake to hot breath against my ear. No, no, no! This can't be happening. Panic sends me scrambling to get away before my eyes are fully open, but there's nowhere to go and Randy's fingers are already squeezing my arm.

"Stupid goddamn bitch. How many times did I warn you?"

He yanks me off the bed so fast and hard, I can't get my feet under me. I'm tangled up in my sheets as I flop onto the floor, my hip taking the painful thump, my right shoulder burning from the strain as he drags me.

"You think I'm fucken playing? Is that it?"

I'm screeching sounds, not forming words, and then I catch sight of Bruce leaning in the doorway, his pupils dilated, hungry mouth hanging wide open. I squeeze my eyes shut, pinch them tight. I don't want to see anymore, hear anymore, be me anymore.

Chapter 22

SHAKE:

It's a bad night. Or a great night. Depending.
What do I need? Escape.

I meet up with Rex, and Escape is for sale. I
snort a line and become a brand new monster. I fly.

I don't know where I go or how I get from the
Crypt to Willow Drive, but I land on the yellow stripe
down the center of the road. Arms stretched wide, I
scream at the guilty voice in my head, spit my anger
and brace myself to fight the light. It comes at me
from around the blind curve, all red throbs and bright
white eyes. Yes, yes, yes, I beg. Come and get me.

The chirp of breaks robs me of the impact.
Then somebody shouts, "Freeze!" and I'm smart
enough to run.

I swear there is nothing left of me but my
breath tearing out of my lungs. I feel weightless as I
sprint through dark neighborhoods, climb over fences,
and duck around shrubs and garbage cans. I grow
suddenly heavy as I bang my head off the unforgiving
overhang and tumble to the bottom of the stairs. I
pass out where I land, sprawled on the basement
floor at Grandma's.

At some point, I strip down to underwear and crawl into bed. Whatever was soaring through my veins now skitters. It is mean and hungry, and as I scratch at my skin, it chases me down into a sweaty pit of loss that is never ending and beyond awful.

In the basement, there is no difference from one hour to the next. Light or dark, I am in hell. I only drag myself out of it long enough to piss, puke and drink water. When my phone rings, I shut it off. I may never leave my bed again. I will atrophy here and moss will grow over me.

The pounding wakes me up. I pinch my eyes shut, promise NEVER AGAIN, and wait for whoever is at the door to go away. How long does the average person knock? Three minutes is a long time. Five minutes is overkill. Nine minutes is demented. A psychopath continues to pound. WTF?

I don't bother putting on pants. Mainly because I can't pry my eyes wide enough to find them. I can't even stand up straight. Climbing the stairs requires both hands and is almost the end of me. Halfway up, I pause to dry heave. Need. Coffee.

I yank the door, flinching away from the stab of sunshine and wobble on my feet. If the basement is hell, I've now crossed into the deepest circle of Dante's Inferno.

Allie Kindle bounces on her heels and is way too animated for my sluggish brain. "Ermigawd! Ermigawd! I love your boxers. Make sure to pack those for our honeymoon. Just those."

In my fragile state, I can't handle the attack of her loudness, enthusiasm, and clashing colors. There is a very real danger of me spewing all over her hot pink Hello Kitty sneakers.

"What're you doing here?" I croak.

"It's so bad." With those three words, her shoulders sag. "Terrible, horrible bad."

My stomach clenches. Then I remember there is no bad news I care about anymore. So I wait her out, figuring Taylor Swift probably has a zit or something.

"Cleo didn't come to school today."

"So?"

"Cleo is always at school."

"Don't care."

"Cleo is always at school."

"I'll cancel the perfect attendance award."

"Cleo is ALWAYS at school."

"Probably got the runs."

"No!" Allie shrieks, cracking my hangover in half. "Cleo is …"

"Always at school," I say with her. "Did you call her?"

"No."

"Do that." I wait. I think my teeth are sweating. I need to concentrate to swallow. She stares at me. Time to move this along. "Call her," I suggest the obvious.

"No phone."

I debate options. I want her gone. "You can use mine."

"You're a wonderful, beautiful person. Our children will be
amazing. I'm hoping for six. Four boys and two girls. We need to set a date for the wedding. Most venues book up quickly."

"Stop." I cut her off, motioning with both hands and squeezing my eyes shut for a second. I swear there's tiny elves, with tiny pitchforks, stabbing my frontal lobe. "Wait. Right there." I point at the welcome mat. "Right there. Don't move."

"I love it when you're all bossy."

Downstairs, I pull on jeans and shirt, scrounge around until I locate my phone and come back to find Allie where I left her. I'm disappointed. I was hoping she was a hallucination. "Here."

She snatches my phone, pets it like a baby gerbil and smiles.

"Call her," I prompt.

"Can't."

"Why?"

"I told you. No phone. But you were so eager to help, I didn't want to discourage you."

I must still be sleeping. Only a nightmare could be this bizarre. "What?"

"Cleo doesn't have a phone." She hands mine back.

What the hell?

"Look, this has been a real blast, Allie, but I give less than a kernel of a shit about Cleo. And I've got a busy day of getting baked and sleeping for, like ever, so..." I start to shut the door. She slaps a hand the size of Captain America's shield against it. The vibrations nearly tear my arm from the socket. Her strength is impressive. I wonder if she can ice skate. She'd make quite a defenseman.

"It's your fault!" The volume of her shout shakes my thoughts like maracas and my eyes cross.

I wait for the vibration to settle down and then, even though I know better, I ask, "What's my fault?"

"OK, it's sorta my fault too. I told her to be the fish. Seemed like a good idea at the time. She totally ended up saving your beautiful butt, so you owe her. And I've decided you're going to live up to my expectations."

"Fish?"

"You're! Gonna! Help! Cleo!"

Across the street, Mr. Polvino stands on his porch, looking this way. Two houses down, Mrs. Eastman emerges onto her front step. The neighbors are gathering like frightened meerkats sensing a threat at the watering hole. I can't have this, whatever this is, coming back on me, getting mentioned to my grandmother and becoming an excuse for her to get rid of me.

"I'm not doing this right now," I tell Allie, keeping my voice low and even, hoping to lead by example. "I'll see you at school."

She explodes into a seismic blast. "Don't you get it? There's nobody else!"

I sigh, pinching the bridge of my nose between my thumb and index finger. My head throbs as if it's about to give birth. "Christ."

"Nope. He ignores both me and Cleo."

I am confused. "What do you want from me?"

"Is that a trick question?"

"Focus Allie. What do you expect me to do?"

"We gotta go to her house."

I glance up. "Cleo's?"

She nods.

Oh hells no. I shake my head. "Not a chance."

She amps up the shouting, or maybe she's acting out a dramatic musical number about a flock of geese getting fed through a wood chipper. She's flapping her arms, stomping her feet and honking accusations at me. Apparently I've done something unforgivable to Cleo. Nevermind that Cleo gave my ass up to Sanderson, stole my hoodie and made herself at home in my bed. And lets not forget the Oreos and my Donatello in fourth grade. Yet I'm somehow the bad guy who gets stuck with Allie jumping his shit.

The neighbors flee to safety. Birds take to the skies. Small children all over the world cry for their mommies as Allie goes into alarming detail over what she's going to do to my balls if her miniature friend is not found ASAP. I hold my skull together with both hands as my stomach climbs to thirteen thousand feet and jumps without a parachute. I am willing to say anything to make it stop.

Allie and I walk to Cleo's.

We are barely off the porch when she tells me, "This is your first step in the right direction."

I have no response. I am in brain-frying hell.
Bruised and sore from my humpty-dumpty down the
basement stairs, sick, and sweating in the heat, I
wonder when it got hot as dick outside. My hangover
oozes from my pores, and I swear I smell tequila. I
don't even remember drinking tequila.

Allie eventually slows to a stop. She points
ahead, to the last and crappiest house on a dead end
excuse for a road. I've heard of the yellow house,
everybody has, but I've never been to this
neighborhood before. I don't plan to ever come here
again. This is where hopes and dreams breed mold.

"This it?" I wait for her nod. "OK. We knock. We
check on her. Then I'm done."

She takes a deliberate step backward.

"What? You're not coming with me?"

Allie is silent. Let me repeat, Allie is silent.
Should I dial 911? Perform the Heimlich? I stare at
her for a second and wonder if I'm actually awake. I'm
hungry, so I must be, right? But her eyes are all big
and … Is she scared? Holy shit. What the hell have I
signed up for?

"I'm not welcome there. That's why I need
you," she finally tells me, and for once, her voice is
nearly a whisper.

"Not welcome? What the …"

"You go."

I scrub at the sweat on the back of my neck,
not happy. "Fine. Whatever."

The final length of road crumbles from
pavement to dirt under my sneakers. Cleo's house

takes a pinch of ass-ugly, blends it with rundown and creates a total shithole. It's small, sags in the middle, leans to the east and was painted egg yolk yellow sometime before disco tanked. There are broken windows, boarded up windows and a nasty looking vine creeping up the side. The lawn is a chaos of knee-high weeds overtaking a vacuum cleaner, toilet seat, roofing shingles and a bunch of old tires. White trash has never looked so hopeless. All that's missing is caution tape and a condemned sign.

I try to picture Cleo here and can't do it.

I follow a worn path, catch the glitter of broken glass and get nervous about a line of wasps nests globbed onto the roof's overhang. Instead of a front step, there is a risky combination of cement blocks. I'm tall enough to ignore them and stand on the ground. A bare wire dangles where the doorbell should be. I knock and old paint flies off the door in a handful of unhappy confetti.

I cross my fingers, hope nobody answers but hear movement inside. When Rex opens up, he grins and says, "Hey man, wassup? Need a taste?"

Here's the thing. I promised myself. No more. But I was lying.

I wet my lips and glance back toward where I left Allie. She's no longer there. I debate, but knowing she will literally barbecue my ass over an open fire, I finally ask, "Cleo around?"

Rex drops the smile. I get it. It's his little sister, and I'm an escalating mess. Nobody knows that better than Rex.

"Not here."

"She wasn't in school." Dumb thing to say. Neither was I. Rex doesn't give a shit.

"Can't help you man."

I nod. Satisfied. Did what I could.

"What's this?" A red-haired dude leans into the doorway, joint smoldering between knobby fingers, brown stains down the front of a yellowed wife-beater. I couldn't dream up a better cliche.

"Hemmie's brother," Rex tells him.

"Like seeing a ghost."

I don't look that much like my brother. This guy is full of shit and straight out of a Guns-n-Roses video. He's wiry and inked, with a face sharp as a machete blade. His eyes are so pale, they are almost transparent.

He jerks his chin at me, grinning with pointy teeth. "Scamming your brother's leftovers?"

I don't answer.

"Nothing here for you."

"Whatever." I start to turn away.

"Hey kid," he calls after me. "Piece of advice. Don't be dipping your dick in my shit."

I swing around. I don't even know what the hell that means, but it pisses me off. "What's your problem?"

Rex flashes a palm at me, wraps his other hand over the guy's shoulder. "It's all good. Shake's a friend in need. Just bidness, man." Rex then tells me, "Hang on a sec, yeah?" He disappears into the house.

I lock eyes with the dude leaning in the doorway. I give him a minute to change my mind, but nope, I'm sticking with my first impression. He is a total douche.

"Your brother owed me money," says the Douche.

"Good luck with that."

"Maybe I collect from you."

"Like I said, good luck with that."

"You don't wanna push me kid." His lips curl up, and his eyes are nothing but mean. I bet he makes a hobby of popping birthday balloons.

Rex comes back and tosses me a packet of blow. I start to fish in my pockets, but he says, "No worries. On me, dude. Take the edge off. Get yer head straight, yeah?"

I glance one last time at the Douche, then walk back up the road. I get it now, why Cleo is always in school, why she might want to sleep in an abandoned car with a busted window or crawl into my bed. Anything's gotta be better than dealing with the Douche in that shitty house. Which is nothing to do with me. Even if it leaves a bad taste in my mouth and has me sort of agitated and feeling like I need to wash my hands.

It takes a while to find Allie, maybe because I'm not looking for her. I'm hoping to ditch her. She jumps out at me as I turn onto Main Street and scares the bejesus out of me. Grabbing me by both arms, she pulls me in and insists, "We go look for Cleo now."

"Hold up. Isn't that what I just did?"

Allie shakes her head. "She's never at her house."

"So why'd we go there?"

"To show you."

"Show me what?"

"Why she needs you."

No, no, oh hell no.

This scavenger hunt needs to end. Right here. Right now. Cleo is nothing but trouble, and she's sort of addictive. Every since telling her off in detention, I've been making it a point not to think about her. I need to remind myself every twenty minutes and like a bug bite, not scratching doesn't make it itch any less.

I open my mouth to shut Allie down when she says, "Your brother looked after Cleo. He'd be glad she has you now."

Aw Crap.

Chapter 23

SHAKE:

We find Cleo curled into the back seat of the abandoned car near the creek. Until that moment, I wasn't taking Allie seriously. But it's bad. And I admit it. I care. I just don't know what to do about it.

I get the door open, lean into the car and touch Cleo with just my fingertips on her shoulder. She opens her eyes slowly but doesn't look at me.

"Cleo?"

No response.

"How bad are you hurt?"

Still nothing. There's blood crusted around her nose and mouth. She's got a fat lip, bruised cheek and who knows what else. Her hair is sweaty and in places, stuck to the blood on her face. I can't decide if she needs soap and water or X-rays, but everything in me knots and twists and I'm suddenly standing at the bottom of a very deep pit and having trouble catching my breath. I inhale real slow and exhale pure fire.

"Cleo? How bad?"

"Leave me alone," she whispers.

"Can't do that."

"I don't need your help."

"Yeah, you do."

She closes her eyes, squeezes them shut and a shiver passes through her. "Go away."

I sigh, grip my neck and come to the realization that Cleo is the straw who will most likely break this camel into a million pieces.

"You gotta pick," I tell her. Her eyes finally flick to mine. I recognize her expression. I've faced the same hopelessness in the mirror. Seeing it on her is worse. "Emergency room or home with me?"

"Stay. The fuck. Away. From me."

Yeah, I said the same thing to her. Yesterday. I don't know how someone so small manages to be such a giant pain in the ass. But I remember she got me home from the Crypt that night. And looked after me when I got blitzed in detention the other day. She didn't walk away, even when I acted like a toolbag and cracked her head against the floor. Somewhere along the way, she's managed to burrow under my skin.

Crawling into the car, so I'm only inches from her face, I say, "And though she be but little, she is fierce."

Quoting Shakespeare isn't playing fair, but I win. She gets soft for a second, then gives me a little nod. I start to ask if she's OK to walk but notice her bare feet. There's no sign of her boots and something so goddamn sad about her dirty little feet. Of course, she's still wearing the raggedy-ass flannel. I'd like to burn it.

"C'mon." I slide one arm around her back, one under her ass and gently, carefully lift her out. She weighs less than my hockey bag.

"I can walk," she argues.

"Nope."

"Put me down."

"Not gonna happen."

"Shake."

"Wasting your breath."

I've never carried my hockey bag for five miles, in the heat, some of it uphill, hungover as hell. I carry Cleo all the way to my grandma's house. She wraps one arm around my neck, tucks her head into my shoulder and fists her other hand in my shirt. This version is called Hurt Cleo. Glancing down at Hurt Cleo, feeling her tremble, I'm already in so deep I should have left a trail of breadcrumbs. I'll never find my way back.

My arms, shoulders and spine are screaming by the final mile. Allie offers to take Cleo, begs to actually, but I'm unwilling to hand her over. I don't analyze it. I'm not ready to face whatever it means but every time Allie reaches for the little package in my arms, I tighten my hold and shake my head no. I did the same thing to Hemmie when I got a remote control car for my seventh birthday and he wanted to take it for a spin. He eventually knocked me down and stole it. I keep an eye on Allie.

We make an interesting parade. Cars slow for a second look. Nobody offers us a ride.

Allie stops at the threshold of grandma's house, refusing to step inside. She's suddenly in a panic over her mom being left home alone, warning me not to tell anybody Cleo's here, and making me promise I won't let anything bad happen to our tiny friend, which seems too little too late, but I give my word, for what it's worth.

By the time I trudge down the basement stairs, I'm a sweaty mess. I forget to duck AGAIN and bang my head off the fucken, goddamn, mother-effen, low ceiling.

"Every freakin time," I grumble, clutching Cleo to my chest and tripping down the last few steps.

I ease Cleo onto the bed, step back and rub at my forehead. I'm too keyed up to sit or be still, and I stare at her like she's a weird exhibit at the zoo.

"Tell me," I say sharper than I planned.

She curls into pillbug mode.

"Cleo!" I'm half yelling at her. I try to soften my voice but can't manage it. "Tell me what happened."

"Fell down the stairs."

"The stairs?" Wow. This girl is the worst liar on the planet. If she was trying to make a living at it, she'd starve to death. Her lie is so transparent, I can clearly see the truth on the other side. "What stairs?"

"At my house."

"Your one story house."

"Basement."

"When?"

"After school yesterday."

I take a second and chew on my tongue. I wait as my brain uploads this fresh batch of crap.

"Let me see if I've got this right. You fell down the stairs, then walked barefoot, approximately five miles, to that junk car in the weeds? Where you spent all last night and all day today? With no food? No water? For no apparent reason other than to worry the piss out of Allie and torture yourself? Jesus Christ Cleo, if you're gonna bullshit me, at least put in a little effort."

"What do you care?"

What the hell do I do with this? With her? With whoever beat on her? Cuz somebody did. I'm blaming The Douche and imagine squeezing his scrawny neck with one hand and wailing the snot out of him with other.

"Who did it?" I form the words slowly.

"Let it go, Shake."

"It was that red-headed douche, right?"

"Stop."

"That slimy piece of shit."

"Shake."

"I will decimate his worthless ass."

"Quit!"

"That fuckwad is a dead man."

"Shake!" It registers that she's shouting at me.

"What?" I finally look at her. I've been avoiding it because the sight of her shoves me straight off the edge of my temper and breaks me apart.

"Stop pacing. You're driving me batshit."

I breathe in, breathe out and try to slow my pulse rate. I plant my ass on the basement stairs but have trouble sitting still. My knee bounces. My hands clench. The air in my lungs is the open flame and my heart is roasting on the spit. Somebody grab some marshmallows because guilt, regret and a whole stack of self-loathing is building a raging inferno. Cuz see, I'm feeling like I've let Cleo down. I definitely let her down.

I walked away from her, and it reminds me way too much of sneaking out of my house and coming back to disaster.

"How do you know about Randy," she half-whispers.

"Who's Randy?"

"My mom's boyfriend. The red-headed guy."

"The Douche," I clarify. "I went to your house looking for you."

She moans and curls up even tighter, hugging herself. I wait for her to tell me something, give me something, a string I can pull on.

"Don't look at me like that," she snarls.

"Like what?"

"Like you just found your kitten splattered all over the highway."

Cleo is not a kitten. She's a rabid wolverine. Yet somebody splattered her.

"I fell down the basement stairs yesterday," I tell her. "I'm sore. I'm bruised. You look more like somebody's punching bag. Tell me. I'll take care of it. I swear to you, it won't ever happen again."

She sits up carefully, tugs her flannel over bent knees and stares at her dirty toes. Her body takes up no space at all on the bed. She's tiny, delicate, defenseless. I know how bad it sucks to have no chance of fighting back, but it doesn't have to be like that for her. I might be a giant moron, but I do have my uses.

"You can't fix this, Shake. If you try, you'll make it worse. So you're off the hook. Not your job. Not your problem. This is just how it is for me."

"Just how it is? Are you fucken serious with that?"

"Stay out of it."

"Is this the no judging each other rule again? Because I haven't forgotten you ratting me out to Sanderson. I'm wondering how come you get to interfere with me, but I'm not allowed to help you?"

"That's different. You're out of control and hurting yourself. She was just supposed to step in, pull you back a little, do something useful. And it was a mistake. I shouldn't have done it, and I'm sorry."

"Why'd you do it?"

She glances up. "Truth?"

I blow out a breath. Isn't that what I've been begging for? "Yeah, Cleo, even if I look fat in these jeans, I always want the truth. Always. No lies between us, yeah?"

For a second, she kind of looks like I slapped her. Then she switches gears and chews right into me. "Because you're a dumbass. This is how it is for me. But not for you. You're wrecking your chance for something better. A chance at a life I'd give anything to have. I can't just sit back and watch. Since I can't figure out how to fix your stupid ass by myself, I hoped Sandersuck would do it for me. But it's not up to me. Not my choice what happens to you. So I shouldn't have done it. It's obvious talking to Sandersuck didn't do you any good anyway. I can smell the hangover on you."

Other than the dumbass comment, that's not what I expected from her. I don't know how to argue, so I say, "I'm stuck in counseling."

"Good."

"With Ms. Robbins."

"Hope you were a boy scout."

I tilt my head, not following.

"Be prepared," she tells me. "Wrap it before you tap it."

Ms. Robbins is a hot mess. Not going there. "What now then? We both settle for the broken pieces of each other?"

Cleo startles. Her big dark eyes grow even bigger. What did I say?

She dips her chin. "I'm pretty sure you don't want any of my pieces."

"I definitely want your pieces. Especially when they're wrapped in that yellow bath towel." I try to lighten things up a little, maybe get her to trust me. I even attempt a smile, but my mouth can't manage it. The look on my face probably scares her. She gives me nothing back but wary silence. "Tell me what to do, Cleo. What do you need?"

She glances away, her cheeks a little pink, her mouth pinched into a flat line. "I need ..."

I'm hoping for something profound. A solution. If I can't figure out what the hell I need, it would be nice to give her what she needs.

"A shower," she says so quietly I barely hear her. "Some clothes."

I swallow the equivalent of a full-grown porcupine and jerk a nod. "Yup. Sure. Hang on."

I dig through my stuff, rushing like there's a time limit, and find a pair of boxers and the NY Dolls shirt. Not quite the same as slaying the dragon, but I am her champion. "Good to go."

She starts to get up. I reach for her, but she stops me and says, "Don't." She looks scared, and I'm suddenly very aware of how big I am, how threatening I might seem.

So I follow her up the stairs, hanging back but not too far. We're nearly to the top when she sways backward. I catch her, fold her against my chest and keep her there. I'm two steps below her but my chin rests lightly on the top of her head. For one second, I don't look back, don't look ahead. I just breathe in and feel good about being here for her. In eight months, it might be the one thing I've done right.

"It's OK," I tell her. "I won't ever hurt you. You know that right?"

Cleo doesn't answer but lets me hold her.

"Just dehydrated," she finally mumbles. "And hungry. And humiliated. And I probably smell bad."

"You've seen and smelled me worse." I pick her up, even though she tells me I don't have to, and decide I like carrying her. She's so itty-bitty, it's a huge ego boost. Maybe I should carry her all the time. I settle for transporting her as far as the kitchen and place her on a chair.

I search the fridge. There's so much food crammed onto the shelves, extracting anything is like a game of Jenga. Unless Grandma is hoarding for the zombie apocalypse, I don't understand it. She rarely eats here. I grab orange juice, strawberry yogurt, bread, peanut butter, jelly and I'm not sure what Cleo likes, so I add applesauce, mustard, salami, a carton of potato salad and consider the eggs. I suddenly remember she likes eggs and pull them out too. I hunt around for bacon. I can replace it all tomorrow.

"Hey."

I spin around. Cleo holds the yogurt. "You aren't feeding Adam Turner and the entire tuba section. This is good. And maybe water."

"Oh. Yeah." I get her a spoon, load a glass with ice and water and put everything else away. Then I stand there with my hands in my back pockets while she eats, feeling inadequate and trying to ignore the trembling in my gut. I'm not sure if it's hunger or not. I can't remember when I last ate, but my stomach is churning hard enough to turn cream into butter.

"How come you don't eat any of it?" she asks.

"What?"

"All the food. There's so much. How come you never eat it?"

I shrug. I don't tell her I'm unwilling to risk my squatting rights in the basement by stealing food. I'd rather go hungry than homeless, and I'm pretty sure my grandmother is looking for a reason to get rid of me.

"How come?" she pushes.

"It's not mine."

Cleo is better after the yogurt and drinking a glass of water. Steady on her feet. Once I get her into the bathroom, I find a fresh towel, turn on the water in the shower and adjust the temperature. Then I stare at her some more. I'm detailing the damage, storing it away so I can be sure someone someday pays the full amount for it.

"Shake?"

"Yeah?"

"Little privacy?"

"Oh. Right. Are you OK to …" I flap my hands at her, but she seems to decipher it.

"I'm bruised. I'm sore. Nothing's broken."

I wonder how she can be so sure, but then I get it. She knows the same way I know if I'm offsides without checking the blue line. In this case, experience is not a good thing.

"Not gonna faint or fall down or anything?"

"I'm good."

No she's not. She's so far from good, it's not even visible on her horizon, but I've been saying the same thing since the night of the fire. I understand, it's code for leave me the fuck alone.

I step into the hallway, tip my head back against the wall and listen to the shower. Since Grandma's car is gone from the driveway, we're clear for now. I don't want to get caught with this. I've caused enough trouble for my grandmother and her patience is probably nearing the end. I need to get Cleo cleaned up, hidden in the basement and then figure out what comes next.

What comes next? Shit. I'm so over my head here. I've got no plan. Most days, I can't even get my ass out of bed for school in the morning. It's a good day if I brush my teeth. And this is a little more complicated than hiding a bag of weed under my mattress.

"Shake?" Cleo calls from the bathroom. Her voice is thin and quivery and doesn't sound like her.

I'm holding the boxers and shirt. I duck back around the corner. The room is steamy, smells like shampoo, and she's wrapped in a towel. I don't know if she looks better or worse, but she seems way smaller than usual. Like she'd fit in my pocket.

Seeing the black-and-blue smudges against her pale skin reminds of the first time I noticed her bruises, when I couldn't be bothered to care, and I hate myself. I'm this combination of ashamed and angry, and I don't want her to see it, so I glance away, down at the floor. Her flannel is lying there crumpled up. There's nothing else. No other clothes.

Chapter 24

CLEO:

I hear the change in his breathing. I watch his chest rise and fall and his shoulders squeeze. His hands are doing the thing where they fist and stretch. Each time his fingers straighten, they tremble.

He doesn't need to say anything. I get it. He's making this into something big and awful.

Yeah, it's super big and awful. The Mount Everest of shitty. The Himalayas of suck. But I'm working hard to pretend it never happened, and he's gotta let it go. He's gotta stop making me think about it, or it will take a broom and dustpan to gather what's left of me.

"Shake." His eyes drift to mine. They are so blue, I swear I can look into them and hear the ocean. But they don't see me. They see bruises and swelling and nothing but a shirt on the floor. They see a mess he can't clean up. I shouldn't be here. He doesn't need this. He's not strong enough to handle it. That doesn't doesn't stop me from wanting to stay and having nowhere else to go.

"Hey." I slide his NY dolls shirt over my head and drop the towel. I put on a brave face and convincing performance. "Shake," I try again as I pull on the boxers. They are way too big and hang hammock-style between my legs. "Take a shower."

"Huh?"

"Dude, you stink like a friggin' goat after a frat party. Make friends with a bar of soap. I'll be downstairs."

I leave him in the bathroom. I'd like to run from whatever is happening behind his eyes but take my time, because everywhere hurts, even my hair follicles, because that fucker yanked so hard. But I don't think about that. Nope, nope, nope.

Sliding into Shake's bed helps more than it should. His shirt, sheets and pillow all have his smell. But then I start to freak out. I pull my knees tight to my chest, stare at nothing but the corner where the walls meet the ceiling, and my skin squirms over my bones. I rock and shiver.

I need Shake down here. I want him right goddamn now.

By the time I hear him start down the stairs, I am in full blown panic mode. I hate basements. I really do. I call, "Hurry!" My hero thunders down and bashes his head off the overhang. Just like always. Just about knocking himself down and out. Someone should buy the boy a helmet.

"Fuck!" He slaps one hand against his forehead and uses the other to clutch the bath towel around his hips. "Every goddamn time."

"You're like having a pet giraffe," I tell him. Just the sight of him calms me down. "A blind, retarded, pet giraffe."

He finally focuses on me. "You OK?"

I am now.

I look him over in detail, because he's wet and wearing nothing but a towel. The towel is slipping and seriously, he should be listed as one of the seven wonders of the world. He could replace the Grand Canyon, because even though I've never been there, I am confident he'd be way more fun to explore. I'd start with the muscles framing his belly button, forming an arrow and pointing under the towel. Wherever it leads, I would like to go there, see the show and ride the ride.

I jab my finger toward the ceiling. "You gotta kill it. Right now."

"What?"

"The spider. Right now, Shake. Before it gets away. And I need to see proof of the kill. Hurry!"

"Spider?" he echoes. He's definitely bonked his head off the ceiling once too often.

I point more forcefully. There is a spider the size of a Volkswagen lurking in the corner, and it's definitely staring at me, waiting for me to look away, so it can drop on my head and crawl around in my hair. I shudder and sniff back a tear and blame the spider.

Shake squints at it, glances around and finally just reaches up and smashes the thing with his thumb. I hear it squoosh, and it's beyond gross. Which I tell him.

"You said to kill it."

"Not with your bare hands. That was freakin' brutal."

"You said hurry." He wipes his thumb on the towel. "Cleo Lee is afraid of spiders?"

"No."

"It's called arachnophobia."

"It's not arachnophobia." The spider is dead. I'm still afraid. I wonder if there is such a thing as Randy-phobia. "Spiders are dirty. They live in a web they literally shit out of their asses."

He paws through the clothes stuffed into his tote and finally digs out a pair of boxers. "You're so scared of a harmless little spider, you made me kill Carl. And it isn't shit. It's silk. It comes out of their spinneret, not technically their ass. Just so you're impressed, certain species of spiders are really into foreplay."

"First of all, that spider wasn't harmless or little. Second, spider foreplay is not something I want to think about. And third … Carl?"

"He's been rooming with me for three days. I thought we should be on a first name basis." He gives the boxers the sniff-test, then tugs them up his legs, under the towel. Tossing the towel at the washer, he misses and it slides to the floor. I suspect Shake is a slob who's hiding his true colors from his grandmother.

He's now standing in nothing but boxers with hands on hips. Droplets of water cling to his hair and slide down his chest. I don't trust the look he's giving me, and he definitely shouldn't trust the look I'm giving him. Him being here and just being him, so totally and wonderfully Shake, shouldn't make me feel so much better.

"Is anybody going to be worried, start looking for you, Cleo? Somebody I should call?"

"No. How do you know so much about spiders?"

"Fifth grade animal project. What about your mom? Or how about the cops?"

"I said no," I snap. "The word ferret is Latin and means little thief. I got an A on mine."

"You're a lot like a ferret." He grabs a pair of jeans and drops down on the edge of the bed. "Should we get some of your stuff from your house?"

"I can't."

"I can."

I envy his fearlessness. "Stay out of it. Did you hear me? I need those four words to somehow sink into your thick skull. Stay. Out. Of. It."

"I'll get your stuff. Your boots. Your shorts. Your ... " It's dawning on him, I have no other clothes. "Whatever you need."

I crawl forward and wrap my knuckles off his forehead four times. "Stay! Out! Of! It!"

He catches me by the wrist and rubs his thumb over my bracelet of deep purple bruises. "No."

"There's no stuff, OK? Nothing for you to get." I hate the sound of my voice, the sudden tremble in it. And Shake hears it. His whole face hardens quicker than poured cement in the sun.

"God, Cleo." He squeezes his eyes shut. "Let me handle this for you. I'll make sure it doesn't ever happen again."

"I owe you a hoodie."

"Please."

"I stole your hoodie, and it's gone."

"Cleo?"

"I'll replace it."

"I know I'm a fucken disaster. But whatever happened, I can deal with it for you."

No, no, no. We aren't talking about this, ever. He will not know this about me and carry all my nasty shit around forever. I will not think it, let it in, revisit it. Because I can't do anything about it. He sure as shit can't do anything about it. Nothing. Ever. I was warned not to hang around him. But I didn't listen, so it spun around and kicked me in the teeth. Yet here I am again. So I mash all the ugliness way, way down, stare hard at Shake and wait for him to give up. Like everybody does.

But this is Shakespeare LeCasse. He is a species I've never come across before. He looks at me. Keeps on looking. Really looks, right into me, in a way no one ever has. It all starts to rise up and take me over.

Randy dragging me across the floor. The rug scraping against my skin. Him ordering me around like a dog, hurting and humiliating me to make a point. I have nothing he doesn't let me have. He let me have my flannel. After I begged and did every awful thing he asked. Only the flannel, and then he burned the rest. He made me light the fire and watch the flames.

Shit, shit, goddamn, shit. I am trembling. Badly.

"Aw no," Shake whispers. "I'm sorry."

When I feel the tears, I'm so surprised, I don't catch them in time. They get away. They spill down my face, and I make this sound, this suckerpunched in the gut yowl, and then I'm gasping, tasting my tears, sobbing, hiccuping. I am the equivalent of an emotional tsunami. I can't stop. I haven't cried like this since I was ten.

Shake drops the jeans, grabs a towel and hands it to me, because I am leaking all down my face.

"Not the one with spider smoosh," I manage to croak between sobs.

He trades the towel for one of his T-shirts, and I swipe my nose and eyes while he climbs up next to me on the bed. In nothing but his boxers. There is so much of him.

"Get away." I shove at his chest. This is how I thank him for carrying me home, feeding me and giving me clothes.

I'm glad he doesn't listen to me. He pulls me into him, spooning me as he slips his left hand under the pillow and splays his right over my ribs. One leg bends up behind mine. The other hooks over me, and I feel him from my head to my toes. I am surrounded by his warmth, his scent and the beat of his heart pounding into my back.

He tells me everything will be OK, that I am safe, and I don't believe him. But I am not scared for the first time in forever. It is the best place in the whole world. He is the cocoon. I am the caterpillar. I will never become a butterfly, but if I dig in deep enough, maybe he'll keep me for a little while.

Chapter 25

CLEO:

I cry so hard and long, I drench his pillow. I am every guy's worst nightmare, and I'm guessing Shake would rather listen to Celine Dion's entire discography. When I finally quit, he pets my hair and whispers a quote from his namesake in my ear. "Our remedies oft in ourselves do lie, which we ascribe to heaven."

He is my hero.

We sleep, bundled together and our broken edges somehow fit together to make something nearly whole. At least for a little while.

Shake's phone wakes us up, still set to the most girlie ringtone I could find. For the second time ever, I skip school. Shake yanks on jeans and a shirt and heads out without saying a word. I hope he's going to school but sort of wish he'd stayed with me. He comes back an hour later with donuts and coffee. Did I mention, he's my hero?

We spend the day playing weird games. We toss underwear and try to snag the leg holes on laundry detergent bottles. We build towers out of random stuff in the basement, guess songs from humming a few notes and watch videos of cute animals on his phone. I am now determined to own a miniature pig. We also match every kid in our class with the animal they most resemble. Brandon Hintz totally looks like a badger. Actually, he looks like George Clooney when he was a kid, if George was really homely, sort of pudgy and not overly bright.

Shake doesn't ask anymore tough questions. I think he learned his lesson after last night's crying palooza. He even smiles a couple of times and chuckles a little without freaking out. I hurt everywhere, and yet it is maybe the best day of my whole life. Which is extra cool since it follows one of the worst. Only one of the worst, because nothing compares to losing Hemmie.

It's about three o'clock in the afternoon when we hear something upstairs. We both glance at the ceiling and go Anne Frank quiet. Slow footsteps and low voices drift toward us.

"You couldn't find her clit with both hands and a flashlight taped to your dick."

"This from a guy who hasn't gotten laid since Blair threw him a pity fuck."

"Blow me, Sam-I-Am. Hey doucherella, you down there?"

"Aw shit," Shake growls and pops up off the bed. He looks at me with a touch of panic in his eyes and says, "Whatever happens next, I'm sorry."

That doesn't sound good.

"Bet he's jerking off," says a deep voice on the way down the stairs. "Hey assburger!"

Two pairs of legs come into view. Two heads clunk off the overhang. It should be funny, but I'm too busy trying to crawl into the wall and disappear.

After some stumbling and swearing, four of us share the suddenly cramped basement. Sam Henley, Terek West, Shakespeare LeCasse and yours truly. Which one doesn't belong? I'll give you a hint. The only one wearing borrowed underwear, who cut her own hair and has never been to a homecoming dance, let alone been crowned school royalty.

Sam gives me the same look I give my calculus homework. Terek's grin takes over his whole face and blasts into a quick laugh. Because me being with Shake is a joke. How hilarious. I sit on my hands so I don't punch him in the face.

As I glare at him, Terek suddenly zeroes in on me. He shoves his nose an inch from mine. "What happened to you?"

I cringe back but still smell flowers. Why in crazy hell does Terek West smell like a prom corsage?

"Rat," Shake warns.

"Who did this?" Terek demands, pinching my chin in his big hand and tilting my bruises for a better view. Without the grin, he's a little terrifying.

"Fell down the stairs," I mumble and hear Shake swear under his breath.

"Bullshit but OK." Terek plops down next to me, right next to me, with his thigh pressed against mine. "Lemme know if there's somebody we need to fuck up." His grin is back. He has a chipped tooth. "Is there?"

"What?"

"Somebody we need to fuck up? Please say there is. I'm bored. Other than Shake going all gorilla on Adam, we might as well grow pussy lips and buy tampons."

"Watch the mouth," Shake snaps as Sam remarks, "Only one of us smells like a vaginal wash."

"Lavender, dude."

"That's just another word for pussy," Sam argues.

"Exactly. As in it gets me lots of it."

"Hey," Shake tries again, pointing at me.

"We've got a girl here."

"I'm aware," says Terek, giving me a slow once-over.

Along with lavender, I get a sniff of the brown bag he's holding, and the smell reminds me, I haven't eaten since a glazed donut eight hours ago. I hope he doesn't hear my stomach growl. Terek seems like the type of guy who'd point it out.

"So?" he prompts me.

"What?" I have no idea what we're talking about. I've had this same sort of conversation with Shake. Maybe popular boys speak their own language.

"Whose ass can I hammer?"

"Um. Uh. Nobody. Like I said. Fell down the stairs."

"When I know you better, that story won't fly anymore."

Sam sets a six-pack of Molson Canadian on the floor and rips it open. He cracks the top on a bottle, offers it to Shake and says, "blowhole." He hands off a second bottle to Terek and says, "bittydick." He hesitates, then holds a bottle out to me without a word. I'm thankful, because I don't want to know what he'd call me. When I shake my head no, Terek takes the beer, opens it and shoves it at me.

"No thanks."

His grin tips to the right. So does the bottle. I take the beer, because he's threatening to spill it on me. He's also bouncing a little, like a kid in a hurry to get somewhere, and I realize he is just a happy camper. At the few hockey games I made it to, I remember Terek as half out of control and mostly sitting in the penalty box.

Shake sips his beer and seems to be considering ways to kill his buddies. Or maybe he's thinking about that video of the world's most adorable miniature pig. With Shake, it's hard to tell sometimes.

Sam angles away, nods his head toward me and speaks under his breath to Shake. "You sure you know what you're getting into here?"

I'm not supposed to hear him.

Shake shrugs. Sam must be better at reading him than I am, because he says, "Hey, bite me. Whatever dude, but you've blown off two days in a row." He drops down on the stairs and dangles the Molson between his knees. "Jesus Shake. Yer goddamn head's so far up your butt, your coughs smell like farts."

"You suck that nugget directly out of Sanderson's ass or did she buy you dinner first?"

Terek spits beer on a laugh. "Shake speaks! More than two words in a row. Hallelujah! It's a goddamn miracle. This must be your doing," he says to me, bumping my shoulder and nearly knocking me over. Beer slops over my fingers. He then points at his buddies. "About once a month, these two scrotes gotta measure their dicks. It's a sad little debate over a pitiful few millimeters." He looks at Shake. "Sooo ... My dad actually sent us over here for a command performance. Said for Sam and me to straighten your nuts out or we'd all answer to him."

"Your dad?" Shake tips his head back to stare at the ceiling. "Fuck me!"

"Worse than that," Sam tells him. "Fuck all three of us. So fucken listen to Rat."

"Night before last, dad gets called to Willow Drive. Seems some douchebag was standing in the middle of the road, howling at the moon, smoked outta his mind. After hitting him with the spotlight, my dad chased the dude for two blocks. A freakishly tall blonde dude. For two blocks, through a hedgerow, with prickers, which pissed him off more than just a little. Ripped his uniform pants, which my mom had to sew, which also pissed her off. So my dad pulled me over on my way home from work, full lights and sirens, and made an evening out of carving me a new asshole. Oh and my mom sent this." Terek hefts the bag that smells like baked heaven. "Chicken enchiladas. Mom says if you don't show up for dinner in the next week, she's going to turn my life into a hell reserved for firstborns. She threatened an eternity of Friday night babysitting, suspended use of my Twat, and tickets to Tully's ballet recital."

"Three tickets," Sam supplies.

"Three tickets, Shake. Have you ever been to a ballet recital? They make you hand over your balls at the door."

As Terek speaks, Sam stink eyes me. I understand. My brother sells drugs for Randy. I am evil and must be destroyed. I am worse for Shake than gingivitis, violent video games and swimming right after eating. *Gasp!* Sam doesn't like me. I smile and give him the finger.

Terek catches me at it, chuckles and nudges my shoulder again. I wipe the fresh spill of beer off my fingers as he blurts, "I bet you're fun to wrestle."

I blink. He's just about wagging his tail. His shirt and jeans look like they've been dragged behind a bus from Miami to Buffalo. His sandy blonde hair is shaggy enough to earn him a part in the Scooby Doo movie. He really is adorable. He reminds me of Hemmie, and I like him.

"I'm meaner than I look," I answer.

"God I hope so."

"Rat," Shake warns again.

Terek ignores him and tells me, "You're fourth on the BAR."

Shake and Sam both groan.

"Bar?" I echo.

"Best Ass Rating. I came up with it. Asses are rated on size, shape, and fermentation."

"Jesus Rat," Shake snarls.

"He means firmness," Sam supplies.

"Right," Terek nods. "Like a ripe apple."

"And I'm fourth?"

"Nevermind him," Sam tells me. "He has the verbal control of a two year old."

Terek is unfazed. "Joy Stephenson is number one."

"The girl who wears plaid skirts with tights?" I clarify. "Who leads a morning prayer before school? And wouldn't spit on your dick if it was on fire?"

Terek adds a head bob to his grin and his eyes actually sparkle. "Those tights, am I right? I bet her puss tastes like angel tears."

Shake makes a sound like, "Grahhh."

Sam explains, "Rat's got the shits, but from the mouth. Feel free to slap him, repeatedly and hard."

"Number two is Allie Kindle," Terek plows ahead.

"Allie?" I echo. Yes, she is my best friend. My only friend. She has many fine qualities. I didn't realize her ass was one of them.

"Nobody can compete with the magnitude of that ass." Terek holds his hands about four feet apart and sighs. "To be honest, it's more ass than I can figure out what to do with. And I've thought about it. A lot. It's like the Mount Kilimanjaro of asses. Like the Pyramids of fucken Giza of asses. A natural wonder of the world. Makes me wanna be the first to climb up, explore every crack and crevice and plant my flag."

"Filter," Sam blurts.

"I'm just saying. Anyway, third is Blair Fredrickson." He now waves his hands. "I know. I know. Her ass isn't bronze medal material, but she's graded on a curve cuz she lets me do all sorts of freaky shit with her. This one time, I had this pixie stick and ..."

"Rat!" Shake barks. Sam drops his head into his hands.

"So yeah, you're fourth," Terek explains. "But you know, if you're willing to put in the effort, there's the possibility of promotion. Be imaginative. Don't be afraid to experiment. And know I'm always here to help."

"I'll keep it in mind." I'm stoked to rate higher than Dripass.

Sam flicks his bottle cap so it snaps off Terek's forehead. "Subject change, dude. Quick, before the girl has grounds to press charges for sexual harassment. Give me an acronym."

"FBI," Terek says immediately. Then adds, "Fellacio By Intervenous."

"French Blowjob Improvisation," Sam supplies.

"Racist, dude."

"No friggin way. How is that racist?"

"Shake is half French. You just insulted his frog heritage."

"OK, fine. Fairy Breast Implants."

"Lame."

"Fugly Ball Infection," Shake joins in.

They all look at me. I think I've figured out the game. Keep it simple. Keep it gross. "Farting Butt Intercourse."

Terek jabs a thumb in my direction. "I dig this chick. SAT," he challenges me.

"Sucking Anus Triathlon," I supply,

"Saliva Asshole Tattoo," he says back.

"You took the SAT's?" Sam directs at Shake.

"Uh-huh."

"You gotta get some applications out, man. Get your ducks in a row."

"I've got early admission and free tuition at Fredonia State, cuz my mom was on staff." Shake is pulled tighter than Usain Bolt's shoelaces and definitely on the verge of taking off. "But it doesn't change shit. Cuz I don't give a shit. So fuck your ducks and stay outta my shit."

The quiet is prickly. When Sam seems about to fill it, Shake looks at Terek and says, "I need your Twat. Tomorrow. All day."

Twat? I'm confused and a little worried.

"If you want my Twat, I need to know what you plan to do with her."

"Just got shit to do."

"I can't just let you bang my Twat all over hell. C'mon Shake, you can do better than that."

"I need to um, take Cleo … she needs some, um stuff."

"Like?" He waits. When Shake spends too long drinking his beer, Terek is more animated than

Mickey Mouse. He bounces up and down. "You're going to the mall, right? Please oh please, if there is a Santa Claus, tell me you're taking Cleo shopping!"

Shake's shoulders hike up. His chin tips down. "Don't say it, Rat. I'm fucken warning ya."

Sam is suddenly all smiles as he winks at me. "Have fun."

"Jesus Christ!" Shake explodes. He actually kicks the dryer. "You guys are such jackasses. I need a car. Don't make it a big deal."

Sam and Terek make eye contact, both say, "Shakeffect!" and explode into laughter.

"Shut the hell up," Shakes snarls.

Now I'm really confused. Terek jabs me with his elbow. "We call it Shakeffect. Happens every time the dude enters the mall. Trust me, you'll figure out what we mean."

Sam reminds Shake, "School tomorrow, dude."

"Taking another personal day. Can I have the Twat or what?"

"Well I don't know Shake," Terek answers, pinching off snickers behind his shit-eating grin. "Are you gonna come to dinner at my house or not?"

"You're such a fucken tool, Rat."

"A fucken tool with a car."

Chapter 26

CLEO:

In the morning, Shake and I meet up with Terek in the high school parking lot and take possession of the Twat. Describing the Twat as ugly is an insult to ugly cars. I still wish it was mine.

Once upon a time, the Twat was probably blue, but now has a red door, black hood, and rust everywhere. The interior combines the smell of sweaty boy and funeral flowers. There's gotta be two dozen water bottles rolling around in the footwell and at least a hundred Pixie Sticks. Remembering the story about Blair, I'm careful not to touch them.

Terek gives us the rules for borrowing his car.

"Give my Twat gas."

"If she feels dirty, get my Twat wet."

"If you eat in my Twat, don't leave her sticky."

He continues until Shake threatens to hurt him.

Terek's sister, Tia, hands me a bag of clothes. I'm not sure who arranged this, but I'm so surprised I almost forget to thank her. She gives me underwear, shorts, tank, bra and flip flops. I crawl into the backseat to put them on. It's obvious her bra won't work for me, which is super embarrassing, even if she is nice about it.

Shake then takes me to breakfast while we wait for the mall to open. We sit at a table and the waitress brings us menus. This is a first for me. I wonder if Shake remembers my list of things I've never done before. I don't know what our plan is for the day, but I'm stoked when my food shows up on a plate instead of in a bag. It's not even a paper plate.

The service is terrible because our waitress is young, has a pulse, and Shake is more adorable than a miniature pig. Her thumb drags through my scrambled eggs. My glare is wasted. Our waitress gives Shake the same half-starved attention he gives his waffles. I worry she'll pour maple syrup over his head and lick him.

Once we hit the mall, Shake has a list of stores in his phone, supplied by Terek's sister. Tia and I are hardly the same species, so I expect this to be more awkward than dressing the family dog in doll clothes. I figure wrong. It's worse.

We start by standing in front of a directory of the mall. We are there less than six seconds before a twenty-something brunette, with legs from here to the moon, wraps herself right around Shake. She doesn't seem to notice my presence but generously offers to guide Shake to his destination. Thank God for Little Miss Magellan's hand hanging off his bicep, otherwise he might never have found his way around the pretzel kiosk.

As we enter a store so pink it steals IQ points, the sales girls all look up at once. Their lips fall open and they actually pant.

Shakeffect. Might as well toss a pork chop into a Jenny Craig convention.

Shake squirms and hunches but only manages to look even more delicious. And these salesgirls haven't eaten more than a grape in the last week. They toss their hair and find reasons to touch his curls, rub against his ass and make a giggle fest of it. I am surprised no one drops to their knees and grabs his zipper in their teeth.

I wish he'd struggle a little harder. Instead, Shake explains how I'm a needy, helpless, pathetic piece of used chewing gum stuck to his shoe. I'm paraphrasing, but the girls all make sexy pouty faces, toss their hair some more and pretend to feel sorry for me, like they care and are dying to outfit me, when they and I both know they'd step on my face for a chance to dry hump him.

My eyeballs hurt from rolling them. When I start to spout off, the girls stuff me into a changing room and take turns standing guard. I catch my reflection in the mirror and wonder why no one has baited me into a trap, tagged my ear and returned me to the wild.

I am forced to try on panties that cost more than I earn in a week, bras that cost more than I earn in a month, sweatpants with dumbass words on the ass, T-shirts with dumbass words on the chest and zip-ups woven out of baby seal whiskers. When the life-sized Barbies threaten me with a bikini smaller than a pair of nickels, I bare my teeth and growl. When I finally escape and tell Shake I don't want all this, he stands at the register, swipes his card and ignores me.

The sasquatch then bullies me from store to store, and every place we go is the same. Any female between the ages of thirteen and forty creams her panties at the sight of him, and he continues to buy shit I don't want. Over fifty dollars worth of makeup fits in a bag the size of a … a … I have nothing to compare it to. I didn't know shopping bags came that small, and I have no idea what to do with an eyelash curler or a lip plumper. Maybe it's an eyelash plumper and lip curler. But it's still not enough. We proceed to add jeans, shirts, socks and TWO PAIR OF SHOES, even though I have one pair of feet, to the growing pile.

I turn into a potato. Let me explain. This one time, Rex zapped a potato in the microwave. It hissed and whistled and suddenly burst into a sticky, steaming mess. Sounded like a bomb. We actually thought we were getting raided by SWAT. Rex flushed a perfectly good dime bag, and I crawled into the cupboard under the sink, just in case.

Shake and I are in the shoe store when I drop the shopping bags on the floor and explode. My shouts spray everybody standing within a ten foot radius.

"I don't want any of this! I don't need it! I can't afford it! I've been saving to get out of the yellow house! I can't be stuck there. So tell me how I pay you back? Tell me, Shake! Explain it to me! There's no fucken way. You gotta take all this shit back! All of it!" I kick at the bags, catch my foot in the handle of one and hop sideways, utterly spastic as I scream, "Take it back! Take it back! Take it back!"

Shake grabs my arm to steady me, but I swat at him. He opens his mouth. I yell, "No! No! I told you. Stay outta my shit! I fucken told you! Why don't you ever listen?" I wait two and half whole seconds for his answer and his silence turns me purple. "Well? Say something!"

"Cleo … "

"No!" Before he can argue, I screech "Just fuck the FUCK OFF!"

Yes, I am a delicate flower, but I've reached my limit. So with Shake and his posse of horny salesgirls gaping like I peed on the carpet, I run.

I'm dressed in a whole new outfit. Nobody's ever worn these clothes before, which is just so goddamn weird, and they make me smell like a fairy princess prostitute who drinks perfume and farts rainbows. I am not me anymore. I'm this thing pretending to belong with Shake, when it's so obvious he's meant for those gorgeous Barbies in the underwear store.

The Barbies aren't bruised and broken and dirty in a way that won't scrub off. They don't need mini pillows to fill the cups of their bras. I bet they've never dug a half-eaten hot dog out of the garbage at a high school hockey game and happily called it dinner.

I wouldn't even choose me. Why would he? And why do I want him to, when I know I'm not allowed and don't deserve to have him?

So I stomp and snarl and swear my way from one end of the mall to the other, searching for an escape hatch, and finally burst outside into the sunshine. I'd like to kick a kitten, knock an icecream cone out of a little kid's hand and maybe junk-punch a birthday clown for an encore. I'm steaming.

I yank at the neckline of my new shirt, craning my chin, breathing hard and getting even angrier as stupid tears leak down my cheeks. What is with all the crying lately? It's all Shake's fault. Goddamn Sasquatch. What was he thinking? Borrowing the Twat and blowing off school! Taking me to breakfast and the mall! Buying me a crapload of new stuff! What an assjack, right?

So what do I do now? I have nowhere to go. I have no way to get there. No money, no cell phone and no one to call for a ride anyway. Goddamnit! Goddamnit! Fuckity, fuck, fuck, fuck! I crouch down in a squat on the sidewalk, hide my face in my hands and just scream for a minute. I scare an old lady with blue hair.

If Shake took off and left me, I'm screwed.

But of course he didn't. Because he's not only insanely hot and ridiculously popular, he's NICE. And he's good to me. Why? What's he getting out of it? It pisses me off.

I find him waiting in the parking lot, leaning against the Twat, ankles crossed, arms folded over

189

his chest. My imagination isn't capable of coming up with a fantasy as good as the reality that is Shakespeare LeCasse. His blonde head gleams brighter than the treasure at the end of the rainbow. His gray T-shirt is something special because his broad shoulders are inside. He makes my mouth dry, my Netherlands wet and my feet heavy.

My new sneakers scuff across the enormous parking lot. I then stand in front of him, stare at the ground and bite my lip.

"Done freaking out?" he asks calmly.

I nod, sniff and nudge a candy wrapper with my toe.

"Gonna let me talk now?"

Another nod.

"C'mere," he says.

I take a step.

"C'mon."

I take another step.

"Little further."

I don't budge. He hooks his long fingers into the waist of my pants and pulls me in so our hips almost touch. My nose bumps his chest. God, he smells like something I want to eat with a glass of milk before bed.

He brushes the knuckles of his left hand along my cheek and I might cry ... or purr. I've seen him do this exact move with Dripass, and another girl named Jennifer, and Amara, and Maddison, and at least two of the Ashley's. Those girls all have something in common. They are not me. What is he doing with me?

If he's trying to bang me, maybe I should tell him he doesn't need to work so hard at it.

"Cleo?"

He nudges my chin. I look up, up, up, and those blue eyes completely own me.

"I don't care about the money. Doing this for you, it keeps me from hating myself for a little while, OK? It makes me feel good. I want to do it. So you don't owe me anything."

With him touching me, I can't remember why I was freaking out. Did he just admit he feels sorry for me? Is this charity? I don't want that. But I can't remember my last name, much less argue.

His hand curves around the back of my head. His long fingers slide into my hair, and he does the thing tall people do, dipping his knees until his face is level with mine. I hold my breath. He kissed those other girls and they melted. What if he kisses me? He will need to suck me up through a straw.

He tips his forehead so it rests against mine. His breath fans my lips. His hair spills around my face. "Are you gonna cooperate? I've got more I want to do with you today."

Shakeffect.

Chapter 27

SHAKE:

My head whips forward. I slap my hands against the dash. The seatbelt grabs me, throws me back and something in my spine pops.

"Doing good," I manage.

Cleo cuts a glare my way. Her hands sit precisely at ten and two. She can barely see over the wheel. If looks could maim, I'd be bleeding from every orifice.

"You're getting the hang of it," I tell her.

I'm teaching her to drive, checking off another item on her never-done-before list. She is slightly aggressive with the pedals. OK, I'm lying. She's more aggressive than a street racer. She is a pint sized Vin Diesel. Pedestrians and squirrels should be very afraid.

My neck hurts from the starts and stops. That's a minor problem compared to my pants, which are cinched tighter than a tourniquet. Cuz I'm horny. As hell. One way or another, Cleo Lee is going to kill me.

After sleeping, or rather surviving the torture of her warm body bumped up against mine in a narrow twin bed for five hours, I finally snuck upstairs and jerked off in the shower. Then we started the day with Cleo braless in a thin, clingy tank top. I spent our breakfast staring at my waffles, trying to avoid the sight of her perky little nips. I wasn't entirely successful. So then, with half-a-hard-on, I ignored her as much as possible while we bought lace bras and panties in a rainbow of colors. Lace is my kryptonite and even worse, I'm pretty sure Cleo is wearing the red ones. At least, I'm picturing her in the red ones. I like red.

"I think I'll do better going faster," Cleo tells me. She's a little breathless, and I bet that's real close to what she'd sound like if I went down on her. Maybe not, but my imagination is running with it.

"Yup," I croak, just to say something as she pilots the Twat in a jerky circle.

She answers back with either, "You're the worcestershire on the plant," or "You are the worst teacher on the planet." I'm not sure. I'm not really listening. I've had an epiphany.

My hands are big. Her ass is not. I'll need to test my theory, but I am suddenly convinced each ass cheek would fit nicely in my palms, and I could support her weight with her back against the wall and her legs wrapped around my waist.

Yes, I am a sick prick. After what she's been through, the last thing she needs is me slobbering all over her. So I will be the friend she needs, do whatever she needs, but shit, I really want to toss her in the backseat and slobber. All. Over. Her.

I haven't been laid in eight months. I've had girls crawling all over me, eager to help, yet somehow so needy, I felt like they might suck me dry. I could've picked any one of them. Easy. No effort. Instead, I'm panting after Cleo Lee. Might as well cuddle a cactus, step on a rusty nail, stick my dick in the blender because the girl is brutal.

"I like going faster," she tells me in a soft voice.

Sweet Christ. At the end of this, we'll be spooned into my twin mattress in the basement again, and I'm ninety-nine percent sure my balls might actually explode.

"Try to park again," I instruct. See, I'm paying attention to the driving lesson. I'm not eye-fucking this new Cleo, who is dressed in actual girl-clothes, that fit her and show off her tight little ass, sweet little tits and make her look so goddamn cute I nearly kissed her when we were standing outside the mall, until the sight of her fat lip and purple bruises slowed me down.

I stick my snout out the passenger window and suck air that is not cold enough. The arctic circle would not be cold enough. We are currently driving around the empty parking lot of an out-of-business Kmart. Cleo eases the Twat between the yellow lines, then stomps the break as if she's trying to kill it. Our heads slingshot forward and back.

She opens her door to check her park job. "I'm on top of the lines again. How is that possible?" Narrowing her eyes at me, she snarls, "You suck at this."

I want her to say suck a few more times. "Doing great."

She jams the Twat into park and now stares straight ahead. Her knuckles go white on the wheel. "What're you doing?"

I think she's caught me perving on her, and I'm speechless with panic.

"Shake?"

"Um."

"Why are you doing this?"

"Doing what?"

She circles a hand in the air. "Breakfast. Shopping. Driving. All of it. Cuz it kind of feels like a big pity party."

I probably shouldn't tell her I want to get into her pants. And that's not even true. Well, it's true, but that's not why. I don't understand it, so I sure as shit can't explain it. But I try. "I want to give you a good day."

"Don't feel sorry for me. I don't want that."

She reminds me of one of those pissy cats. The more I try to pet her, the harder she makes me work for it. Whenever I'm nice to Cleo, I can almost see her ears flatten and her tail swish, like she's getting ready to bite. Which gets me thinking about Cleo biting, maybe licking, because I am entirely under the command of my dick and deserve to be taken out and shot.

"Didn't we already hash this out?" I try. "Back at the mall?"

"I'm not buying it. What is Shakespeare LeCasse doing with me? I'm not exactly your style."

"I have a style?"

"You're answering my questions with questions. It's super aggravating. Cut the shit."

"Maybe I like you."

"Maybe?"

"I like you."

"Like me how?"

"How do I like you?"

"Yeah, Shake, that's what I asked. Just switching the words around doesn't count as an answer."

"Um."

"I know I'm a disaster, but whatever's going on, I can handle it."

I'm fairly sure I said something similar to her the other night. I hate it when she throws my own asinine bullshit back at me.

"Cleo." She finally looks over at me. "Could we just enjoy each other without picking at it? I could use a good day too."

"Are you hoping to bang me?" she snaps.

"I'll take that as a no."

"Should I take that as a yes?"

"Trick question."

She tilts her head, narrows her eyes, and the claws are out.

"If you're asking if I want to hook up," I start. "The answer is yes. A very definite, please put me out of my misery, yes. But if you're asking if that's why I'm spending time with you, then no, that's not the reason. Even if you tell me there's zero chance of anything beyond us hanging out, it won't change anything. I like you. I really like you. We're friends, right?"

Cleo stares back at me, expressionless for a few seconds, and then her lips curve up just a little. "OK," she tells me.

I don't know if "OK" means I'm getting more than friends or not. I do know better than to ask for clarification.

She shifts back into drive, hits the gas without letting her foot off the break and spins the tires like she's Danny Zuko racing for pink slips.

"Off the break," I blurt. She suddenly shoots us forward, then stomps down hard, and we say hello to whiplash. Rat would have a friggin aneurysm if he were here.

"Fuck-a-duck!"

"Just use one foot," I advise.

"You said to always use both."

"Both hands. One foot."

"Grrrrr."

Her growling just reminds me of Rat's comment about the rabid wolverine, and I squirm in my seat.

We circle the parking lot for another half hour. She's still dangerous to herself and others, and I will never share this story with Rat, but she gets a hell of a lot better.

I know she's had enough when she pounds the horn and half shouts, "I think there's something wrong with this car!" We switch seats, and I drive us to the ice rink. It feels like I'm dragging my guts along the pavement behind us. I want to do this for her, but it's my first time back here in eight months, and just the sight of the building is a brain freeze.

I park the Twat, and we start across the parking lot. I make it halfway before I'm shivering so badly, I need to stop and clench my fists for a second. Cleo turns in a circle, probably wondering what the hell we're doing here. Hopefully I'll teach her to ice skate, but I might just curl into the larva state.

I open the door to the rink for Cleo. The chill in the air reaches toward me. It has a unique smell. It smells like home to me. I used to crave it. Now, the familiarity is sucking me into a panic attack.

I wait for my heart to drop back into my chest. I wait for my lungs to remember their purpose. Then I lead Cleo to the pro shop. The place is pretty much empty in the middle of the school day. Bobby is behind the counter, sporting a man bun and a ripped sweatshirt that reads "If you think my attitude stinks, smell my bag." He manages the place, does everything from driving the zamboni to scrubbing toilets, and just about shits a brick when he sees me. His face splits into a megawatt grin.

"Hey, man." He comes around to give me a back slap, then grabs my hair. "What the hell is this, Goldilocks?"

I shrug and can't quite look him in the eye. A fresh crop of white sparkles explode in my brain.

"You coming back to work or what?" he asks.

"I um, ah, not right yet I guess."

"Yeah, no worries man. Whenever. I've always got hours you can snag." We stand in awkward silence for a few seconds. He head bobs, which is why everybody calls him Bobby. His real name is Mark. "You're still gonna run Learn-to-skate this summer, right?"

"Yeah well, um, I'm not sure what I'm doing just right now, or yet, or even you know, over the summer."

He stares at me, taking a second to translate my mumbles into coherent English, then nods a few times. "Sam and Rat are handling sign-ups, but you're the sanity, man. I can't leave the little dudes at the mercy of those two knobs."

Now it's my turn to bob my head.

"Cool?" he asks and I'm not sure if I just agreed to something. "So yeah, hey, take a look. The new Grafs came in." He swerves back around the counter, digs through a pile of boxes on the floor and shoves one at me.

I stare at him.

"C'mon, fucken take 'em, dude. Nobody else has a hoof big enough, and I already sharpened 'em, did something a little different with the edge that I think you'll like." He nods a few more times. "Try 'em. Let me know how they feel."

"I … I can't just, ah … "

"They're yours, man. Say no more. It's done." He catches sight of Cleo. "Who's this?"

Cleo finger waves.

"Cleo, Bobby." I make the intros. My tongue flops in my mouth like a stale gummy worm. I swallow, squeeze my fingers and try to calm my shit the hell down. "I'm um, teaching her to, you know, skate. You got some skates she can maybe use? Any open ice?"

"Sure, man. There's some college intro to ice or some shit on the main rink. Practice rink is empty. Have at it."

He locates a pair of rentals in Cleo's size. I take the brand new Graf's that retail for over four hundred bucks, the ones he's been keeping for me so long the box is dusty. They are nearly identical to the skates I lost in the fire eight months ago. Along with my stick, bag, gear and everything in life that ever mattered to me. Yet here I am, back at the rink as if nothing happened.

Just under a year ago, I was still hoping to play on this ice for the local college team. I spoke to a recruiter, made some promises and then got the absolutely-not from my parents. It pissed me off so badly I threw down f-bombs, ended up grounded and climbed out my window for the last time.

I sit Cleo down on the bench outside the locker rooms and lace her skates for her. Tying my own takes longer because they're brand new, stiff and my hands fumblefuck.

"You work here?" she asks.

"Used to."

"Why not now?"

"Needed a break."

"Maybe you should get back at it."

"Maybe not," I snap and feel bad about it.

I concentrate on my laces. Just skating, I tell myself. Not playing hockey. Not stepping back into my old life. Because I shouldn't be here, not just at the rink, but here, alive on the planet. And if I don't keep suffering at max capacity, it's like I've forgotten.

What do I need?

I need pain. PAIN. Yes, the kind of pain that comes in all caps.

"Shake. Hey." Cleo tugs on my arm. "You OK?"

"Huh? Yup. I'm good."

"We don't have to do this," she tells me.

Sitting next to her on the bench, elbows on my knees, I stare down at my feet in the new skates. My breath gets stuck in my throat and I nearly choke on it. Fuck. Can I do this?

"You know what?" she says, suddenly standing up. "We can go back to your grandma's, paint each other's nails, bitch about period cramps and watch the Notebook on Netflix. Or, how about you man up and get your fancy ass on the ice?"

I glance up at her. She's standing on skates. I'm sitting. I'm still taller than her, and she's bullying me.

"I want to learn to skate," she rags at me. "Hopefully you're better at this than teaching me how to drive." She grabs my hand and pulls. "My feet already hurt, and I'm getting cold, so hurry the hell up."

When we step onto the ice, I just stand there.
This used to be my favorite place to be. My parents
constantly bitched about how much time I spent at the
rink, and maybe I neglected some homework and
chores for the sake of hockey. I can now pitch a tent
on the ice and no one will give a single crap.

"Go ahead," Cleo urges. She clings to the
boards with one hand and gestures in a circle with
other. "Skate around. Wiggle your ass for me,
Sasquatch. Show off your awesome skills."

She waits, but I'm paralyzed.

"Hey! Shake! Stop thinking." When I look at
her, she lets go of the boards and tries to shove me.
Her skates slip out from under her, head in opposite
directions, and she ends up in sort of a split hanging
off my shirt. I catch her by the hips and prop her up.

"Why is this ice so frickin slippery?" she snarls.
Her chin jabs me in the sternum as she tips her head
back. "Hey. Look at me. You're making this into
something it isn't."

"It's just …."

"No," she cuts me off. "It's just skating. Strap
your big boy pants on. C'mon, race me, Buttface."

Then she spins and shuffles away, moving
slower than a three-legged turtle. I could catch her
with Allie riding on my shoulders. Brave little Cleo, all
battered and bruised, daring me to grow a pair.

So I push off, hyper-aware of muscles I've
ignored too long, the rub of new skates and cool air
on my face. I dig in, knees bent, and fly past Cleo. My
lungs expand and my heart wakes up in my chest. I

hear the sweet cut of my blades as one foot crosses over the other. The rink is a blurr. There is nothing but the familiar sensation and I realize how bad I've missed this. So I keep pumping, circling the ice, until sweat runs down my face, until I'm sucking air, and I'm burned down to nothing. God, it feels so good and so awful, and just maybe I can let myself have this.

Curled forward at the waist, I glide up beside Cleo. Between pants, I peek at her through my hair. "Buttface?"

"Ha! Well, it got your ass moving."

I swing around to skate backwards in front of her and take her hands. "Bend your knees and try this." I weave my skates in and out. "Pumpkins."

"Pumpkins?" She smiles as she gets the hang of it. "You run a Learn-to-Skate program?"

"For a couple of years. It's mainly little kids, four-year-olds up to about ten. We teach them the basics."

"But not this year?"

I hike a shoulder. "We'll see." I don't want to think or talk about it. A few laps around the ice is a world away from jumping back into regular hours at the rink. Catching the stubborn look I'm getting from Cleo, I rush into a subject change. "You look different in your new clothes."

"Different is a good thing?"

"Well um, you look really good."

"As in I didn't look good before?"

Uh-oh. Abort. Abort. "That's not what I'm saying." I point my toes in. "This is called a snowplow. Try it. See if you can snowplow to a stop."

"You were saying? How I looked like a ball of snot before you bought me new clothes? How all of sudden you might manage to pork me with a half-a-hard-on? I'm so flattered I can barely keep from jumping you right here on the ice."

"Jesus, Cleo." I tug on her hands and almost send her sprawling. She hisses at me. "Why are you so quick to bust my nuts? The truth is, I like you best in nothing but a towel. OK? So it doesn't matter if you're wearing that uglyass flannel or your tight new girl clothes. Either way, it's all I can do to stay hands off. Happy?"

"Good for you." She smirks and tips her head to the side. "That was a really great answer."

"I've got skills."

Her eyes roam over me, and I like it.

"Cleo? Thanks for this."

"For what?"

"I didn't think I'd ever skate again."

"Why?"

"I have a hard time with anything I used to do."

"You've never done me."

She catches me by surprise, and I combine "What?" and "Huh?" into an imitation of a whale burp.

"Why stay hands off?" she wants to know.

"What?"

"You said it's all you can do to stay hands off. What's the problem? Can't stand the thought of getting your pretty paws dirty?"

"No, Cleo, that's got nothing to do with anything." I transition to skate beside her and take hold of her right hand. I'm holding hands with Cleo Lee, and it somehow feels right and bizarre at the same time. "I didn't figure you'd want me to push, after you know, whatever happened to you."

Just like that, her face changes, and I wish I could take the words back. Her chin dips down and her lashes throw shadows on her cheeks.

"I'm cold," she mumbles.

"Ready to call it quits?"

She nods and tugs her fingers free from mine. Whatever we had going between us, I wrecked it.

"OK. Yeah. You did really good."

We skate off the ice and once she sits down on the bench, I kneel to take off her skates. I try to come up with something to say to smooth things over, but I've got nothing. I don't know what went down with her, or what she wants, or if maybe her and I are an epic disaster waiting to happen. I just know I'm not half as insane when she's around. So that's a good thing, right?

I bend over her laces, pluck at the knot and feel her fingers slide into my hair. I go still.

"I don't want to tell you what happened," she says, her voice so soft I hold my breath to hear her. "If you need to know, I will. But I don't want you to picture me or think of me that way. You don't get it, but I can't change how my life is. Not yet. So it's best to just leave it alone."

I keep my eyes down and just wait and listen.

"It's not what you think." She hesitates, then says, "He didn't, you know."

It should be a relief. It is. But hearing the way she says it and knowing that motherfucker hurt her, the anger gets even bigger and harder to manage. I'm going to annihilate him, reach down his throat, pull out his intestines and strangle the son of a bitch with them. Just a matter of time.

"Shake?"

I finally look at Cleo, into those big, dark eyes and wonder how I went so long without noticing her.

Her fingers are still tangled in my hair and they tug. I answer by sliding my hands up her legs and around her waist. She shivers. Maybe from the chill of the rink. Hopefully because I find the bare skin between her shirt and pants. Then Cleo leans forward and presses her lips to mine.

Chapter 28

CLEO:

I don't know where I find the guts to kiss Shake, but when I do, he smiles. His lips curve against mine, and it's enough to hatch falcons from my heart. Yes, falcons. They are bigger and more badass than butterflies. And when his fingers prance across my bare skin, shivers shoot up my spine and startle those birds into flight.

It's just an innocent meeting of mouths, but this is Shake's mouth we're talking about, with that yummy lower lip, and there's a promise of naughty things ahead. Since throwing him down and turning him into my personal merry-go-round, right here next to the ice, is probably against rink rules ... it says *No Horseplay* on the sign ... I settle for the kiss. Settle is the wrong word. I might not have a ton to compare it to, but this kiss is sipping champagne when I've had nothing but tap water.

Shake pulls back slowly, and we lock eyes. I have no idea what's going on in that blonde, curly head. Maybe he wants me. Maybe he's doing long division. But he said he likes me. He said he wants to hook up. I didn't imagine that.

And the reason I'm sporting a fat lip is because I keep buzzing around Shake. I'm not imagining that either.

Today or tomorrow, I'll be headed back to the yellow house. Randy has probably cooled off by now, maybe even feels guilty, and there's a fine line between that and him getting pissed all over again. I'll need to lie my sneaky ass off about where I've been.

Shake holds my face in his big hands and gives me one more soft kiss at the corner of my mouth. Unhappy thoughts are no match for him. The way he looks at me, I'm not sure I can live up to whatever he sees, but I'd like to try.

He returns my skates to the pro shop. He and I don't say much as we leave the rink and drive to his grandmother's. Things have shifted between us, and it's awkward. I'm worried. So far, every time a little bud of happiness has sprouted, the sasquatch has stomped the shit out of it. He's the smart one. He and I don't belong in the same zip code, much less swapping spit.

I sneak peeks at him while he drives.

Shakespeare LeCassse scares me stupid. Just thinking about him spreads my fears faster than the Ebola virus. Because he's off limits. Because I'm falling, or maybe it's too late and I've already tumbled head over heels for him. Another first for me. I've never cared about anybody. Nobody has ever cared about me. Everything about my past, present and future is as stinky and sticky as vulture guts. So what am I doing here?

Shake deserves someone with college plans, family photo albums and a middle name. That's right. Along with no lunch money, no birthday gifts and more sleazoid boyfriends than there are types of cancer, dear old mom only gave me four measly letters. And that's one more than my brother got.

What happens if I tell him about the night of the fire? What happens if I don't? Keeping such a big secret is like hiding a tiger in the closet, and no matter what I do, there's a really good chance it's gonna get out and one of us is getting bit.

We park in the street in front of his grandma's house, sit in the car for a minute and say a whole lot of nothing. Shake finally climbs out first and carries my shopping bags down to the basement. "Duck!" I shout and save him from bonking his head off the overhang. He throws me a grateful look, drops the bags on the floor, and as he digs around for a hoodie, I make three important decisions.

Number one: Walking away from Shake is the right thing to do, because it is best and safer for both of us.

Number two: The sooner I end this madness the better.

Number three: Screw that, I want him.

"Shake?"

He looks up. I roll onto the sides of my feet and just stare at him with my teeth dragging at my lower lip. I don't know how to say or do the right thing to claim him. I'm way better at pushing people away. But Shake gets me.

His eyes zero in as he prowls toward me. I'm still not used to it. The sight, sound and smell of Shakespeare LeCasse makes me feel like a tourist in Rome. He's so beautiful, he's overwhelming. I keep expecting someone to warn me not to touch. There should be velvet ropes around him and signs forbidding flash photography.

I almost back away. Almost. He bends down, takes my hands and links them around his neck, where my fingertips tangle in hair so unbelievably soft, it's like petting a bunny. Then he grabs me by the hips. As he picks me up, my legs wrap around his waist and my chest crushes to his. He is a slab of granite. His head tilts, dark lashes resting against his cheeks, lips parting and ... hello ... Shake is kissing me, really and thoroughly kissing me. This is insane. Unbelievable. Amazing.

This kiss is like no other. We're creating something brand new and just ours. Like a snowflake, maybe millions of them all swirling so gently. It's magical. Then his tongue sweeps in, leads mine in a slow dance, and we escalate into a frenzy of want.

There's no thought of coming up for air. His hands find my ass and squeeze. My fingers dig into his curls and give them a tug. A rumbly growl spills from his mouth into mine, shoots a tingle through my veins and my thighs cinch him tighter. I could kiss this boy for hours and never get enough. I might spontaneously combust, but I swear my panties are wet enough to put out the flames.

I'm nipping at his lips, his jaw, kissing every square inch I can reach when Shake abruptly sets me down and steps back. I start to move in, but he holds me in place with hands at my hips. Maybe he doesn't want me? Maybe I have bad breath, suck at kissing, or he's done the math, and my four measly letters just aren't enough. But no, he's got a whole Big Bad Wolf thing going on, huffing, puffing and looking hungry. His eyes are eating me up. For once, I know what he's thinking. I'm thinking it too. When he licks his bottom lip, my knees turn to pudding.

"I wanna take my time with you," he says, and I'm convinced this boy is a genius. He has the best ideas. I am totally on board and would love to hear the details of this plan. "You'll be here when I get back?"

Does a fish have fins? That's a yes, so I just nod. I think I nod. He is an ocean wave and I'm upside down in the undertow.

He takes my face in his long fingers, gentle as can be, and the receiving end of his attention is a wonderful place. After one more brief kiss, Shake charges up the stairs, heading to mandatory dinner at Terek's. I hope he eats fast.

Chapter 29

CLEO:

I can count the number of people who've been good to me on one hand, with fingers left over. Shake is one of them. Minnie Reid is another.

When I hear Minnie moving around in the kitchen, I debate for about three seconds, then tromp upstairs. Shake would not be happy. He didn't warn me to stay hidden, but I'm pretty sure I'm a secret. Doesn't matter. If his grandma doesn't want me staying at her house, I'll leave. She deserves the choice.

"Hey."

At the sound of my voice, Minnie swings around with a bark. I'm ready for it and still need to peel my heart off the ceiling. She is almost as tall as Shake and broad in the shoulders, with wide hands and strong fingers from mixing and kneading heavy batches of dough. She is as subtle as a bulldozer. When I first started working for her, I caught hiccups every time she spoke.

"Cleo! Holy Christ in a canoe, way to stick a cold thumb up my ass. What're you doing here? And what's with the face?"

I help myself to a kitchen chair, straddle it backwards and rest my arms over the top. "I fell down some stairs and got banged up. Shake is letting me stay here until I feel better. Just a couple of days."

She mangles a laugh. "Don't sell me taco farts in a bottle and call it perfume. Try again."

I roll my eyes. "OK. That's my version of the truth, and it's all you're gonna get."

"Does this look like a hotel?"

"Do you hear me offering to pay rent or bitching about the spiders in the basement?"

"Cheeky little shit." She picks up a mug of coffee, leans back against the counter and takes a sip. Her eyes stay on me and don't miss a thing.

I try to sit still but curl my toes so tight, they start to cramp. "Me being here isn't an invitation to dig around in my life," I tell her oh so quietly. "Just leave it be."

"You're in my house."

"As Shake's guest and I can go. Just say the word."

"Cleo, tell me I'm not looking at a tetanus shot from sitting on a rusty dick."

"Now there's a lovely image," I mutter. "This won't come back on you. Promise."

"You'd tell me if you needed some help?"

"Yup." Total lie.

"Is Shake stirred up in this shit stew?"

"No," I answer, and it's not technically a lie.

"He do that?" She gestures at my face.

"No!" Has she not met her grandson?

"So who did?"

"The tooth fairy. What does it matter?"

"I wanna know what's going on."

"I told you. Shake's letting me stay in the basement."

"You're all of a sudden shacking up with my grandson? Making yourself as hard to get as fleas in the monkey cage?"

"Right."

Minnie's eyes narrow. "How is he? Is he good?"

"Um. I haven't slept with him yet so … "

"Jesus Henry Christ, that's not what I meant. Let's boil the dirty out of those thoughts and put on our good girl panties. How is my grandson doing?"

OK. That's embarrassing. "Ask him."

She hesitates. "Is Shake downstairs?"

"Having dinner at a buddy's."

She nods and visibly relaxes. "The school keeps calling. He keeps ditching. Three days in a row this week."

That's my fault, which I don't tell her. "What does he say about that?"

"Ask him," she says my words back at me.

"That's your job," I blurt. After my backfired attempt with Principal Sandersuck, I should know to keep my nose out of his business. Yet I hear myself start to say, "You gotta talk to him. He's got nobody in his corner. You need to help … "

"Yeah well, maybe I'll shit little green apples as an encore." Minnie cuts me off with whatever that means and now won't even glance at me.

So I announce, "I'm hungry."

"I'll alert the media."

"How about pancakes?"

"I'll play your silly game. How about pancakes?"

We both stare at each other for a while. Until she prompts, "I'm not getting any younger here."

"Wait. What? Me? I can't make 'em."

"Christ, you're as helpful as a hole in a bucket."

"And you're meaner than a werewolf with gingivitis."

"Grab the eggs. Those round, white thingies."

I scrounge through the packed fridge, trying to reach the eggs without causing an avalanche. At the yellow house, I get excited when there's more than an old bottle of mustard on the shelf. I've made a meal out of ketchup and crackers more times than I want to admit. "What's with all the food?"

"What do I know about what teenage boys eat? I've bought everything I can think of. Even bring treats home from the bakery and leave them out on the counters. Like bait. He won't eat it."

Now that's interesting.

She sets up the griddle, grabs a big mixing bowl, and tosses together ingredients without measuring. She lets me stir but yells at me the whole time. God, I love her.

"Don't overwork the batter," she bitches. "Treat it like your job at the bakery."

"Do all the work for no thanks and shitty pay?"

"Half-assed and quit early."

The pancakes are paradise on a plate. I eat until I'm almost sick. We're still sitting at the kitchen table, sipping coffee, trading insults and opinions, talking about everything but Shake, when he walks in. My sasquatch is almost unrecognizable.

Pale. Sweaty. Twitchy. Breathing in shallow pants. He is a flameless dragon. His eyes dart every which way but never land anywhere. One hand flexes and clenches at his side while the other squeezes the back of his neck. When he catches sight of us in the kitchen, he stumbles backward and bumps off the door hard enough to rattle the hinges. WTF?

I think maybe he's in the middle of a panic attack but have no clue what to do about it. I look to Minnie for assistance. She's the responsible adult here, right?

She makes a noise that sounds like "Whelp" and jumps up so fast she upends her chair. Grabbing her mug and plate, she dumps the dishes in the sink and something breaks. When she turns back around, her face is pulled into an expression I've never seen before.

"Everything OK?" she demands with all the gentle compassion of a drill sergeant with irritable bowel syndrome. "Do you need something?"

I'm no expert but the boy is not in the same solar system as OK, and the force and speed of her questions throw him into a whole-body flinch. It's quite a performance by grandmother and grandson. I wish I had a whistle so I could referee, send them to neutral corners and declare a winner. I thought things were hinky at the yellow house.

I start to say something to Shake, but he bolts, thumping down the basement stairs and bashing his head off the overhang. I feel the vibrations under my feet.

"That's either a concussion or structural damage to the house," I remark.

"Gotta start my ovens," Minnie mutters, snatching her keys off the counter and practically jumping out the front door.

Well hell. I'm left alone in the kitchen, wondering what just happened. I take a last sip of coffee, pick up Minnie's chair, brush my teeth and hop in the shower. Giving Shake a breather seems like a good idea. Whatever happened between when he left and came back, I don't think I'm his solution.

Let's face it, adding my mess to his problems is like trying to mop up spilled milk with a dirty sock. Who knows if we're making it better or worse, but one thing's for sure, nothing's getting clean.

I finally tiptoe downstairs, only to find an empty basement. I get dressed, sit on the bed and think and wait, wait and debate. Where did he go? Each minute takes its sweet time. I finally flop backward, scan the ceiling for spiders and get worried. Shake looked desperate. I lift his mattress. The baggie is gone. Sonofabitch.

I slip outside into a chilly night full of stars and walk and walk and walk. I should've stolen another hoodie from Shake. My aches, pains and shivers slow me down. I hug myself, count the row of twelve willow trees on Willow Drive and think back to the last time I was inside house number 14532. Hemmie said to stay in the basement but the stairs didn't even creak. The carpets were so thick, my bare toes completely disappeared.

I just wanted to see what it was like. Being inside that big beautiful house with family pictures and the smell of happiness in the air, it seemed safe, like nothing bad was allowed inside. Boy was I wrong.

I only stole one little thing.

Keeping an eye on the twist in the road, I now walk up and stand over the giant disaster sitting on the yellow line. Shake's knees are bent up, head sagging between them, and his blonde mop is silvered by an adoring moon. It's a miracle no one has run him over yet.

"You can't sit here, Shake."

"I'm sorry," he whispers and starts to rock.

"We need to go."

"I need ..."

I wait. Rushing this boy never goes well, but I prompt him, "Tell me what you need."

The silence stretches. The road stays dark, but my heart thumps with dread.

He finally says, "There's nothing. Nothing. I shouldn't still be here."

I can't decide if he means here in this road or on this earth, but admitting it doesn't do him any good. His breath is nothing but a series of loud, fast inhales that collapse into a wet choking sound.

"I want them back," he moans. "I don't want to be left here without them."

That cracking sound is my heart splitting in half.

"I know." I slide my hand across his shoulders and feel the quivers beneath my fingers. What do I say to him? How can I make it any better? I could tell him the truth, right here, right now, and rip the lid right off him.

When he looks up, his cheeks are wet. Tears drip off his chin. The whites of his eyes are stained pink, and there's only a thin rim of blue around the big black holes of his pupils. I wonder what he's on. And how much. Goddamn Bruce.

There's very good reasons why I no longer dabble in illegal substances. Living in the yellow house, I've seen rock bottom. Hell, I've hit it. Shake is jackhammering a hole in the earth's core.

"You can't stay here, Shake. Somebody will run you over, and it will mess 'em up. You're going to wreck some innocent guy driving home from the night-shift. Is that what you want?"

"I can't do this anymore."

He's not hearing me, and I can't really understand him. His words are quiet and tumble over each other. "Let's go. Let's get out of the road. Then we can get your sorted out."

"No more. No further. I just can't."

I squeeze my eyes shut for a second. Then I grab him by the arm and tug. "C'mon." I can't budge him.

"No more," he whispers.

I yank on him. "No, Shake. Just … No! We'll get you some help. We can figure this out."

He spills backward, spreading across the road like a stain, and since I'm hanging on, he jerks me down with him. I hit both knees, adding new scrapes to my bruises.

"Goddamnit!" I screech. "Don't do this. Please!"

I've spent most of my life in the middle of a shitstorm. I've been selfish with my survival. I've covered my head, squeezed my heart down to the size of a lemon seed and left no room in my hidey hole for anything or anybody. I take care of me, only me and barely get by.

So how did I get here? I tell myself I'm making up for failing Hemmie, repaying Shake for saving me, but know I'm lying. This catastrophe of a boy has claimed a piece of me as his own. With every hard thump against my chest, that piece just gets bigger and more determined.

I get my feet back under me, grit my teeth, haul on his arm and move him half an inch. Flat on his back, he stares at the sky, and he's such a broken, wasted mess, all the king's horses and all the king's men couldn't put him back together again. Doesn't mean I'm giving up.

"Get up!" I shout, then lower my voice, because holy horny toads, the last thing we need is the cops showing up. "Get up. Right goddamn now, Shake."

I scuttle around to crouch between his feet, wrap my hands around his ankles and catch the glow of headlights. Fuuuuuck! Pulling, heaving, huffing, I literally drag his dead weight across the pavement. Just to be clear, he doesn't help AT ALL.

I back pedal so fast, when we hit the curb, his head bounces and I stumble, flop backwards and crack my elbow on the sidewalk. I scramble to get him out of the road, because he's a monster, limbs all over the place, and the headlights are right there. Then I throw myself down on top of him as the car flies by. The wind of it blows my hair, road grit dusts my face, and I taste exhaust.

If Shake survives this night, I'm going to kill him. Then I'm going to revive his ass, just so I can kill him again. In-between, I will hug him so tight I might crush his ribs.

"Shake. Hey!" I prod at him. I'm not gentle. He won't answer, won't look at me, even though his eyes are wide open. I consider pinching that sensitive fleshy part between his nostrils.

"If you don't talk to me, I'm calling an ambulance! And the cops! And the fire department!" I don't have a phone, don't trust anybody wearing a uniform, not even the mailman or bus drivers, but he's shoved me out of the airplane without a parachute. "Shake! I'm not bluffing."

He finally mutters, "Leave me alone."

Grrr. A sharp cleaver would come in handy right now. I could chop him into manageable pieces, because there's no way I can get two hundred pounds of Shakespeare to his feet. And we can't stay here. If somebody hasn't already called the cops, it's not far off. With my luck, Sergeant West will show up. He knows my mom, knows me, and would LOVE to throw me into the system. He's already got Shake on his radar. So what do I do? What do I do? What do I goddamn do? Shit. Fuck. Crap.

Wait! Shake has a phone! I'm so excited by this epiphany, I run in a stupid, tail-chasing circle around him, accomplishing absolutely nothing. I finally drop down and dig the phone from his pocket. My hands tremble so badly I drop it. It skitters across the sidewalk. Snatching it back, I scroll through his contacts and can't find anything under Terek or West. I start to hyperventilate, consider trying Sam but don't want to. Then I come across Rat. Someday someone needs to explain why that super cute boy has a rodent's nickname and smells like feminine products.

"What's up Shitstain?" Terek answers.

I sob. And beg. If this is another side effect of Shakeffect, I'm done.

Chapter 30

SHAKE:

I wake up in hell. It looks like my grandma's basement, but it's definitely hell. How else can I explain the taste of donkey piss in my mouth, glass splinters in my eyes and tiny sweaters on each of my teeth?

It gets worse.

I am not alone in my bed. The body next to me is warm but definitely not Cleo. It's too big. And heavy. I'm scared to look, terrified to uncover what species of swamp creature I dragged home with me.

I turn my head a millimeter at a time, starting to sweat, and find Rat drooling on my pillow. His flower stink is all over my sheets. Thank Christ, he's wearing pants. I don't want his junk anywhere near me or my bed. I know where it's been.

"Hey." My voice is one octave above what dogs can hear.

Rat remains comatose. He's flopped on his stomach, mouth wide open, breathing hard enough to turn three little pigs homeless. I jab him with an elbow and realize too late, I should not move. I'd puke but I lack the strength.

His eyes pop open one at a time, focus, then blink. "Morning buttmunch."

"Don't shout," I mouth the words.

"Who's shouting?"

"Shhhhhh."

"Hungover?"

"Stop shouting."

"I'MMMM NOT SHOU … TING!"

"Oh God." My brain dives into a hole and dies.

"Stupid shit," Rat mutters, scrubbing at his hair as he sits up. The mattress bounces and my insides curl over in waves.

"What… " It takes a second to manage each word. "Happened?"

"A whole lotta crazy."

"Where's… " I lick my dry lips. "Cleo?"

"Gone."

Gone? As in not in the basement? Or she's done with me?

Rat turns so his back is against the wall, knees bent up. He braces one giant foot on my shoulder, the other on my hip and shoves. Hard. I roll just like one of those hot dogs at the gas station, flop off the bed and smack onto my back. Everything hurts. Even my thoughts. If I could stand, I'd kick his ass. I doubt my whimpers are gonna scare him off.

"Hey," Rat says. "Princess Peach is up." He's on his phone. I wonder if he's talking to Cleo. "Not so good. Looks like something Sam spewed up, licked up and shit back out." A pause. "Not you, asswipe.

Sam the dog." Another pause. "That's the plan. Bring 'em over."

Definitely not Cleo. Why does he keep shouting? I use both hands to press my head together and inhale small, careful breaths. I think there's a very real possibility of my chest splitting open. I seem on the verge of hatching something slimy and really smelly.

Rat's shadow looms over me. I peel my lids just far enough to see him. The look on his face isn't friendly.

"Go away," I manage.

He nudges me in the ribs with his toes. I cry a little bit.

"Me and Sam have tried waiting you out. We've tried ignoring your stupid shit. We thought maybe you were coming around. But last night, you majorly effed up. Again. So we've come up with a new idea."

Whatever he's talking about, I don't care. I'm just thankful when he heads upstairs. I celebrate by holding perfectly still and staying right where I landed. I decide to stay here forever. It is the best spot in the whole world. I love this floor. If only it would stop tilting. And spinning. Why is fuzz growing on my tongue?

I don't remember much from my night. Pretty sure I puked in the street, made Cleo cry, puked on the sidewalk, lost a shoe, puked in the Twat and maybe wrestled a giant spider named Carl. That last bit was probably a hallucination. I hope the whole thing was, but since I reek of stale vomit …

When Rat comes tromping back down the stairs, he seems to have grown ten thousand feet, and they're all using my brain for soccer practice.

"Stop," I whisper.

"C'mon Sleeping Beauty. Up, up, up we go!"

"No, no, don't, don't," I chant as hands grab me everywhere and haul me up. My muscles are soggy. My hair is too heavy. Blinking nearly kills me.

When I finally glance around, I see Sam, Drew, Adam, Thad, Nate, Carter, Mitch, Ozzie and Rat. They're wearing their jerseys and hockey gloves. Bizarre. Maybe my teammates are another hallucination. I wonder if they've met Carl.

Then Sam stuffs my hands into a pair of gnarly team gloves, forces a mouthguard between my lips and mutters, "Sorry buddy." Oh shit.

When there's a problem with the team, we solve it in the locker room, without Coach. We call it Locker Boxing. It's brutal but effective.

"Here's the deal." Rat points at me. "You wanna stand in the middle of the road, lose yer shit? Have at it. Long as one of us is standing next to you. But go nuts all by yourself, buy shit from fucken Rex or Bruce, get toasted outta your mind again, and we're gonna beat the ever loving piss outta you. Got it?"

"What is this?"

"You heard me. We're here to fix your ass. The new plan starts now."

"Ganging up on me?"

"That's right," Adam answers.

"Leave me the fuck alone." I'm half falling on my ass, before I even throw or take a punch. Not good.

"We're a team, Shake. Your team," Sam snarls at me. "So no. We're not gonna leave you the fuck alone."

"We're brothers, man," Thad tells me. I swivel to glare at him and my eyes cross. "Go ahead, asshole. Blow your wad. Fight me on it. I'll still be standing right here."

"Consider this a team intervention." This from Ozzie, a junior left winger.

"Fuckers," I mumble, bringing my hands up, knowing I'm gonna get my ass handed to me.

Sam shakes his head.

"OK dickwad, you deserve this." Rat taunts cuffs me across the face. Little white sparkles scatter behind my eyes, and I taste my stomach lining.

"You scared Cleo last night!" For all his smiling and joking around, Rat's the meanest son of a bitch on the team. He holds the school record for penalty minutes and spends half his time at a kickboxing gym. "The only chick willing to put up with your shit called me, crying, begging for help. After she almost got hit by a car, dragging your ass out of the road!"

Bracing my hands on my knees, spit slides out of my mouth. My cheek stings from the scrape of the glove. Doesn't compare to the sting of realization. I messed up. Again. Yet I still hear myself saying, "What do you care about Cleo?"

"Seriously dude?" he barks. "Ask yourself why she cares about your idiot ass."

"Tell me she didn't go back to the yellow house." Waiting for his answer pulverizes my insides. "Rat?" I glance up. He lets me stew in my own juices for a minute. "Please?"

I see it in his face when he takes pity on me. "She's at work."

Without warning, he swats me again. A backhand this time and I flop backwards onto the bed.

"Get him up."

Hands yank me back to my feet. Blood trickles from my nose. I don't usually suck this bad at Locker Boxing.

"Somebody beat the hell outta that little girl!" Rat is shouting again. "Instead of stepping up, taking care of her, you wigged out and gave her more shit to deal with, you selfish ass. And you hurled in my fucken Twat."

He's right. Which really pisses me off. Since I can't punch myself, I take a swing at him, miss and stagger into Mitch.

"Jesus dude, your breath smells like you've been licking a cat's ass." He props me back up.

"Just take your lumps, man," Drew tells me, steadying me with a hand on my arm. "It'll go easier if you don't keep fighting."

"Piss off." I tear away from him but there's nowhere to go. I've been running from these guys all these long months, unwilling to let myself have their support, afraid they'd figure out what a mess I am. Yet here they stand.

Sam drops his gloved mitt on top of my head and holds me in place as he leans in. "You need your friends, you fucken moron. Open your goddamn eyes. Get your head outta yer ass. You need us, and we're right here." He pats me with heavy thumps. "Better get your hands up. This is gonna hurt."

What do I need? Friends.

Chapter 31

SHAKE:

I can't come up with the last time I cared what a girl thought. Maybe never. But right now, I'm so nervous I'm chewing my thumbnail like it's a competitive sport.

I don't know how long Cleo works, so I wait. And sweat. It's hot as balls outside, and I'm dying a slow painful death.

Leaning against the brick wall of a hardware store, I lurk in a narrow strip of shade. I'm not sure if I'm loitering, stalking, trespassing, or just plain creepy, but I grab more attention than Batman in drag. Apparently every car needs to slow down and confirm I am totally pussywhipped.

This is why I've kept to myself. Not the pussywhipped part. The part where I keep screwing Cleo over. Not literally screwing. If that were the case, you wouldn't hear me complaining. But well, shit, I totally messed everything up.

Anyway, my point is ... yes, there is a point. If I'm not making sense, blame my hangover. My points are about as sharp as a kindergartener's crayon this morning. Right. The point, the point ... Cleo doesn't need to witness or participate in the shitshow I starred in last night. I am an ass. A moron. A lifeform lower than a worm. A selfish worm who deserves to be ripped in half by a pair of starving robins.

Yup. My teammates knocked some sense into me. But that's not what has me taking a hard look at myself. The thought of Cleo going back to the yellow house, because I am too far up my own buttcrack to take care of her, is worse than an acid enema.

Cleo Lee actually needs me, looks at me with something besides pity, and I blew it. If I sucked any harder, I could vacuum the carpets. So why would she give me another chance?

As I think it, Cleo and Allie push out the back door of my grandma's bakery. The miniature girl carries a couple of white paper bags and her scowl is all for me. Her sidekick is decked out in rainbow spandex and sparkles, and as she runs toward me, she throws in a few leaps and a twirl that go badly. What she lacks in grace, she makes up for in enthusiasm.

"There's my cream puff!" Her shout clubs me like a baby seal. Why is everybody shouting today? "Just puff and I'll cream."

I'm going to ignore that comment.

Allie carries her giant purse. In her purse are magic pills to smooth out my hangover, quiet my brain, help me forget. I know I can't have them. Doesn't mean I don't want them.

I chew at my lip and look from the purse to Cleo's eyes. They are narrowed and nearly black with anger.

"No!" She barrels into me with both hands against my chest. I think she's trying to knock me down. She is the size of a mosquito. I am a gorilla. Instead of moving me, she bounces backward and nearly falls. When I steady her, she yanks free and shouts, "No more meds! No more blow. No more weed. No more of that shit! No! No! No!"

"Shhh," I beg. I even hold my index finger against my lips.

Allie then stabs a verbal icepick directly into my ear. "Your face!"

"Don't touch me, don't touch me, don't touch me," I chant as she sweeps one giant paw around my ribs and catches a handful of ass in the other. I squeal, literally squeal, sounding exactly like a nine-year-old girl finding a toad in her book bag. I know this because of a prank on Blair Fredrickson that sent me to the principal's office.

"Ermigawed! Ermigawed! Your perfect, beautiful, precious face! We can't have you looking like this in the wedding album!" Allie's full-body hug is a cross between square dancing and a too-small sweater. Either way, it's awkward, sweaty, sorta charming, and there's no getting out of it.

"Who did this? How could they? Why not just spray paint a ferret's esophagus!"

"Pharaoh's sarcophagus," Cleo translates.

"Or Michelangelo's pita!"

"Pieta," Cleo corrects.

"Isn't that the bread pocket thingie?"

"You've got it backwards."

Allie gives me a parting squeeze I feel in my molars and tells me, "Hugs are good for the soul. You're welcome."

I twist side to side and test my body for damage. My ass cheek hurts from the rough treatment but my back and shoulders feel fantastic. She has a future as a chiropractor.

Cleo catalogues my injuries but not with the same eyes as yesterday. I look nasty, but it's just the team's idea of a group hug, which I don't explain, because I'm hoping for pity.

Unfortunately, this version of Cleo is Badass.

Time to win her over. Good thing I planned my strategy the whole walk here. Tucking my hands into my front pockets, dipping my chin, I lead with, "Hey." I force a smile. I'm so goddamn smooth, I don't know why she isn't throwing herself into my arms.

"The sight of you pisses me off," she tells me.

That's not a good start.

"Just let me," I try but she talks over me.

"Hearing your voice makes it worse." She whirls away. "I've gotta feed my strays."

She's swimming in my New York Dolls shirt. My ear buds dangle around her neck. If she's still stealing my stuff, maybe we're OK. So I trot after her. Badass Cleo hustles to stay six feet in front of me. Allie is my own personal barnacle.

"How come Cleo won't walk with me?" I ask.

"She warned me not to tell you ANYTHING," Allie blares. "Even if you act all cute, drop to one knee and offer a diamond. Just so you know, I prefer princess cut and will expect to be carried over the threshold."

She bats her lashes and blows a kiss at me.

"You um ..." I now prove I have no shame. "You look particularly ... uh ... hmmm ... colorful today, Allie."

"I've been experimenting with body paint."

"That's um, cool."

"It's edible. I plan to use your skin as my canvas and my tongue as the brush."

I choke on my own spit. I never know if she's serious or fucking with me. "So, yeah, hey." My voice jumps up and down as if I'm stuck in puberty. "You know that redheaded douchebag at the yellow house?"

"Randy." She makes a face.

"Yeah. Randy. I'm guessing he doesn't want me around Cleo. Am I right?"

"She's supposed to stay away from you. But she couldn't help herself."

"Why is that?"

"Have you looked in the mirror? Seen your hair? Your eyes? That bottom lip? Your butt? Ermigawd, that butt." Her volume throws my brain into a metal garbage can and kicks it downhill. "The girl isn't made of stone."

"Allie! Allie," I cut her off. Why is she listing random body parts? "Shhhh," I plead. "Why's it a big deal if she hangs out with me?"

Cleo swings around and walks backward, pointing at me. "You're a giant ass weasel. You know that right?"

I've been called a moron, dickstick, asshole, dumbshit and now a giant ass weasel, all in a matter of hours. Doesn't matter if I've earned it, I'm getting a little tired of it. But this is me being a good boy, so I keep my mouth shut as I follow her all the way around to the back parking lot of the grocery store.

When Cleo heads down the path through the weeds, Allie grabs my arm and hauls me back. "I gotta check on my mom."

"OK." I try to tug free. Nope.

"You could be good for Cleo."

"Uh-huh." I tug again, harder. Still no.

"Let's just remember, everyone in Cleo's whole life has let her down. Hurt her. She's had enough of that. If you become a problem instead of the solution, I'll eliminate you from her situation."

She squeezes my arm. My balls shrivel in fear. We really need to get her on the ice. She'd make a ferocious defenseman.

"Are we clear?" she checks.

I nod. Vigorously.

"OK. Go grovel and win her back. I'm counting on you."

I nod some more and leave Allie standing in the parking lot, burning holes into my back. I thunder down the path and burst into the clearing, in a hella hurry and stumbling like a spastic jackass. A dog with a missing eye, half an ear, and a bald ass growls at me.

Cleo makes a big show of rolling her eyes and ignoring me. I watch her dole out pieces of muffin to her reject animals and wait for my turn. She then tries to brush me off without so much as a scratch behind the ears. WTF? So I block her exit. Her eyes give the WTF right back at me, and she's better at it than I am.

"Wait." I hold up my hands, half expecting her to hit me.

"I'm still working out where to dispose of your body," she tells me, fists planted on her hips. Badass Cleo is adorable. "But I've figured out how I'm going to kill you."

"How?"

"Slow. With a plastic bag, duct tape, and tweezers."

I don't doubt her. "Sounds kinky."

I give her an eyebrow waggle.

She doesn't soften. Without warning, Cleo fakes right, dodges left, and nearly gets by me. She's quick, but I'm big. My accidental hip check drops her like a dead cat from the Empire State Building. Perfect.

Could I screw this up any worse? I guess I could puke on her shoes. Oh wait, I did that last night.

I stand over her, hold out my hand to help her up, and surprise, surprise, she flips me off. So I sit down next to her, feet spread and knees wide. Last night I was five minutes from getting in her pants. Today, I'm five seconds from getting charged with assault.

"You OK?" I try.

No answer. I watch her brush the dirt off her hands.

"Are we gonna be OK?"

Still no answer.

"C'mon, Cleo."

"You suck."

Is that progress?

She sits up, wraps her arms around her knees. There's a leaf stuck in her hair but I don't dare pluck at it. Her scowl could cut glass. I try a smile. "What's it gonna take to fix this?"

"Explain what went wrong last night," she demands.

"I don't ... um ... ah ... " I stammer.

"You don't and that's the problem. I dragged your sorry carcass out of the road last night, Shake. You nearly got us both run over. Tell me why or I'm out."

I'd rather spend six hours locker boxing than this. Shit. I pull at a dandelion between my feet and try to come up with something to say. Cleo is not patient. She waits approximately three seconds then jumps up. "Screw it. You have a nice life."

"Hold on." I snag her by the shirt.

"Why can't you tell me?"

I close my eyes. "Because I don't want you to know how pathetic I am."

"I already know."

I glance at her. She spreads her hands, lifts her shoulders and says, "Hey, you found me sleeping in a car, carried me cuz I didn't have shoes and listened to me cry for hours. It doesn't get much worse. So you know what? I can't afford to mess with some dumbass who won't even try to fix himself."

I hang my head. "Talking about it messes me up. So I don't."

"Great strategy. How's that working so far?"

"Yeah." I nod and pat the ground beside me. "Please Cleo?"

She lowers herself back down. We sit in silence until I swear I hear her bristle. I finally tell her, "Rat's got six younger brothers and sisters. It's chaos at their house. Loud, messy and so friggin normal. And his mom and dad and everybody pretends I'm just another kid, like I'm family, and here's some bread and pass the peas. But ..." My voice snags. Heat spreads across my face. "I'm not their son or their brother. I'll never be that again."

Cleo tips her head against my shoulder. I close my eyes and wonder if the sharp beat of my heart will slice me open and spill my guts right here in the dirt.

"Before I left, Rat's mom hugged me." My voice thins to a whisper as I remember the way her arms gathered me in. Even though I'm way bigger than her, it was a mom's hug. She pulled my head into her shoulder, rubbed my back and whispered, "It's gonna be OK, honey. We're here for you."

She turned me utterly helpless. It was all I could do not to sob all over her.

My hands now stretch, clench, stretch, clench. I watch them, can't stop them. I'm about five seconds from a colossal meltdown when Cleo crawls between my spread knees, wraps her fingers over mine, and holds tight. Her face is no more than six inches from mine. I'm tempted to grab her and just kiss the hell out of her, make us both forget this conversation. But I know better.

She never lets me get away with anything.

"Tell me," she pushes.

I bob my chin, swallow, nod some more and work my way up to it.

"She said she'd be there for me, whatever I need." I don't admit that figuring out what I need is a destination I can't reach. So I decided there is nothing I need, because nothing can change the truth. I should have been home the night of the fire. Even if I couldn't have saved my family, I should have died with them. Because no matter what I do with my life, I will never equal out the loss of theirs, and I don't want to be here without them.

I finally meet Cleo's big dark eyes and say, "When I left Rat's, I started thinking about you waiting for me in the basement."

"That was a bad thing?"

"Yes. No." I grind my teeth for a second and all sorts of sticky emotions get clogged in my throat.

She lifts one hand to cup my face. "It's OK. Tell me."

"My feet always try to take me home, to Willow Drive. Every time. Except last night. I turned straight toward my grandma's house. I was in a big hurry to get to you. I wasn't thinking about anything else." Each minute of the last eight months lands on me, and my chest starts to collapse.

She waits. And waits. And then says, "I don't understand."

"I forgot." Those two words are harder to pull than teeth, and when they fall off my lips, there's a raw empty hole left behind.

"Oh Shake," she whispers.

"How could I? How could I forget?"

"Seriously?" Her eyes nail me. "That's why you're beating yourself up? Because for one minute you forgot to hate your life and felt a teeny bit of happiness?"

I look away. My whole body shudders.

"Wow. You're an idiot. That's what's wrong with you. I miss Hemmie every goddamn day. I want him back, and I don't know when or if it will ever get any easier to take. Probably not. But nobody's counting our smiles or weighing our tears." She thumps her chest. "The hurt's in here. It's big and awful, and it's ours. We don't need to feel it at max capacity every second to prove it. And I hate to tell you this, but your pain doesn't change a friggin thing for them. If they were here, they wouldn't want it. They'd want a better life for you. They'd be totally pissed that you're making yourself miserable and blaming it on them. So all you're doing is hurting yourself."

She stares at me.

I've got no words.

She stares some more, then says, "Now is no time to think of what you do not have. Think of what you can do with what there is."

A Hemingway quote. My brother must have taught her that.

She gives me a chance to say something. I can't. I can't even look at her, because she'll see the kamikaze tears spilling down my face. I sniff, rub my face against my shoulder and my breath hitches.

Her arms slide around my neck, and as I tuck my forehead against her chest, she kisses my hair. "It's gonna get easier. I promise, Shake. Little by little. You're gonna do OK and manage to have a life. You're allowed. OK? Being happy isn't failing but succeeding. And you don't need to go through the hard stuff by yourself. So if you wanna shout, fight, fuck, skate, dance, laugh, whatever, it's all right. Doesn't mean you aren't hurting enough."

I swallow. Something indefinable lifts off my chest. Why does having someone's permission to be happy make such a difference?

We stay there, wrapped together, while I soak up the feeling of her, the words she spoke, the relief loosening the knots in my gut. She smells like the bakery, like a sugary treat, which has me wondering how she'd taste. Eventually, I manage to murmur, "You said fuck."

"I what?"

I pull back, hoping there's no fresh wet on my cheeks. "You said whatever I wanna do. And you said fuck."

Her eyes roll up, and she smiles a little. "Yes horndog, I did. Leave it to you to pick out that one nugget."

"Did I ruin it?" I ask her. "Whatever we started between us."

She tilts her head but doesn't answer. So here goes. It's the overtime shootout and I've got the puck. Translation: I've got one chance to win or lose.

"I'm gonna get my shit together, Cleo. Because of you." This is my epiphany from my walk to the bakery. "No way I'm letting you down again. I will be what you need."

Her face crinkles up as if I just pinched her. Great. I go for it anyway. "Cleo, do you want to be with me?"

She hesitates. The life cycle of a mayfly expires. A rare species of treefrog becomes extinct. The ugly stray dog with the missing eye whines. He's got a bald, raw ass but feels sorry for me. I am that level of pathetic.

I'm having a threesome with disappointment and humiliation by the time she finally admits in a teeny voice, "I want you more than I've ever wanted anything."

It takes a second for me to catch on. This version of Cleo is Mine. I stop just short of tearing the wrapping off my new toy. Only because fear is written all over her.

Cupping her sweet little face in my giant hands, I promise her, "I won't let anybody hurt you, Cleo. That's not how it is for you anymore."

"I need to go back to the yellow house."

"No."

"But ..."

"No."

"I just gotta ..."

"Cleo." This is non-negotiable, and I fight dirty to get my way. I slide my knuckles along her cheek and quote Shakespeare. "She is mine own, and I as rich in having such a jewel as twenty seas, if all their sand were pearl, the water nectar, and the rocks pure gold."

Do I sound like a douche? Yup. Am I whipped? No doubt. But she goes all pink in the cheeks, soft in all the right ways and smiles. For that, for Cleo, I'll be a whipped douche.

"That might have been overkill," she tells me.

"Did it work?"

"Hells yeah."

I wrap her up and pull her to her feet, digging how small she is, the feel of her tight little body, the shape of her under my hands. Threading my fingers into her hair, I hunch way down and kiss her. Her mouth opens for me, letting me inside, and she's hot and sweet and maybe as eager for this as I am, because she lifts to tiptoes for a better fit.

A zing of awareness shoots up my spine, and I'm instantly so goddamn hard I could pound nails. I think about laying her down on the ground and going for it. But she's already got some weird complex, thinking she's not good enough, and deserves way better than getting banged in the dirt. So I step back, breathing hard, calculating the time and distance to my grandma's house. I'm suddenly in a big effing hurry to get there. Maybe if we sprint.

"Ready to go?" I tug on her hand, trying not to drag her caveman-style, but really tempted to just throw her over my shoulder. I'm worried her short legs are already going to slow us down.

"Wait. Wait." She digs in her heels.

Shit. Goddamnit. If she tells me no, I might die. My balls might literally detonate. Down boy, I tell myself and take a deep breath.

"I want to … I've got something for you." She holds up a white paper bakery bag. If all I'm getting here is a cookie, I need to pretend I'm cool with it. I try out a nod, but I'm so revved up I'm sure I come off looking like a bobblehead.

"I was at your house a couple of times," she tells me. "In the basement and uh, I snuck upstairs. Hemmie said not to, but I wanted to look around. And, well …"

The bag is flat and actually looks empty. I'm confused and a little wary. I inch backward.

"I stole something," Cleo admits. "I wanted a little piece of your life. I'm sorry."

She reaches inside the bag and hands me a photograph. My lungs deflate and I can't fill them back up. I go completely still. Even my thoughts are suspended, as if I'm outside of myself, looking at this moment from a long way away.

I remember this photo on the bookcase behind the piano. I picture it there and smell wood polish and the very faint scent of my mother's perfume. I feel the worn spot in the carpet from so many hours of sitting on the piano bench and scuffing my feet. I hear my brother in the basement, his music seeping up through the floorboards and my dad not realizing he's humming along to it. For all the time I've stood on the centerline of Willow Drive, this is the first time I've truly been back to my house.

The photograph is of my family, standing on a beach in southern France, and I'm probably nine or ten. My dad has his arm slung over my mom's shoulder, looking at her, while she tilts her head back and laughs. I stare up at Hemmie and he's grinning straight at the camera. We are happy. My mom is beautiful, and my dad loves her. Hemmie is the big brother who taught me a wrist shot. It is a memory I haven't allowed myself to have in eight months. Instead of pain and loss and anger, it's warmth and comfort and familiar. I am suddenly thankful for what I had, for the good things.

I look from Cleo to the photo and back. I don't know how to tell her what this means to me.

What do I need? To remember.

Cleo has given my memories back.

Chapter 32

CLEO:

Shake takes me home with him. We hold hands. Me and Shakespeare LeCasse. Me and Shake. Shake and me. Hold hands. Yeah, it's more exciting than watching David Beckham bend over and tie his shoe. A shirtless David Beckham.

Actually, Shake drags me. He walks so fast, I run to keep up. I didn't know cardio was gonna be part of this deal. We've kicked the tortoise aside, lapped the hare and are setting world speed records.

I'm not sure about the hurry, but maybe Shake understands we shouldn't be seen together. I half expect Dripass to jump out of the bushes and dump pig's blood over my head. I know Randy will do way worse than boil my bunny for this. But whatever, nobody's gonna piss on my parade today.

"Watch it!" I warn, and Shake dips his head just in time to avoid the basement ceiling.

The second we arrive at the bottom of the stairs, he grabs the hem of my shirt, which is actually his shirt, and gives me a look. It's quite a look. He's so hot, I could fry eggs on his abs. I might dissolve into a sticky puddle just standing near him.

"Is this OK, Cleo?"

He waits. I raise my arms to help him and my shirt lands on the floor.

"Red?" he whispers. He sounds like he's in pain. Or is that disappointment?

The red bra and panties aren't enough to change this duckling into a swan. So I fold my lips between my teeth and wonder if I should quack, just to make sure he knows what he's getting here. But there's no second thoughts when he scoops his hands under my butt and lifts me.

"You drive me crazy," he tells me.

I wrap my legs around his waist, arms around his neck, and he kisses me. But it's more than that. Shake doesn't just kiss me. He makes me his. He turns my whole world upside down. Parted lips, soft tongue and there's nothing but his taste, his smell, his heat. My fingers crawl into his hair, grabbing handfuls of the silky mess, wanting him closer and just plain wanting him.

He shuffles across the floor, carrying my weight, and then we suddenly fall. He drops backward onto the bed, and it's a long way down. I sprawl on top, my laughter spilling into his mouth as he rolls me onto my back and stretches out beside me. Propping up on one elbow, he fans a big hand across my ribs and grins down at me.

I wish I could take a picture of him. He's all lit up. But I don't need it. I'll never forget this moment. I might never have another to even come close. His smile is proof, anything is possible.

Now I'm nervous. I've had sex a couple times, but never straight and sober or because I really wanted to. I've done it to get drugs and booze. I've done it to stay safe, picking a guy so scarier, meaner dudes leave me alone. I usually just close my eyes and ride it out.

But this is Shake. This is different. He is different.

"Still OK?" he asks.

I remember the first time I was in his bed, when I walked a blitzed Shake home from the Crypt, and he was all over me faster than an exploding bottle of baby powder. Color me surprised when he waits for my nod and treats me careful and gentle, like this is something worth taking his time with. As if I am worth it.

Starting with the curve where neck meets my shoulder, he kisses a slow and thorough path all the way to my ear. My eyes roll back as he pulls my lobe between his teeth. And sucks. And tugs. His fingers find the answering shivers and follow them up to the edge of my bra stroking me through the lace. I'm so glad I have new, pretty underthings for this.

He cups me in his palm, thumb brushing over my nipple, while his lips press soft and moist against my temple. I'm starting to squirm, ready for more, when he releases the front clasp of my bra.

Shake's eyes sweep over me, over a body only a ten-year old might envy, and then raise to meet mine. I don't know what I'm expecting. Definitely not his whispered, "I've been thinking about this, wanting you so much. You're more beautiful than I pictured."

Pushing the fabric aside, his blonde head tips forward. Soft curls spill over my chest as his tongue, lips and teeth take turns on my nipple. My toes curl. I didn't know anything could feel this good. And I ... And I ... can't think. At all. Obviously. Because Shake is right there, and instead of touching him, I'm clutching the sheets with both hands.

Just when I might manage something more than sponging up his attention, his hand slides down over my belly and dips under the waistband of my pants. My surprised "ah" gets cut off when he strokes between my legs.

"Mmmmm," he hums against my skin. "You're wet."

I jerk when he pushes one finger inside.

"Yes?"

I think I nod.

His fingers are long. He adds a second, and curls them in a way that makes my knees fall open and my hips buck. Then he takes me for a ride. Kissing, touching, faster, faster, and oh, dear God, I just grab him by the hair and hang on.

The sensations build on top of each other. They pull me like a string he's winding around his hand until I can't go any further. I completely unravel, making these panting little shrieks and slapping a palm against his chest. I don't know if I'm trying to push him away or reel him in, but I clutch his shirt and need it gone. I need to feel him, right goddamn now.

Searching my fingers under the fabric, I am rewarded by his naked skin, the jump of his stomach muscles and a hiss through his teeth.

"Shirt off," I beg. Is that my voice? All breathless and hoarse. "Now."

He breaks away just long enough to rip his shirt over his head. Then he's right on me again, looking in my eyes for the OK, hooking his fingers in my pants and panties and dragging them down my legs. He tosses my clothes aside, takes me by the ankles, and tugs my legs further apart. His dark, dark blue eyes heat into a low flame as he crawls up over me, bracing an arm on either side and settling his hips between my thighs. The brush of denim against my sensitive skin makes me suck a sharp breath, makes me want more, want it now, want it so bad my hips shove up toward his.

"Jesus, Cleo. I'm trying to take it slow here, but I'm barely hanging on."

Slow? No, no. Let's go fast.

I reach for him, yank him into a kiss and set us on a new pace. We are frantic, tongues searching, hips meeting, and my hands learn the shape of his jaw, the line of his throat, the hard planes of his chest. I spread my fingers wide, hoping to touch as much of him as possible, then curl in, scratching over him with my fingernails.

He throws his head back with a rough "ahhhh," and watches me, lashes heavy, lips falling open and breath coming faster as I detail his nipples, map his ribs and travel the path of rigid muscles down to the waistband of his jeans. I reach around to the small of his back, slide into his boxers and find the smooth skin of his ass. He jerks.

"I don't know if I can take it." His eyes squeeze shut. "I swear I'm gonna lose it before I get inside."

I tug on the button of his jeans. "Let's get these off quick."

In the seconds it takes him to get out of his jeans and briefs I forget to breathe. I hear him tear open a condom. I feel his weight settle back between my thighs.

"You're so small. I don't wanna hurt you."

I start to reassure him but lose my words as he eases in, fills me and starts to move. And then I lose myself.

Chapter 33

SHAKE:

Her hair is dark and spiky, maybe the softest thing I've ever felt, and it's just long enough for me to tangle my fingers in and tug her head back. When I do, her spine arches, angling her hips just right.

Holy fuck. Holy fuck. I might say this out loud because Cleo breathes a laugh.

We are on round two. As in, after banging her once, it wasn't enough. Less than fifteen minutes later, I was desperate for her again. So I rolled her over, got her on hands and knees, and now ... well, she's making these little "huh, huh, huh," sounds and driving me right off the motherfucking cliff.

I'm trying not to break her in half as I slam into her from behind, but I'm pretty much out of control. All I can think about is getting deeper, and the sight of her perfect ass pushes me to pump harder, faster, while I reach around to stroke her clit with my fingertips.

Her sounds pick up speed, morph into a chant of my name, and I suddenly love hearing my name. Then her hands twist into the sheets. She shoves her ass back against me and her pussy tightens around me.

Jesus Christ, this girl is going to kill me. And it's gonna be the best death ever. I wish I could die over and over again in the exact same way. Because it's so good it actually fucken hurts. So I don't want it to end, and I'm doing everything I can to make this last. But I am close. Too close, and there's no stopping or even slowing down. My body draws so tight, with every muscle squeezing into a physical vibrato, and I feel the release all the way down to my friggin' toes. Maybe I even black out for a second.

It takes a while to remember where I am. I find myself collapsed flat on top of Cleo. I am dead weight and probably crushing her.

"Did I hurt you?" I mumble against her ear.

She waggles her head back and forth.

"Are you OK?"

She nods.

"Why aren't you answering?"

"Cuz you're squishing me, but it feels so good, I don't want you to move. Ever." Her voice is muffled against the mattress.

"I can't move. You've paralyzed me." And then, for no other reason than sex-induced stupidity, I blurt, "Rat was right."

"What?"

"Uh …"

"Right about what?"

I exhale with my mouth buried in her neck. Shit, shit, shit. I'm such a moron. I could have a labotomy and not lose any IQ points. "Could you please just let it go? Just this once?"

"Not a chance." She bucks her hips, and since I'm in the hypersensitive, post-orgasm state, her little bounce sets off shockwaves and electrocutes my balls.

"Aaaah, no, no, don't do that."

She does it again. Spasms radiate from my gut to my fingertips. Did I mention, Cleo Lee is going to kill me?

"OK, OK, stop." I pull out and ease off her with barely enough strength to get rid of the condom. My legs wobble. "It's just something Rat said. He's a dumbass."

She glances over her shoulder at me. Perfect little face, round little ass, and she's naked in my bed. I wouldn't change a thing and could get used to this.

"What did he say?" She must read my expression, because she adds, "If you don't tell me, you shouldn't feel safe falling asleep."

I look away and admit, "He said you … ah … that you might possibly, maybe bang like a rabid wolverine."

Cleo snorts. "Should I be pissed or happy about that?"

"I'm sure as shit happy about it."

I flop onto my stomach, wrap an arm around her and snug her warm little body tight to mine. I'm so exhausted, breathing takes effort, but I'm hoping for a quick recovery. I want to play with Cleo some more.

She props her head in her hand and starts running her fingers up and down the valley of my spine, from neck to ass. It's heaven.

"Cleo?"

"Yeah?"

"I'm going to fall asleep now. Don't go anywhere, OK?"

"Will you feed me at some point?"

"Whatever you want."

"Then I'll be right here."

Fuck counseling. I've found the one thing that makes me forget everything else. And I think repetition is the key. Hopefully, Cleo will cooperate with this theory.

Chapter 34

CLEO:

"Purple?"

I look over my shoulder to see Shake watching me. I'm wearing the purple bra and painties, pawing through shopping bags for pants and shirt to wear to school. I'm nervous about going back there. New clothes, new guy, same old me. A tag on my underwear proves I'm a total zero.

I don't understand the look Shake gives me, but I recognize it. The slight curve of his lips, tip of his chin and concentrated attention of darkened eyes are becoming familiar. It never fails to saturate me in shivers.

It's Monday morning. We spent Saturday and Sunday trying new places to screw around. Bent over the clothes dryer, on the stairs, on the picnic table, under the picnic table, next to the picnic table, in the shower … the boy is creative. We only came up for air long enough to eat. I also made it to my shifts at the bakery. He walked me to and from, like my own personal guard dog, and I barely made it back into the basement before the horny puppy was all over me again.

I'm not complaining. He is sex on a stick. By this point, his stick should be worn out. But with a T-shirt snagged around his neck and unzipped jeans sagging off his hips, Shake's smoldering baby blues are again plotting ways to jump my bones.

"Shake," I warn.

"Cleo."

"School."

He prowls toward me. This playful Shake is a brand new animal. "I like purple."

"That's what you said about the red undies. And the blue. And the black." I take a step backward. "You're a horndog."

"I'm focused. Goal-oriented. Found something I really want." He steps closer. He towers over me. "I can't get enough."

"Oh, ah ... " My graceful self steps backward and tumbles into the dryer. My heart tries a pirouette but trips and cracks against my ribs. I've never felt like this before. I didn't know anything like this was possible. It's amazing. And scary. I need a handbook with directions, warnings, maybe diagrams, because I don't know the next step or what the hell I'm doing. I'm bound to mess it up. Leaving this basement is the first step toward my downfall, but there's no choice. We can't stay down here forever. Can we?

"Be a good boy," I tell him.

"I'm trying. It's hard. Soooo hard. Kind of a shame to waste it, right?" His smile is all sly boots and as warm as the hands curving round my hips. "How bout I show you just how hard I can try?"

Who needs school? Especially since there's a whole big, bad world waiting outside, and no one wants to see Shake and me in it together. And once he takes a good look around, he's gonna agree with them.

"Wait, wait," I try again. "Sandersuck's been tattling to your grandma. You're on the verge. School, dude. You gotta go."

He groans, head tipping back, palms cupping my ass. "Cleo."

"Shake."

"Couldn't we be a little late?"

He turns those amazing eyes on me, licks his lower lip and catches it under his teeth. Does he know how dangerous he is? It should be illegal. No boy should be this potent. I can't think straight when he … it doesn't matter what he does. Shake brushing his teeth is better than porn.

"I've got something I wanna try with you." His voice drops, goes husky, and he waggles his eyebrows.

I'm hooked. If I were a fish, he'd already have me in the boat. "What?"

"I wanna see if I can make you cum with my mouth. Then, when you're all nice and wet, I'm gonna try fucking you standing up."

Am I supposed to be shocked? Embarrassed? Offended? You have me mistaken for somebody else. I'm already nice and wet, just at the sound of his voice. Just looking at him. In case you're wondering if he can make good on his promises, the answer is yes. To both. Yes, he can.

Shake's talented tongue takes me on a magic carpet ride. Aladdin's a poser. This is a whole new world. Those biceps of his are good for more than filling out his shirt. I might have a scrape from the wall on my back. He might have scratches from my fingernails on his shoulders. Maybe a bite mark or two.

We're naughty and late leaving for school.

When we hit the sidewalk outside his grandma's, Shake holds out his hand. I stare at it. He waits, and I know he'll stand there all goddamn day. He is one stubborn sasquatch.

"What's the word that means a one-time thing?" I ask. "Like an accident that shouldn't happen again? Anim … Anam … Anom … "

"Anomaly?"

I point at him. "Yes."

"No." His eyes freeze over.

"This." I gesture at his big hand, still floating between us. "Bad idea."

"Why, Cleo?"

I'm not ready to tell him why.

"Shut up and take my hand, Cleo. Unless you're ashamed or scared to be seen with me for some reason?"

I zip it and grab his hand. His wide palm and long fingers overtake mine, and it's weird how I am tickled and terrified at the same time.

I've braved his hand before, even let him carry me, right through town. It should get easier. But I'm that frantic squirrel, running back and forth across a busy intersection. Eventually I'm going to get crushed. The only question is which direction it's coming from.

Walking up the steps to school, panic gets the best of me and I tug against Shake's hold. "I can't. We, us, this just isn't … "

With arguments like that, I should probably give up on law school. But Shake gets it. He tightens his grip and tells me, "Fuck em. Nobody matters but me and you. And you know I've got your back."

Easy for him. He's not seeing the dump truck full of TNT headed straight at us. At me. Mr. Popularity will be just fine.

Dripass won't poison HIS apple. And what if Bruce sees us? Hears about us? He'll trip over his boner running to Randy. Oh God.

At least we've timed it so the halls are empty. But we need tardy passes, and because we skipped three days in a row, we're at Sandersuck's mercy. She starts with Shake and spends a long time, because his rehabilitation, salvation and graduation are soooo important. I hear her ragging on him through the closed door, picture his shoulders hiked to his ears, and wonder why nobody gets how to handle him. I guarantee he's got a spaced out expression on his face, dead eyes, and isn't hearing a word of it.

When it's my turn, Sandersuck and I both pretend the scrapes, bruises and swelling on my face are no worse than a bad haircut. Nothing that hasn't happened before and no permanent damage. She isn't all that interested in lost causes and knows I'll tell whatever lies she needs to hear. She just wants me to hurry up, graduate already and get out of her hair. So I hold up the rug, and she sweeps my life under it.

Shake's waiting for me outside of Sandersuck's office. Of course he is. The look on his face says it all. The sasquatch claims my hand again, and since I'm about as lucky as Friday the thirteenth, the bell rings as we walk to my locker. The hall floods with shocked bystanders. Teenagers freeze in their tracks and clutch at their hearts. The female population drops to their collective knees and weeps. Might as well wear sealskin boots to a PETA convention. Sing Marilyn Manson in church. Grab a piece of the flag for toilet paper. When Cleo Lee and Shake LeCasse hold hands, it's the end of the world as we know it. Any second, locusts will fall from the sky, mountains will crumble to dust, the devil will need a wool coat, and wolves will mate with bunnies.

It's not enough for Shake.

Oh no. The crazy idiot puts on a performance. With all eyes on us, he traps me at my locker, braces his hands on either side and leans over me. He treats me to his legendary grin. He actually finds this amusing. I'm trying hard not to pee myself and consider pinching his nipple, just to wipe the smirk off his face.

"Why?" I beg, poised to run.

"You're not a secret, Cleo. You're mine."

Pittypat goes my heart. Then the universe shifts, because Shakespeare LeCasse dips his blonde curly head and pulls me into his orbit.

Chapter 35

SHAKE:

I was content with eating, sleeping and banging in the basement. I like that world. Alone with Cleo, I am not THAT kid. The tragedy. The story. The pity case. The fuckup. Until Monday morning. As much as I'd like to skip again, school is a big part of me getting my shit together. Doesn't mean it's easy.

I need Cleo's hand for the walk back into reality. I need it badly, but she'd rather not give it to me. She's got her own mess going on, doesn't want to be seen with me for some unknown reason and fails to understand we are stronger together. So I bully her. I win.

And lose. Because I'm at school. Where I'm public property and claiming Cleo has given everybody permission to ride me like the local bus and graffiti their shit all over me.

Principal Sanderson lectures me about keeping bad company, doesn't mention Cleo by name, but makes it clear she is more dangerous to my future than salmonella. I tune out for most of it. I've got every detail of that stupid chicken poster memorized.

Rat, Sam and various teammates take turns meowing and whip-cracking whenever they spot me. Deanna, Blair and any chick I've ever glanced at twice, get in my face and throw out words like slutty, cheap, trashy, nasty and you get the picture. They seem to be under the impression that they're doing me a huge favor. They somehow think slandering the girl I've chosen makes them look more appealing. Deanna even cries a little bit.

By the time I'm heading to fifth period counseling, my brain has turned as soggy and sticky as overcooked oatmeal. I'm also deliberately late. For a couple of reasons. One, the empty hallway is a better option. Nobody is staring at me, so I'm not tempted to bash their faces in. And two, I fucken hate counseling.

Ms. Robbins says moronic shit about wandering uncharted land, lacking direction and blah de-friggin blah. Since she is not a sherpa guiding me through, I don't need her help or want her hands on me. She touches me in ways I don't like and way too much. Her messy bun makes her look like she just got screwed on her desk. At least, that's Rat's theory, and he's dying to test it. He's been trying to dick his way into counseling since ninth grade.

I'm wishing I could trade places with him when I round the corner and nearly smack into Bruce. He's waiting for somebody. Maybe me. If he's hoping to score a sale, in school, this is definitely not cool. I promised both Cleo and my teammates I'd be a good

boy, sooooo … I'm done with that shit. I give Bruce a
nod, mutter "hey," and make to drift around him.

Bruce holds up his hands and says, "We
good?"

"Huh?"

"We cool?"

I'm not following but wanna get away, so I play
it off with a, "Yup."

His shoulders relax. "Whatever shit Cleo told
ya, we both know how it is, right dude?"

This stops me. I don't know how it is, so I give
him my full attention and wonder how old he is. Bruce
looks forty, has been shaving since sixth grade, and
I'm doubtful he needs a high school diploma to
achieve his future plans.

"Nasty little bitches." His tongue slides across
his teeth as he hooks his thumbs in his pockets.
"They all got lots a bullshit to spread, until ya stuff up
their holes. Then they'll suck like friggin' leaf blowers."

I go still. His poison is so thick and oily, it takes
a few moments for it to fully penetrate. He takes my
blank stare as a green light.

He eases closer. We're alone in the hall but he
lowers his voice. "Fucken Cleo. That's one angry
bitch, am I right?"

He waits. I nod because I want to hear what he
has to say. I'm not so much curious as masochistic.

"Man-o-man, when her ass is against the wall,
she can deepthroat like a world class ho. Am I right?"

I need to repeat his words in my head to be
sure. Then I actually hear a ping. And I lose my shit.

I lunge forward, grab him off his feet and throw him against the lockers hard enough to leave a dent. He staggers and tries to say something. I don't know what. He never manages it, because my fist meets his nose for the first time and maybe his face breaks the bones in my hand. I register white hot pain in my fingers, wet splatters on my cheeks and not much else.

I duck down and jab at his stomach, hoping to drive my fist right through his friggin spine. When he curls forward, I uppercut with a quick, hard left. His knees buckle. I hit him again as he slides to the floor. I don't stop. I kick him in the ribs, hip, thigh and vibrations zing from my foot to knee. Bruce finally squirms into the fetal position, so I drop down, grip him by the shirt and keep wailing away.

His face splits. My knuckles turn slimy. My ears buzz with adrenaline, and I hear screams gathering behind me. Someone is yelling my name. Hands haul at my shirt. It doesn't slow me down. If anything, I amp up the punishment, because I know I'm running out of time.

Chapter 36

CLEO:

"You and Shake? What a joke!"

The idea is so hilarious, Dripass bursts into musical giggles. I squint against the sparkle of her pearly whites, watch her hair flow around her shoulders and expect an ambush from singing mice and rabbits. There's no way this princess ever farts, burps or gets a pimple.

I am envious of her shoes, shirt, smell, glossy lips and everything about her. For once, she's jealous of me too. Which is the only reason I don't ram her face into the toilet.

I'm sucking a cigarette, spending my lunch period in the girls' bathroom, hiding in the stink of urine to avoid shit from Bruce. I heard he's been looking for me.

"It'll wear off." Dripass corners me in the stall. She folds her arms, cocks a hip and tilts her head. "Shake will get tired of slumming."

I blow smoke at her.

She waves pretty pink fingertips and squinches her little dab of a nose. "Just because you're sleeping with him, doesn't make him yours."

I smile. "Yeah, but I still get to fuck him."

She flinches. Score.

"I get that you want him," she fights back. "Shake is a really good guy. But he's hurting, and you're not what he needs. You're just something he'll regret someday."

I inhale her words on a long, slow drag. They burn all the way down my throat and painful heat spreads across my chest. Is this bitch psychic or did she just get lucky? She nailed the bullseye on her first try.

With her arrow right through the middle of it, my heart struggles to beat. I bleed from my own vulnerability. Nothing ever changes. I've spent my whole life running, hiding, bowing down to anybody bigger, meaner, richer, more popular.

I tap my ash in the toilet, exhaling toward the floor. When I look up, I see Dripass's disgust. I also see panic and pain. Her insecurities are like quarters dropping into a vending machine, and I answer with a snack-sized bitchslap.

"He's made it pretty damn clear. I'm exactly what he wants and needs," I snap. "Just ask him."

She spits something back, but I don't listen. I'm having a lightbulb moment. Do I believe what I just said? Slap my ass and call me crazy, but I do. Holy crispy crap. I'm the reason Shake smiled this weekend, even laughed and promised to be a good boy. No more baggies hidden under the mattress. He even came to school today. I did that.

I'm tempted to fist pump, maybe take a victory lap around the stall wearing the American flag as a cape. This is a brand new contest, and I am the winner.

"You don't know do you?" Dripass baits me. "About what happened to Shake last period? Him and Bruce?"

Don't ask, I tell myself. Don't beg. Don't give her the satisfaction. If it's big, I'll get the dirt from somebody. Allie takes her duties as president of Shake's fan club seriously. She'll know. Right? Patience. Deep breath. My brain explodes into a million worst-case scenarios. Oh freckled fuck, I gotta know.

"Tell me."

Dripass doesn't. Of course she doesn't. Her lips curve and her silence is worse than Bieber blubbering love songs. I wish I was chewing gum, just so I could spit it into her hair. Flipping all those fabulous waves over her shoulder, she leaves me with, "Stay out of my way, loser. Shake is mine."

Meh. She could have done better.

I ditch my butt, make myself count five Mississippi's, then chase Dripass out of the bathroom. She and Blair-bitch stand together, scoping out the nurse's office, and their animated reaction causes mine. Sweaty palms. Quick inhales that don't add up to enough air. Taste of rot in my mouth. I may spew my cookies before I even know what the hell is going on.

What put Shake and Bruce together in the same sentence? They probably weren't going halfsies on a pizza or pairing up to study French vocab. There's one common denominator here. Me. That's very, very bad.

When the twin bitches rush toward the main office, I move slow, slower, barely trudging to finally peek into the open doorway of the nurse's office. A guy sits on the end of a cot, left arm wrapped tight around his middle, right hand holding an ice bag against what's left of his face. I think it's Bruce. I recognize his shirt. His face is swollen into a bloated, bloody massacre, and his eyes hold me to blame.

I nearly turn inside out in my panic to get away.

Chapter 37

SHAKE:

    I'm parked in one of the chairs outside Principal Sanderson's office. Whoever designed the chair should win an award, get a listing in the Book of World Records. No way anything could be more uncomfortable, except maybe a trip to the proctologist.

    I've been cooling my jets for twenty friggin minutes, ass going numb, jaw clenched so tightly I'm cracking fillings. I rest my elbows on my knees, hold an ice bag against my shredded knuckles and ignore Mrs. K's worried glances while replaying the beating of Bruce on a steady loop. Anger drills for oil in my brain.

    Sanderson's got Rat and Sam quarantined in her office, trying to figure out what led up to my two linemates pulling me off Bruce. It's tempting to get up, walk out and be done with this shit. I'm trying here, but school has become worse than a waste of time, and I need to get to Cleo.

    "Shake." I glance up. Sanderson stands in her doorway. Lips pinched into a flat line, bright red spots riding her cheeks, she jerks her chin to get me moving. I pass Sam and Rat on their way out. I limp. I majorly effed up my foot kicking that assturd.

Sam slaps my back. He's got a split lip and blood on his chin. Did I do that? Rat leans in, winks and whispers, "Self defense, man. Dude had a knife."

"Terek West, what did I tell you not two seconds ago?" Sanderson's voice is less fun than lemon juice in a paper cut. "There's no discussion taking place right now. You two boys sit. Don't move. Don't speak. Don't twitch. Hope I forget about you."

"Grab Cleo and keep an eye on her," I tell Rat.

"Shakespeare LeCasse! You will not confer with your friends. Get in my office. Right. This. Instant."

I land in my usual chair and force myself to stay put. I'll catch up with Cleo eventually. Eventually just isn't soon enough. I'm worried about her. I've got a whole bunch of questions rolling around in my skull, getting worse and more urgent with every turn, and I can't stop stretching and squeezing my swollen fingers, even though they ache like a bitch.

Feels like some broken bones in my hand and foot. Maybe I should alert somebody. Since I'm not sacrificing more time for medical attention, and I'm pretty sure nobody gives a flying fart, which is downright depressing, there's no point.

Sanderson slams the door. My sprawled legs are in her way. Her glare should incinerate me. I don't move, sort of hoping she goes apeshit. Then I'd have an excuse to storm out. My parents would tear a stripe off my ass for this, but I'm just not in the mood to cooperate.

My high school principal finally steps over my feet. She throws a pen down on her desk. It bounces onto the floor, and she leaves it there. Yup, she's done with me.

Dropping into her swivel chair, she rubs her face, realizes she's smearing black shit around her eyes and turns on me. Whatever she sees, it further pisses her off. Maybe it's the blood splattered across my shirt. Maybe it's the attitude imprinted on my face. I'm done with her too.

She saw the bruises on Cleo this morning. It wasn't the first time. While she's been so busy chasing after me with a leash, why has she never done anything to help Cleo?

"Do you have any idea of the situation you are in?" she starts. "Some mistakes never go away. They hang around like an anchor, dragging you down, and eventually, you end up drowning in regret."

And away we go.

I zone out. Her voice grates on me, reaches the same pitch as the Twat, when the muffler dragged along the road. Rat left it that way, because he was broke and the sparks looked cool. Then his dad threatened to ticket him. So Hemmie helped us rig a coat hanger to fix it, and Sam ended up needing six stitches in his left hand. God, I miss Hemmie. He's the reason for my right hook. I think he might be the reason for whatever the Douche did to Cleo.

I come back in time to hear Sanderson say, "You have the potential to be either successful or a total waste of it. I'm concerned your choice of companions is making the decision for you."

She gives me a silence to fill and it lasts for the next three minutes. I hope she's holding her breath.

When the door to the office suddenly bursts open, I actually jump. In my defense, my grandmother is scarier than Hagrid, covered in flour, stomping trolls with every step she takes. She points at me. "Not one goddamn word. Got it?"

I jerk a nod and swallow my Adam's apple.

She turns on Sanderson, spreads her fingertips on the desk and leans over them. "Explain why your inability to manage this circus means I abandon my job to do yours?"

Sanderson startles, her chair crying for mercy and a vein materializes in her forehead, thick as a spring worm. "As I explained on the phone, your grandson physically assaulted another student. If you will please take a seat, perhaps we can agree on the proper course of action for his best interests."

Best interests? Hah. They're just pissed I'm taking up their valuable time. I snort. Both women murder me with irritated glares. I go back to slouching and watching my ice melt.

"Boys get into fights, Viv. You're overreacting."

"Overreacting! This was a bit beyond a fight. Your grandson is a threat to himself and others. He did far more damage than you can even imagine."

"Sam and that shaggy-looking boy," Grandma snarls, jerking a thumb toward the door. "What was his name? Mouse? Sam and Mouse tell me the kid is a known drug dealer. I'm not sure why you're willing to look the other way, but that delinquent attacked Shake with a knife. Seems to me ..."

And this is where shit and fan collide.

"Those are some very serious accusations, and there is no proof of a knife ... "

"Self-goddamn-defense. Ever heard of it?"

"I questioned every witness, searched the entire ..."

"You think one of the inmates might have snatched the knife, Viv?"

"Interesting how only Shake's former teammates are ... "

"Just maybe you're yanking the wrong set of balls?"

"Why I'm certainly not ... "

"You've made a repeat habit of jerking me off!"

"I would hardly call my recommendation of counseling as ..."

"The only thing Miss Titsie ... "

"Ms. Robbins is qualified ... "

"...qualified to give the boy a woody."

On that happy note, the door swings back open. I'm grateful until Rat's dad fills it. He's in full uniform and makes my grandmother look like a slip of a gal. His shoulders are wider than the Grand Canyon. His hands are bigger than deflated basketballs. His eyes grab me so hard I maybe pee a little bit. "I'll talk to Shake alone."

He sounds a lot like Mufasa. I shiver more violently than a hyena with Simba clamped between its teeth. Shit, shit, shit.

Whaddaya know, the two ladies finally agree on something. I swear they link arms and river dance out of the office. I consider wrapping both hands around Grandma's ankle. Saying I really, really don't want to be left alone in the office with Rat's dad is the understatement of the century. I might asphyxiate on my own panic.

He props his hip on the desk, folds his arms and stares me down. My balls shrink down to the size of raisins and I glance toward the door, to the floor, finally focus on my swelling hand and try to clear my throat without him hearing me.

I've known him since Rat and I played on the same team for Mosquito level hockey. I've spent countless nights at his house and used him as a reference when I applied for the job at the rink. He loaned me a suit to wear to my family's funeral, knotted the tie for me and kept his big hand on my shoulder the whole day. Disappointing him sucks.

"Let's hear it," he prompts.

I shrug and work on swallowing the bucket of fishy spit sitting in my mouth.

"That's how you want to play this? Aren't gonna man up?"

I'm effectively reduced to nutless plankton.

"No? Nothing to say? Then I'll tell you how it is.

You're done fucking your life away, Shake." He gives me a second to appreciate my role as his bitch. "You will be in school, on time, every single goddamn day until graduation. You will graduate. You will check in with me weekly for the duration, and I'll be getting reports from both your principal and your counselor. If you screw up, the least little bit, I'll start piss testing you."

He points a thick finger at me. His voice drops to a new level I've never heard before. Compared to this, Darth Vader is Minnie Mouse. "This weekend, you and I will sit down and complete your college acceptance and whatever paperwork you need. We'll talk to the coach, get you onboard for team tryouts, and I'll move you into your dorm in the fall. As per my wife's request, you'll join the West family for dinner on a regular basis. And I consider you part of the tribe, not a guest, so you'll help with the dishes. Take out the trash. Babysit. Same as the rest."

I don't know how I manage to inflate my balls, but I say, "That's not gonna work for me, uh sir."

"On your feet, Shake."

"Huh?"

He hauls me by the arm. I drop the bag of ice and put too much weight on my wrecked foot. I'm barely done whimpering when he slams a cuff on my wrist and locks my hands behind my back. He's not gentle about it, and I start to seriously worry.

"You and I are headed down to the station, son. I'll be processing you for assault and giving you a sample of what you can expect if my plan doesn't work for you."

Awesome.

Chapter 38

SHAKE:

I'm not talking. Bruce isn't talking. Rat and Sam won't shut up. They saw a knife. It's bullshit and everybody knows it, but my teammates have my back.

So the good news: I'm not getting charged with assault.

The bad news: I'm suspended from school for ten days.

Maybe that's good news. Who am I kidding? That's DEFINITELY good news.

So, other than more worthless counseling, I'm off the hook. Except, my knuckles are purple and the size of plums. My foot throbs. My sneaker is getting smaller by the minute. I missed lunch and for the past hour, my stomach has been cannibalizing itself.

Doesn't matter. My biggest bitch is the crap Bruce said. I shut the motherfucker up, but his words won't leave me alone. I hear them. Picture them. There's plenty of time for them to bulldoze my china shop, because Rat's dad leaves me squatting in a holding cell for over four hours. He's proving a point. He's got me by the balls, and he's squeezing. I either play by his rules or get tossed back into the cage. Anytime he wants. For as long as he wants. It's an effective strategy.

What do I need? Consequences.

I'm grimy and deflated by the time my grandmother claims me from the police station. I am as pathetic as the last mutt left at the pound and probably smell worse. There's a little bit of deja vu when I fold into the passenger seat of her car, slam the door and rest my aching head against the window. I was right here eight months ago. It still blows, and I'm guessing Grandma still doesn't want me.

I finally glance over. My grandmother makes no move to start the car. We're parked in front of the police station, the sun dying across the hood. She stares straight ahead, through the windshield. Maybe she's waiting for me to get out of the car and fade into the sunset. My stomach cramps. Hunger? Or having nowhere to go, nobody to take me in? I'll admit, I haven't exactly earned a spot in Grandma's heart or basement these past few months.

"Sorry about this," I mumble. Do I sound sincere? I don't think so. I sound exactly like what I am. A punkass teenager who's pissed off, scared shitless, barely hanging on, with no idea how to ask for help.

She nods once, then says, "Sam and that homeless-looking kid, what was his name? Rabbit? Weasel? Their story was nothing but shit in a shoebox, and nobody's buying it. There was no knife. But I'm going to pretend that other boy earned the beating you gave him. Because I saw the bruises on Cleo, and I'm hoping your mother raised you right."

I bite my lip and wisely decide to say nothing.

"Don't make a habit of being a bully," she says, finally cranking the key in the ignition and easing out of the parking lot. We are halfway to the house before she speaks again.

"When your mom was growing up, I wasn't around enough to know she resented the hell out of me. I was making a living, building a business and neglected what's important. The few times I made an effort, I made a mess of it. So when your mom kept me away from you and your brother, I didn't fight her on it. I understood her reasons." She signals, swings into a right turn, and I think we're done talking. But she goes on.

"Eight months ago, I knew bringing you home with me was probably a mistake and definitely the last thing your mom would want. I could see how unhappy you were with the arrangement, and I don't know jackshit about handling a teenage boy. Especially a kid in your situation. So I left you alone, did what I could to stay out of your way. Figured it was best. But I should have said it then. I should have made sure you understood how it is."

Wow. I saw this coming, and yet I'm surprised by how bad it stings. I've turned into such a worthless piece of shit, my last chance at family is kicking me to the curb. Congratulations to me.

"So here it is," she says. "You matter to me, Shake. You're the most important thing. Losing my daughter, my grandson and your dad ... All I can do is thank whatever sadistic prick is overseeing this zoo for leaving you behind. You're the only reason I still get out of bed every morning. Whatever's going on with you, tell me or don't, but I'm on your side. Always. I'm not going anywhere and I'm going to do better. I promise. And however bad it seems right now, we'll figure it out. You'll be OK. I'll make double damn sure of it."

I just stare at her. Huh?

She finally glances at me. "You just need to speak up. Tell me what you want, what you need, what to do. I'm not a mind reader, but I am your grandma. We're family. Yeah?"

I manage a nod, fight to swallow the hairy coconut lodged in my throat and blink slowly, because I'm basically on the verge of menstruating and might cry.

"You'll stay with me?" she asks.

"I ... um ... I'm not going anywhere."

"You'll go places, Shake," she tells me. "Just wait and see."

What do I need? My grandma.

Chapter 39

CLEO:

I'll miss curling up with Shake's big body, feeling safe in that little twin bed in the basement. But I'll be OK. Yup.

I'm walking down the side of the road, scuffing my feet as slowly as possible toward the yellow house. The sun shoves against my back but fear cripples me.

I just gotta live there for a little while, until mom shows up or I turn eighteen. Or until Randy kills me. If I can smooth this over, somehow make lemonade out of pure piss, I'll be fine.

Just thinking about Randy cranks my panic into high gear and my heart could win at Daytona. How do I explain the new wardrobe? Or where I've been these past few days? What if he's heard all about me and Shake from Bruce? He's going to think I told Shake about the night of the fire. He won't listen or believe a word I say.

I am so screwed. For all of Shake's promises, this is just how it is for me. I can't fight it. I've got nowhere else to go.

I'm just turning onto my street when Terek rumbles up beside me in the Twat. He yells out his open window and offers me a ride. Since I am within sight of the yellow house, I point and refuse. He's not planning on taking me to the yellow house, and I'm not agreeing to go to Shake's house, which means we're at a standoff. But he's bigger than me. So when he jumps out the driver's side, I run, shout at him to go away, leave me alone, go copulate with himself.

I learn Terek West is really friggin' fast on his feet. He catches me so easy it's embarrassing, throws me over his shoulder and does a little dance that nearly ends with me puking down his back. I switch to name calling, and he definitely cops a feel as he wrestles me into the passenger seat. I then pound the dash and threaten to turn his balls into earrings. He warns me to be nice to his Twat, cranks death metal on the stereo and peels out.

It has become a hostage situation.

I end up cross legged on Shake's bed, chewing a thumbnail, nerves bubbling up and fizzing in my brain. Worry drives me half-crazy. Terek drives me the rest of the way.

"C'mon," he whines for the eighteenth millionth time. He stands at the bottom of the stairs, blocking my escape. I already tried to dart around him once, and he literally flipped me back onto the bed. Then he laughed when I screamed at him and performed a super offensive victory dance.

He's currently wearing a laundry basket upside down on his head. He must have gotten his jeans and shirt from the secondhand store. From the dumpster behind the secondhand store. After a naked Eskimo threw them away.

"You do it."

"I told you," he huffs. "Won't fit. And since you're the size of a Polly fucken Pocket ... "

"I'm not riding down the stairs in that basket."

"Why the hell not?"

"Don't wanna get hurt. Not in the mood. And it'll only make one of us happy."

"Did I ask for anal?"

"What? Ew. Jesus, you are one twisted pretzel. Why are you still here?"

He starts singing, kind of. It's the chant from the Wizard of Oz, when the guards march into the castle of the Wicked Witch. But he changes it from "O-Ee-Ya! Eoh-Ah!" to "Cle-O-Ya! Cleo-Ah!"

Holy hepatitis, he's annoying. Terek West is verbal confetti and in his world, it's always midnight on New Year's Eve. How has no one killed him yet?

"Terek! Jeeeez-sus! Stop!" I throw Shake's pillow at him. It bounces off the laundry basket.

"Hey! I'm just saying. You're kind of disappointing."

"Just cuz I wouldn't do naked headstands?"

"It's a cure for hiccups. I'm fucken telling ya."

"Neither one of us has hiccups."

"What's your point?" His head tips left and after half a millisecond of blessed silence, he blurts, "Singing Penis Cums Aggressively."

It takes me a few seconds to catch on. "SPCA?"

He rolls his hand and his eyes. His cuteness has worn off. The smell of lavender is giving me a headache. This is the same boy who ate a bug on a bet in third grade. For a quarter. "Scented Pink Cat Anus."

"Slimy Pussy Crack Allergy."

"Sore … um … Peculiar … ah … " I sniff, blink and WTF, I might cry.

"It's all good, Cleo." For once, Terek's mouth isn't wearing a smirk. "My dad won't let anything happen to our boy. And Shake won't let anything happen to you. That's why I'm here."

"He got hauled out of school in handcuffs! He's in jail!" I wail. "Because of me."

"He's with my dad. Because of him. Shake's a big boy. He made big boy decisions, and I'm guessing he's gonna show up any minute. Then you can suck his face off and live happily ever after."

I snort and swipe at my damp cheeks. "After what Bruce probably told him, that ain't happening."

"Won't matter to Shake. The dude is so loyal, he barks in his sleep. Trust me on that. I've known him a long time."

"But Bruce …"

"Is a wet turd." And the grin returns. "One of those wet turds with corn in it." OK, he's still a little bit cute. That chipped tooth and mess of sandy hair is hard to resist. But then he wrecks it, because there's just too much Terek. Pressing his fists into the small of his back, twisting his hips, he tells me, "Mighta pulled a muscle jerking my pud this morning. But man, I creamed so fucken hard, I painted the ceiling."

"Oh my fucking God."

"Gets ya wet, right?"

He is his own special brand of disgusting. Maybe that's good. Because he's also more distracting than a dildo in a bridal bouquet. Time passes and eventually the basement door opens. I yell "duck" too late. Shake is moving fast. His forehead bounces off the overhang and his eyes glaze as he stumbles down the last few stairs.

"What a spaz," Terek laughs, as if he isn't wearing a fresh bruise from being just as big of a spaz.

Shake's stare finds me. It lands so hard and heavy, I make a noise when I catch it. For a second, I can't breathe.

"So what happened, dude?" Terek wants to know. "How bad you get bent over?"

"Beat it," Shake snarls.

"What the fuck, dude? Aren't you getting laid? Why're you such a whiny bitch? Cleo, why is he still such a whiny little bitch? Are you not taking care of my boy here?"

"I swear to Christ, Rat, if you're not gone in three seconds ..."

"Three seconds?" Terek echoes. "That's random. How about I go pump seven gallons of gas into the Twat, come back in twenty-eight minutes and bring eleven slices of cantaloupe. Better yet, how bout you take three fucken seconds to thank me for saving your nuts and sitting on your girl? Her sweet ass isn't exactly cooperative, and I'm taking major heat from my dad. He's not buying the story about the knife."

Shake deflates. He grinds the heel of a hand into his eyes, tips his head down and nods. "You're right. It's just, whatever. I'm a dick. I appreciate everything, Rat."

"Teammates man. You want some help with whatever set you off on Bruce?"

"Nope."

"Need anything?"

"What do I need?" Shake gives a bad imitation of a laugh and spreads his hands. "Fuck if I know."

"No worries, toolbag. Guess I'll be giving you a ride to Tully's ballet recital." Terek tosses the laundry basket aside, bro hugs Shake, then woofs twice at me.

Too soon, the front door slams and it's just me and Shake.

Just us. Is there an us? I want to grab Shake, wrap my arms around him, but I don't know if I'm allowed to do that anymore. Bruce has probably dirtied his view of me. He's now looking through the grimy windows of the yellow house, seeing a more honest version of me.

Shake stares. I fidget. I wish he'd sit. I get to my feet. He's uncomfortably tall. Looking up at him hurts both my neck and my heart, so I get busy studying the floor. I shift from foot to foot, tempted to run, but he deserves the chance to send me away. I want to cry, but I don't deserve the pity my tears might my earn.

His touch catches me by surprise. I flinch, and he hesitates before spreading his fingertips across my cheeks. I drown in the heat of him, sound of his breath, his clean scent. This is how he wears me down. Just by being every wish I've ever made.

So I finally look up. Shake is waiting, patient but making a face I recognize. He will get his way. He is a stubborn sasquatch.

"No more secrets," he says.

"I'm sorry," I whisper.

"Are you my girl or not Cleo?"

His girl? Wow. That's just … wow. I can't even wrap my head around his voice saying those words. I've never been given a choice, never been chosen, and this boy is so far beyond me, I'm surprised I can see him without a telescope.

"Are you my girl?" he repeats. "There's only two answers here. Give me one."

"Yes," I say, convincing myself, giving him the answer he wants, but it's not enough. He needs more. Always more and I'll never be enough.

"Then tell me. Everything."

"I don't want to give you up," I blurt.

"I'm not walking away."

"You will."

"You know me better."

Do I? Maybe. Yes. I keep expecting him to bail on me, but so far, he just keeps putting up with my shit and waiting for me to prove I'm not worth it.

My shame is pure heat, pumping through my veins, burning my tongue, and my voice is less than smoke. "Bruce told you, right? What a skanky piece of ass I am?"

"Don't do that. Trust me enough to be honest."

I start to tremble. It originates in my legs, travels up my spine, and I'm shaking my head no, trying to step back, when his hands tighten and don't allow it. He quotes Shakespeare.

"Our doubts are traitors, and make us lose the good we oft might win, by fearing to attempt."

And so I begin with the end.

"Randy, when he gets pissed, forces me to do things. To prove a point. As punishment. Because he can. And this last time, he took my clothes, all of my stuff and burned it." My voice drops down into a wet mess that backwashes up my throat. So I blink and blink and swallow and refuse to give in to the tears. "He made me crawl and beg. I didn't cooperate right away, and it pissed him off even more. That's when, you know, you found me in that abandoned car."

"He made you crawl? And beg?"

I nod. I don't recognize his voice. It's scratchy as the old vinyl record albums my mom sometimes plays. His breaths are deep, nostrils flared, teeth clenched. His one palm still gently cradles my head, but the right hand drops away, and those swollen, purple knuckles clutch and stretch, over and over. We are ticking toward detonation.

"Because of me?" he demands.

I close my eyes and nod.

"Why?"

"Cuz of that night." I don't need to clarify. He knows.

"That night," he prompts. He wants me to go on. He thinks the truth will help. He's wrong.

I meet his stare head on. His rage is blinding. And frightening.

"I was there that night," I admit. "At your house. I was wasted. That was the last time for me. But it was rock bottom. I was such a toasted mess. We all were."

"My house?"

I nod.

"Who?"

"Me and Rex, Bruce, Randy and Hemmie." I focus on the feel of Shake's touch, expecting every word to rob me of it. "We hung out in the basement of your house sometimes. But it was bad that night because Hemmie owed Randy money. A lot of money. He took product to sell. Took it on credit and then there was no product, no money, no nothing, and Hemmie just didn't give a shit, you know? Like always. And Randy wasn't happy. He got mean, really mean, really fast. Hemmie told me to go, but I shouldn't have listened. I knew something bad could happen."

His silence is so static, it becomes a demand for me to fill.

"Rex left with me. I don't know what time. The sirens started right before we made it back to the yellow house. I didn't find out about the fire until the next day, and I asked Randy. I asked him what happened." I hesitate, trying to phrase this so he won't keep peeling this onion. "He told me nothing happened, that he and Bruce left right after me, and not to ask again. He said to stay away from you. He made it real clear, but I hung out with you anyway. That was my choice. I knew what I was doing, what would happen. So, you don't need to do anything about it."

"How?"

"What?" I pretend I don't get what he's asking.

"How did he make it clear? What did he do to you, Cleo?"

"You don't need to know this."

"Tell me."

I pull my trembling lip under my teeth and widen my eyes to make room for the tears I won't let fall.

"No more secrets," he pushes.

I shake my head, but he just waits me out, not giving an inch. I will lose him if I don't tell the truth. I will lose him if I do. So I get nasty, because it's all I know how to do.

"He fucken spanked me. Put me over his lap and smacked my naked ass black and blue. OK? Are you picturing it? And then I sucked him off, and he half-choked me to death while I did it, cuz he gets off on that shit. He made me do it to Bruce too. How's that, Shake? Does that get you hard? Make you proud of me? Or maybe you should gargle bleach?

Disinfect your dick? Get a rabies shot! Can we stop now? Huh? Are you done with me?"

He steps back and his hands lift away from me like I knew they would. It still breaks my heart. He can't even look at me, and I'm on the verge of puddling at his feet.

"Sonofabitch," he mutters.

"Fuck it," I snarl to defend myself. "You and I both knew this couldn't last. I'm just sorry you got tangled in my shit, got yourself dirty."

"Jesus Christ, Cleo. Don't apologize." Now his eyes smash into mine, hot and ferocious. "I'm the one who's sorry. I should have seen it. I should have made you tell me. I just... " He bites the inside of his cheek and shakes his head. "I was too busy with my own shit. Which is no goddamn excuse. But you said, you told me he didn't ..."

"He didn't."

"It's the same fucken thing, just as bad. So why do you keep going back there? Where's your goddamn mom? Why not get help? Talk to the cops? Talk to me? That shit's not OK, Cleo."

"I can't end up in the system!" I shoot back, both our voices rising over each other on every turn. I'm actually yelling at him. "I told you! This is how it is. My mom comes and goes. Her boyfriends do what they do, and if anyone finds out, I'll get sent away. It's happened before and it sucks. It's worse. You don't understand. You CAN'T understand. So LET IT GO!"

"No." He grabs me.

I shove away, fighting against the one thing I want above all others, but he's too much to hold off. He traps my flailing hands, wraps me so tight against his chest, it hurts. And heals. It is the only spot where I feel I belong. I am home.

"Nobody gets to touch you like that." His voice vibrates in his chest, against my ear, and I grab the shirt at his back in handfuls. "Never again, Cleo. I promise you. That's done." He tilts back to look down at me. "Understand?"

I nod even though I don't believe him.

"Give me the rest."

No. No. I silently plead, and I know he hears me, but he demands it anyway.

"Cleo? Tell me. The Douche was there when the fire started, right?"

I open my mouth. Nothing comes out.

"Don't protect him, Cleo. Was he still fucking there?"

I don't give a shit what happens to Randy. I'm protecting Shake. This is only about him. He is the one who matters, who is worth so much more than the rest of us combined. My next breath drags tears in its wake. "I don't know."

"God fucken damnit!" he shouts. I flinch. He lets me go, starts pacing, limping and manic. "That night. That night. I can't call it anything else. Did you know that? I can't even say it. It's too fucken painful to even think it. The night I snuck out. The night of the fire. The night I didn't get home in time, didn't save them. The. Night. My. Family. Burned. To. Death. And

I lost EVERYTHING. My dad. My mom. Hemmie. Everybody. So you fucken tell me what that motherfucker did, Cleo."

I've been convincing myself nothing was for sure. I wasn't there when it all went down. I've got no proof. I can't know what happened. But I do know. I know, and I suck so bad for keeping it from Shake. I let him suffer the guilt because I'm a coward.

"I don't know who started it, how it started, but Hemmie was wrecked that night. Too wrecked to get out. Randy was going nuts over the money, and he had a point to make. Nobody gets anything from him for free. And the next day, he acted really weird and was over the top pissed when I questioned him." I don't look him in the eyes, because I can't watch the devastation I'm causing. "I think Randy and Bruce were both there when the fire started."

The sound that spills from his lips is awful. It rips from somewhere deep inside and cuts him in half. With hands braced on his knees, his body heaves. I know what I just did. I told him he didn't lose his family to some tragic accident. It didn't need to happen, shouldn't have happened, and even though there's somebody to blame, I think this only makes it worse.

"Shake."

"Fuck! Fuck! Fuck!" His voice booms in the basement, and I swear the foundation trembles. He finally straightens, head tilting back, fingers grasping at his hair as he staggers sideways. "Ahhhhhh. Fuuuuuck."

This beautiful boy is shattered. I did this. His eyes are broken and he is no longer here with me. He is lost in a place I can't get to.

"I shouldn't have left. I'm sorry. I'm so sorry. I don't really know anything for sure. I don't. I don't know. This isn't ... " My words rush over each other, but I've got nothing. There's no medicine for this kind of hurt.

In a voice scraped raw, he says, "You knew. All this time."

I nod.

"Why didn't ..." He stops. I watch his throat work as he swallows the bitter truth. "You didn't tell me. You let me think it was my fault."

I stand there. My heart catches on the jagged edge of my guilt, and it's painful.

"Why?"

I look away.

"You were afraid," he says it for me. "Of what he'd do to you. But you kept coming around, trying to fix me anyway."

"Scared for both of us."

He starts to shake his head, but I jump in, "You don't know what he's capable of."

"Stay here, Cleo."

"No Shake, wait!"

He hauls ass up the stairs. I chase after him. I'm no match for his long legs. The door slams behind him and in front of me. I jerk on the handle, twist and tug and scream a little. It takes me a minute to realize Shake locked me in.

Chapter 40

SHAKE:

The night of the fire, the Douche and Bruce got themselves out. They got themselves out. Walked away. Safe and sound. No looking back. They left my family behind.

They. Left. My family. Behind.

My mom. My dad. My brother.

My thoughts roll end over end, digging deeper, and the lizard part of my brain squirms in the mud.

I remember the very first moment in the street, when I realized the flames clawing at the sky were feeding on my house. I looked around, searching the faces of neighbors, expecting but not finding my family and unable to understand why. The realization came over me in a wave, and I still kept hoping, kept resisting, even when a pair of firemen dragged me back, wrestled me to the ground. I screamed and raged and fought. I fought against both their hold and the truth. I was no match for either.

There are no words to describe the pain.

I remember how quickly it multiplied, like a parasite, filling me until my skin felt too tight, my skull ready to burst, devouring me from the inside out.

Then came the anger. Anger at myself, at the world still turning around me and even at my family for not waking up, not getting out, leaving me behind. Now, all of a sudden, everything is different.

I've got a name. I don't know what to do with it or about it. I just know where I'm headed.

It's all I've got.

So I hobble on my effed up foot, no longer able to put weight on it. My sneaker is a tourniquet. My toes have five separate heartbeats. The hard throb reaches all the way up to my crotch and every step kicks my ass. My right hand is worse, but it doesn't matter. There's no choice here, no turning back, and my breath sucks from my lungs like a bilge pump fighting a sinking ship.

I trade one part of town for another. The street lights disappear, pavement gives way to dirt, and the sun pisses a shitty mustard taint across the horizon as it fades away. Humidity wraps heavy around my shoulders and sweat slips down my back. The yellow house waits for me in a crease of shadows.

I hammer the door, focusing on a small crack in the wood, and watch it split right down the middle. I am that crack. When the door starts to open, I heave forward with everything in me and shout, "You shit! You goddamn piece of shit!"

My shoulder plows into the Douche, blasting him off his feet, sending him crashing into the kitchen table and chairs. I follow, grabbing him by the shirt and hauling his skinny carcass right back up.

"You shit!" My spit dots his face. I can't put anything else into words. I'm raging, mindless, an animal as I smash my busted right hand against his jaw.

"Ahhhhhh!" There's so much pain, I actually scream back it. I've never felt hurt like this before. It takes my breath away. I don't think it can get any worse, until it does. My weight lands on my bad foot. I'm no match for the agony, no match for the Douche kicking me in the balls.

The impact rattles my kidneys, and I drop knees to the linoleum as bile rushes up my throat. The Douche boots me in the ribs. I curl up quicker than a pig's tail. I am two hundred pounds of helpless idiot, and the Douche is merciless. He kicks me again. His boot splits the skin above my right eye. Bells ring, blood pours down my face and for some reason, I notice the dumbass is wearing cowboy boots. He probably can't even spell Holstein.

"You wanna dance?" he taunts. "C'mon, pussy, let's tango."

The Douche bounces on his feet, working out his neck, smiling through bloodied lips. He's liking this.

So am I. The pain is the perfect marinade for my rage. Lashes wet and sticky, I blink and push to hands and knees and grin.

He skips forward, lining up my skull for a field goal. I watch it coming. Shifting, I take the impact to the chest, wrap my arm around his leg and twist. It's his turn to scream. He lands on his back, and I throw myself on top, bracing my right forearm against his throat.

The little fuck is fast. He pops a quick jab. Same eye. Good for him. He rattles my cage but only manages to let the monster loose. I hammer his face, smart enough to use my left hand, and snarl, "The fire. You did that. Didn't you?"

I swing another left. Another. For me. For my Mom. My Dad. Hemmie. Cleo. Each pound of my fist hurts us both. His skin splits. His bones crack. My heart tears. My soul hemorrhages.

This motherfucker will never touch Cleo again. He will suffer for what he took from me. I may keep hitting him until there's nothing left but a bloody residue on the shitty linoleum.

I barely register the squeak of a sneaker on the floor, right behind me. I don't think or worry about it, until hot pain drives into my back. This brand new agony takes me hostage. It stabs deep. Again. Again. I twist away, but my body doesn't respond like it should, and I can't stop screaming.

Somebody else can't stop laughing.

Chapter 41

CLEO:

I go hair-pulling, foaming-at-the-mouth bonkers. I search every crack and crevice of the basement and find only spiders. They are gigantic, but I kill them because I am brave. I am fierce.

I am worthless.

Minutes tick away and I waste each precious one with no results. Round and round, top to bottom, there's no way out. But I keep looking because I don't know what else to do. I practically slapped a stamp on Shake's forehead and sent him straight to hell.

Goddamnit. Shit. Crap. Holy fuckorama. I'd chew off my own foot if it would help.

When I hear a creak above me, I scramble to the top of the stairs and wrench and tug and go batshit on the door handle. The lock clicks, the door flies back at me and Terek blurts, "Whathehell?"

I definitely require a helmet to get through this life in one piece. And Terek should buy a matching one. As I tip ass over teacup and tumble down the stairs, he rushes after me, whacks his skull off the overhang and trips over his bigass feet. We end up in a pile of stupidity on the floor. He lands on top and weighs more than a baby gorilla, carrying a full grown elephant, wearing lead boots, jumping off a pogo stick.

That hurt. Like really hurt. I can't even decide how bad, because I'm in too big of a hurry. I gotta get to Shake right effing now. If only to beat his hot ass for locking me in the goddamn basement. So I shove and push at Terek, who has way too many arms and legs, and I'm half sobbing, half chanting, "We need to go, we need to go, we need to go."

"Weeny taco?" Terek says back. "Sounds like something I should try with Blair."

He must have bashed his head beyond repair. He's not making sense. So I yell it louder and faster. "Weneetogo! Weneetogo!"

"Stop saying that!"

"C'mon, c'mon, lessgo!"

"What the hell, Cleo? I came back for my phone, and you're locked in the basement?" He grabs hold of me when I try to scramble up the stairs, gets right in my face and hits me with a whole lotta blue eyes. "Cleo! Calm the fuck down. Tell me. Where's Shake?"

"Yellow house!" I finally blurt and that does it. Everybody knows about the yellow house. Or maybe it's my eyes stretched ten miles wide or my voice hitting the pitch of a dolphin getting an enema, but Terek understands we have hit Defcon Five. He snatches up his phone, which was tangled in Shake's bedsheets THE WHOLE TIME and races me to the Twat.

We pile in, not bothering with seat belts. He punches the gas, ignores all traffic signs, and the headlights carve tunnels in the dark. The Twat rattles so badly I'm sure we're pulling a Hansel and Gretel and leaving bits of muffler, fender and rust behind.

Terek quizzes me, and I fill him in, sort of. I can't manage to string more than a pair of words together because my head is a buzzing hive of panic. But he seems to understand and his usual grin is missing. He pushes the Twat even harder, and I lean forward in my seat, as if I can make it go faster.

When I spot the yellow house, I sling the door open.

"Whoa!" Terek shouts, laying the breaks into a skid and trying to catch my arm.

I flop out before the Twat's in park and nearly eat curb. My feet tangle and trip over garbage hidden in high grass, and I hear Randy's voice seeping from inside. I know that tone. It's the delighted evil of a genuine psychopath and sets off warning flares. A happy Randy is a very bad thing.

"Yeah, I fucken started it!" he shouts. "Your dumbfuck brother tried to dick me, told me to pound shit. Me! Nobody fucks with me. Got it? Catching on yet? Or maybe you need another lesson from Bruce?"

I finally see Shake, framed by the open door. I don't know what I expected, but not this. He's on hands and knees and hurt in ways I can't comprehend.

Blood is everywhere. It's splattered on the walls and puddled on the yellowed linoleum. It's all over Shake. Streaming down his face, saturating the front and back of his shirt and dripping off him. Seeing him like this, I can't process it, can't breathe, can't, can't, can't. This is my fault.

Terek suddenly shoves me behind him, shouting, "What the fuck is this?" and then he is inside, rounding on Bruce. He seems to double in size. "C'mon jagoff, let's see what you got." The two immediately knot up like a pair of shoelaces, grunting and trying to kill each other.

Does Terek not see the knife in Bruce's hand? That giant knife belongs in the drawer next to the kitchen sink. Rex once used it to cut PVC pipe for a homemade bong. He wrecked the blade, and we should have thrown it out. Why didn't we? Why is there blood on the knife? What do I do, what do I do?

Shake hauls himself upright. I don't know how he does it. Balanced on one foot, he tosses his head like a wet dog and squares off with Randy. There is no quit in this boy. Unlike me. I have never fought for anything in my life. I've survived this long by tucking tail and flying below the radar, but Shake is the exception to everything I've ever known and Randy is the rule I no longer live by.

So I grab a kitchen chair by the metal legs and swing with everything I've got. For the first time ever, I have something to lose, and I'm not letting that spithit Randy take anything else from me.

I scream. The chair bashes against his face. His head whips sideways. Vibrations sizzle up my arms. Blood sprays wet over my cheeks, gets into my mouth. Randy drops like I killed him. Did I kill him? Is that a good or bad thing? Should I hit him again? I think I should, and I know I want to.

He made me crawl and beg. He laughed. He turned me over to Bruce. He hurt Shake. But he's not laughing now. And I can't seem to let go of the chair.

I'm gagging, revving with adrenaline when I hear Shake whisper, "Cleo?"

I spin toward him. His eyes are all murky. As they roll back, he pitches forward and I trade the chair for grabbing him. His size and weight are too much for me. We go down together, just like I always knew we would, and his blood seeps into my clothes.

Chapter 42

SHAKE:

When Allie's face looms over my hospital bed, I think I'm hallucinating. The blue eye shadow, purple hair and pink lipstick remind of that game I played as a kid. What was it called? Candyland.

"I'm the goose!" she shouts.

I'm confused. Maybe it's the pain meds.

"And you're my golden egg! Wanna get laid?"

Clever.

"No touching, no touching, no touching," I chant, holding up both hands to fend her off. Who am I kidding? There's no stopping the juggernaut that is Allie Kindle. Maybe I don't try as hard as I should. She gives damn good hugs.

One big mitt slides into my hair, the other reaches around my waist, and I'm wrapped up tight. She squeezes and I feel downright dainty.

"Allie! Allie!" I gotta make a show of fighting back. She expects it. Since I'm butt naked under a thin sheet and paper gown, I need to slow her down a bit. "That's enough. Remember, we have a deal. You bring me clothes and I, and I ... " I can't make myself say it.

"Somebody's a Mister Grumpy-pants."

"No. I'm Mister NO-Pants. Where's my stuff?"

She holds up her enormous purse. When I reach for it, she jerks it away and waggles a finger at me. "Not so fast, Shake-a-licious. Our deal?"

Allie is ridiculously easy to manipulate, and since I'm a selfish prick, it works for me. Sort of. I'm getting what I want, but I'm selling my soul for it. I force a nod and clarify, "No pictures. And no video."

"One picture."

"No renegotiating. We agreed. Take it or leave it." I'm bluffing. I'll do just about anything to make this happen. Thank Christ she hasn't caught on. I don't think I could live with myself if I caved to her original demands. She is really into this wedding stuff.

"You're extra pissy today," she huffs back.

Hells yeah, I'm pissy. I hurt EVERYWHERE. I need a shower, a decent meal and how about a pair of goddamn underwear.

Broken foot, broken hand, concussion, some internal shit and miles of stitches add up to a miserable me.

I hate the hospital. Hate it. The place is too white, too bright and smells like mothballs soaked in rubbing alcohol. After eating the food, I've added Poison Control to my contacts. Plus, every time I fall asleep, some natzi nurse wakes me, just to make sure my squash isn't mushed. Since I'm drugged to the gills, and exhausted from their hourly prod and poke, I'm about as coherent as a pile of snot.

So yeah, I'm busting out of here. That's where Allie comes in. She visits every day and is the only one who's willing to help me.

Instead of feeling sorry for me, Grandma and Rat's parents blame me for everything from my injuries to fewer marshmallows in their Lucky Charms. Sometimes, Rat's mom even bursts into tears when she looks at me. Just in case I didn't already feel like a big enough shitheel. If I apologize, she cries harder soooo, I'm clueless.

My teammates showed up yesterday. I figured they'd help me out, have my back, make good on the whole one-for-all promise. Instead, they spent the entire visit razzing me. Apparently, I'm as pussified as a maxi pad because my ass landed in the hospital. To top it off, a daily parade of girls from school keep filling my room with flowers, stuffed animals and hysterics. Who needs doctors, nurses and medication when I've got a giant pink fuzzy dog and wilting daisies?

Did you notice somebody missing from my list? One miniature, ballbusting, sticky-fingered girl who hasn't shown up? Not once. In five days. Nobody will tell me the truth about where she is or what the hell's going on.

Here's what I know, and it's not much. Social Services is involved, and Cleo has been removed from the yellow house. That's a good thing, except she's also been removed from me. In case you're not catching on, that's a very bad thing. Very, very bad. I'm quickly losing my shit over it.

Randy, aka the Douche, is truly fucked. He's somewhere, lurking here in this same hospital, and while he's recovering from a broken face, he's getting investigated for his possible involvement in the fire. Plus, a search of the yellow house turned up a sizeable stash of drugs. So sizeable, he's facing distribution charges. I'd still like to hunt him down, crack his skull and scramble him like an egg. Yes, I'm holding a grudge. He needs to hope he ends up in jail.

Bruce, aka the Douche Weasel, is no less fucked. Physically fucked because Rat beat the holy piss out of him. Legally fucked because of the eight-inch kitchen knife he stabbed into my back. Four times. Repeat after me. FOUR TIMES. IN THE BACK. Which is why my insides are messed up, my feet dangling off the end of a too-short hospital bed, with my ass hanging out. I'm going out of my friggin mind.

So I'm taking matters into my own hands. Also Allie's hands. I'm relying on her to put my plan into action. What could go wrong?

I swing my legs over the side of the bed, then grunt, sweat and maneuver my way into a sitting position. Standing is gonna hurt. I know this because, after begging, pleading and charming my way off the catheter, the whole bedpan thing is a giant no-effing-way for me. Every time I gotta piss, I man-up and walk. Aren't I hardass? Except I've needed the help of an orderly every time and can barely manage my own dick, which is super goddamn embarrassing. So yeah, this solo flight might end up in a crash and burn.

"Lemme help." Allie's hand lands on my thigh, way too close to my junk, and as I squeal like a five-year-old princess, Rat and Sam walk in. And burst out laughing. My misery is hilarious.

"We can come back when you're done?" Rat drawls. "Three minutes sound about right?"

I don't answer. My lime JellO dinner bubbles in my gut, and I might vomit if I move too quickly. There's a ringing in my ears. White spots behind my eyes. My stitches pull, my foot throbs, my hand aches, and my brain is swimming faster than a goldfish after somebody taps on the glass. Other than that, I'm good.

"Hey buttmunch, you supposed to be sitting up?" Sam rags.

Allie does me the solid of telling him, "He gets frisky on the meds, so I'm getting him into some undies and helping him feel proactive."

"Should that make sense?" Sam questions.

"No worries," she says. "We've got a deal, and he won't make it through the ceremony. I'll have him flat on his back again in no time."

"What?" Sam tries.

I'm with Sam on this. What did she just say? Cuz it sounds suspiciously like Allie's playing me. I'm not with it enough to be sure. I zero in on Rat. He's the most informed and the weakest link. "Hear anything new?"

He shakes his head but then admits, "I overheard my dad."

"Jesus, Rat," Sam moans. "We went over this. We agreed. Right out in the hallway, remember? We even fucken practiced. Remember what you're gonna say?"

"No news is good news."

"Right."

Rat presses his mouth shut and nods. The overhead lights hum. The air ducts wheeze. I stare until he folds. He lasts maybe eight seconds, which is probably a record.

"OK, so I'm not supposed to tell you, but I guess my dad tracked down Cleo's mom."

Sam groans.

Rat goes on. "This was a couple days ago. He found her shacked up with some dude with outstanding warrants in Tennessee or Alabama or some fucken place. If she gets her ass back here and convinces everybody she didn't just ditch her kids, and cleans up her act, then maybe Cleo can probably come home."

"Where is Cleo?"

"She's fine," Sam tells me. "Worry about yourself."

"Rat?"

He looks from me to Sam and back. "She's staying with some foster family in Buffalo."

"Goddammit," Sam explodes. "What part of zipping yer shit do you not understand? The big ape's so doped up he's still slurring his words. There's no way he's gonna stay put when ..."

"Hey, fuck that," Rat comes back at him. "He deserves to know, and it's not like I'm gonna let him past the door."

I stop listening. Buffalo. That's only an hour away. It's doable. If I can bully the address out of Rat and borrow the Twat. Maybe take the bus. If I can borrow money. I may need to promise Allie a honeymoon.

"Hey," I start and catch Rat giving Allie his patented nod and wink.

Seriously? Is he scamming in my hospital room?

"You smell yummy," Allie tells him. For once, she's not yelling. She's turned into a Lollipop Kid sucking helium. "Is that lavender?"

"Wanna find out?" Rat grins back. "I taste better than I smell."

"I've got a snorkel mask I'm dying to try."

"So you need me to get ya wet?" He licks his lower lip as Sam smacks him across the back of the head.

I ease my weight onto the balls of my feet. The floor is ice cold and about as steady as a lily pad in a typhoon. What's up with that? I check but nobody else seems to notice.

"Shake," Sam warns. "Don't be a friggin idiot."

"Dude," Rat puts out there. He says a lot with that one word. Is he right? Am I acting like an immature asshole? Yup. Do I care enough to stop and reassess my grand plan? Nope. My brain is chanting Cleo, Cleo, Cleo. I've been on the same loop for five straight days, chasing an itch I can't reach, and it's not gonna quit until I get to her.

She needs me. I've already let her down enough. And I need her.

I stand up all by my selfie. OK, I'm plenty woozy, but I give my teammates the thumbs up, Allie the gimme sign and hold off throwing my arms into the Rocky double fist pump. I'm not quite at the celebration stage just yet.

Allie digs in her purse for my clothes and hands them over. I fumblefuck my boxers. The cast on my hand is the problem. So is the one on my foot. My balance is wonky, and there's definitely something weird going on with the floor. Maybe I'm just unlucky. I catch a toe in the waistband, end up hopping, which is a huge mistake, and pain dives into my guts with a big splash. I'm going down.

Allie catches me. She lands both hands on my naked ass, and once again, I shriek like I've been neutered. Awesome. Just fucken awesome.

"C'mon man," Sam mutters. "Back to bed."

He and Rat each take an arm. My boxers land at my feet. Defeat lands on my shoulders. I actually need the both of them to hold me up. I inhale and squeeze eyes and fists shut. Can't one fucken thing go my way? Could I please just have my girl back? Or at least know she's OK? Because an eight-inch knife is nothing compared to the worries decimating my brain.

I really can't take anymore losses. I need, I need, I need.

The door swings wide and there stands my little rabid wolverine. Is she really here? Does anyone else see her? Does it matter? Either way, I'm tickled. She's wearing my NY Dolls shirt, and she's so hot, I'll need oven mitts to handle her. I grin. I am a giant tool in a paper gown. A happy tool.

When her wide, dark eyes take me in, they get even bigger and she cups a hand over her mouth.

"I'm OK," I tell her. I've seen my face in the mirror. I could score a starring role in the Nightmare Before Christmas.

She sniffs, plunks her fists on her hips and suddenly barks, "Hey! Sasquatch! Get your ass back in that friggin bed!"

It's the sweetest sound I've ever heard.

My smile tests the limits of my face. I pull away from Rat and Sam and make her help me. It's a struggle for both of us. I'm draped all over her, about as helpless as a walrus in quicksand, and I'm pretty sure she's been guzzling Drink Me Potion and chasing white rabbits, cuz she is even more teeny than I remember.

She tucks the covers around me, tries to draw back, but I tug hard enough to land her on top of me. It hurts. I hiss with it. The pain is worth the press of her little body, even when Cleo wiggles to get away and makes everything worse. By everything, I mean both injuries and horniness. It's too bad we're not alone, because I'd be testing the limits of my stitches. I settle for an arm around her waist and slide my knuckles down her cheek.

"Hold still," I whisper against her ear. "Please Cleo. Stay with me."

She pulls back enough to look into my eyes, giving me the stare down, and I tell her again, "I'm OK."

"Truth?"

"You're here. I'm good now."

Sam snorts. "No balls and wearing a dress."

"Need me to run out for tampons? Midol?" Rat offers.

I flip them off. I barely hear them cuz Cleo finally nods and lets me settle her in beside me. She fits just right, and for the first time since heading to the yellow house, I am truly OK. For the first time in eight months, I'm actually OK.

I don't know when Cleo Lee became so important, but it's hard to breathe when she's not around. Sometimes, for completely different reasons, it's even harder to catch my breath when she is.

Tilting to look up at me, she asks, "Do you need anything?"

What do I need?

This version of Cleo is everything I need. I've finally figured it out.

Chapter 43

Cleo:
Five months later

"Honey, I'm home," I call out. That just never gets old.

I hang my jacket on the hook beside the door and turn to find Shake. He sits in the recliner we salvaged from the side of the road. It's diarrhea brown, with a tear in the cushion, a stain we don't question and a spring that tends to poke your right ass cheek. But it was free. So it's ours. And perfect. Just like our tiny, shitty apartment that I just love.

For the first time, I have a home. Even if it smells like Chinese food, weed and wet dog, no matter how much I clean it. I'm just happy our apartment is a short walk to the bakery, because I haven't passed my driver's test yet. There was an itty bitty incident involving some metal garbage cans, a stray cat and a fire hydrant. It was definitely not my fault, but let's just say, Shake is insisting I practice a little more. Once I pass, we're planning a trip which will take me to new states and the ocean. More firsts.

Shake bought an ancient Pontiac Grand Am. He barely fits in it and regularly bashes his knees on the dash. The Grand Am is the Twat's ugly stepsister, but it gets Shake to class. He's enrolled at the college, playing for the hockey team, working at the rink and helping out at the bakery. He's busy. That's a good thing. The quiet times cause him trouble.

"Hey," he finally says back. I hear it in his voice, recognize it in the set of his beautiful mouth. Sometimes, Shake still falls into moments of incredible sadness.

He is no longer in a sinking ship alone. So I climb onto his lap, thread my fingers into his messy blonde curls, which I refuse to let him cut, and guide him back to shore.

I start by nipping at his bottom lip. I have no choice when he frowns. My willpower might be enough to resist Minnie's inventory, but that mouth is tastier than a white chocolate cupcake.

When his big palms cup my ass, I kiss the hell out of my boy. I kiss his cheeks, nose, eyelids, earlobes, mouth and think mine, mine, mine, mine, mine. I make sure we're both breathing hard and his hands make sure I'm thinking naughty thoughts.

Finally, bumping my nose against his, I stare into his eyes. "What do you need?"

"Time," he answers softly, letting his lashes dip to his cheeks.

"What else?"

"You."

"Yup. Anything else?"

"Still you."

"Good answer."

"And colossal amounts of dirty sex."

"Horndog," I tease, but I squeeze him with my thighs.

Then his eyes open. Like an ocean wave in the sunlight, those baby blues roll over me. They are so warm and clear, I float in them.

He swallows, glancing away and back, breathing a little faster, and I realize my sasquatch is nervous. This is new.

"Shake?" I know better than to rush him. I stop talking and wait. And wait. Eggs hatch and grow into mature chickens. Stonehenge crumbles to dust. Somebody watches Titanic from start to finish, then rewinds to watch the good parts again and guess what? Rose could totally scoot her ass over and make room for Leo on that raft! But whatever, I'm still waiting, trying not to scream, "Come onnnnnn!" or pull his hair. Being with Shake teaches me patience, has taught me some things are worth the wait.

We aren't the same people we were a year ago. We're damaged but figuring out how to make something good out of the lives we're sharing.

"Shake?" I push, just a little, cuz otherwise my sexy snail of a boyfriend won't speak up until Halloween candy goes on clearance and the devil is lacing up his ice skates.

"I need, um, to tell you something."

There's a small scar just above his right eyebrow, from where Randy kicked him. I run my fingertip over it, understanding that the bigger scars, the life changing ones, aren't as easy to see.

Should I be worried right now? "OK."

He still hesitates, and I resist my instinct to attack first and say something awful. See, I'm learning. Shake is one of the good guys. He is good for me, good to me, won't hurt me, but, but, but I want to keep him so bad. Sometimes I consider tying him to the bed. OK, we've done that. Talk about fun. But this is now and my insecurities are using my heart as a trampoline.

"I um ..." he starts.

I can't breathe. I might throw up. Which will definitely drive him away. No one wants the girl who vomits on them. Why did I think I could have somebody as hot and amazing as Shake? Does he think I will actually let him go? Cuz I will fight mean and dirty to keep him.

He frames my face with his hands and concentrates on my eyes, his expression so serious. "I love you, Cleo."

What? Not what I was expecting. At all.

This is a first for me. A first and a forever. Wow. Shake LeCasse. Loves. Me.

"You're supposed to say it back," he tells me.

"You just don't wanna feel cheap after last night," I remark. Last night was epic. We put rabbits to shame. I'm sore in the right places.

His smile is a little wary. I keep him waiting for a second, just to savor my own thoughts and then taste their sweetness on my tongue as I say, "I love you too, Shake. Always. No question."

Because, duh, I loved this boy before he knew I was alive.

His arms wrap around me, and he finally smiles for real. What a smile it is. I get a little dizzy.

I plant a kiss on his nose, trail my lips down his neck and get impatient. Grabbing the hem of his shirt, I ease it up and off. The miracle of his hard chest, the abs straight from my fantasies and whole delicious body belongs to me, and I just never get tired of claiming my prize.

"You smell like sugar cookies," he murmurs against my ear, biting at it before stripping my shirt off. "I need to taste."

"Tell me one. Then you can do whatever you want."

He quotes his namesake.

"Doubt that the stars are fire. Doubt that the sun doth move his aides. Doubt truth to be a liar. But never doubt I love."

The End